God Made Sunday

and other stories

Walter Macken, author and dramatist, died in April 1967 in his native Galway at the age of fifty-one. At seventeen he began writing plays and also joined the Galway Gaelic Theatre (the now celebrated Taibhdhearc) as an actor. In 1936 he married and moved to London for two years, returning to become actor-manager-director of the Gaelic Theatre for nine years, during which time he produced many successful translations of plays by Ibsen, Shaw, O'Casey, Capek and Shakespeare. To enable him to have more time for playwriting, he moved to the Abbey Theatre in Dublin. Macken acted on the London stage, on Broadway, and also took a leading part in the film of Brendan Behan's *The Quare Fellow*. Many of his plays have been published, and of his novels the first two, *I Am Alone* (1948) and *Rain on the Wind* (1949), were initially banned in Ireland. Several other novels followed, including *The Bogman*, which first appeared in 1952, and a historical trilogy on Ireland, *Seek the Fair Land*, *The Silent People* and *The Scorching Wind*. *Brown Lord of the Mountain* was published a month before his death.

Also by Walter Macken in Pan Books

Seek the Fair Land
The Silent People
The Scorching Wind
Rain on the Wind
The Coll Doll and other stories
The Bogman
Brown Lord of the Mountain
Quench the Moon
Sullivan

Walter Macken

God Made Sunday

and other stories

Pan Books in association with
Macmillan London

First published 1962 by Macmillan & Company Ltd
This edition published 1973 by Pan Books Ltd,
Cavaye Place, London sw10 9pg,
in association with Macmillan London Ltd
2nd printing 1976
© Walter Macken 1962
isbn 0 330 23502 8
Printed in Great Britain by
Richard Clay (The Chaucer Press) Ltd, Bungay, Suffolk

CONTENTS

God Made Sunday	7
Patter O'Rourke	74
The Big Fish	83
Solo and the Nine Irons	93
The Match Maiden	108
The Conjugator	115
Solo and the Simpleton	124
Light in the Valley	140
This Was my Day	150
Solo and the Sinner	157
No Medal for Matt	175
The Red Rager	182
The Lion	195

God Made Sunday

The Word Beforehand

EVERY summer a man comes to our island in the sea. People call him the Taleteller. It took us a time to get to know him. Many people come to the island in the summer. It is a place of great beauty then, and calm. It is peaceful. The sea is not angry. We do not disclose ourselves easy to casual people. You have to protect your private thoughts from strangers. They come and they go. If you give some of yourself to them they are likely to take it away with them when they go. So this man grew on us, because he came back again and again. He wormed his way into our thoughts, like a sand-eel in the beach-sand. He even got to learn our language and though the way he made his mouth form the words would make you laugh, it showed that he was earnest and sincere.

When he arrived he would look like a sick fish. He was a red-haired man and that made him look worse. He was fond of drink. In the world, he wrote books and things. It was no use giving us these books because we were not masters of the English tongue and could make little of them. But people said he was good at his trade from the way he could tell tales with his mouth. He could make you laugh, or excite you with a story until your breath was short in your chest.

He went around in an old island-knit gansey and old trousers. He looked like a travelling man. He put up a tent in a sheltered place by the sea. Our pigs lived better lives than he, but at the end of a month he looked a better man. The red would be gone from his eyes, and he would be livelier in himself, and when the time came we would be sorry to see him go, and would miss him, and be glad that

7

he was one we could look forward to again next year. He was a married man somewhere but his wife never came with him, nor his children. He didn't talk much of them. He didn't believe. People were sad for him on that account. You would see him sitting lonely on the hill watching the people coming from the chapel on Sundays.

He became my friend. I do not know why I talk in the past about him. It is because I am heavy handed at this writing. He is still my friend, and it is because of him that I am, with great pain in my fingers and sweat on my brow, writing this.

I am the one with a boat, so he often came with me. I liked to see him. When he got better at our tongue we could talk over many things as I laid my long lines. Last summer this nonsense came up and that is why, here in the winter, I am doing this.

Colmain, he said, why do you believe, what makes you believe there is a God? This shocks me. There are things that you know for sure and there are things that you don't know for sure. There are some things you don't talk about at all. There are things that no language can tell, if you spoke all the languages in the world. I just know, I said. You are not stupid, he said. Is what you are sure of, so unsure that you can't tell other people about it? You are confusing me, Pól, I said. Faith is a precious thing, he said, like a pearl in a sea oyster, how have you found this thing? Why can't you let me look at it? Are you afraid if I look at it it will dissolve into a grain of sand?

Most of my life, I said, I have had it. My mother gave it to me, my father, his father and mother and their fathers and mothers, as far back as the memory of dead ancestors can go.

That can't be true, he said, because each man in his own life has to pass through a period of great doubt. It's a personal thing. God cannot be an obscure something dealing with millions in the mass. He must be personal to each man. Therefore each single person, the black man in the jungle, the yellow man in the rice fields, the white man like

8

me living buried in a hole in great concrete cliffs that men call cities, must be individually challenged. It's not that easy.

His words confused me. I thought about them. Maybe they made wisdom. I said, I am not a well-educated man. I did not go beyond seventh book. If you want answers to your questions you must go to a man who knows. Go to the priest.

No, he said, I go to you. You are important. You live with the nerve of life. You are what's known as the common man, but you live on the bosom of the sea and over your head there is a great sky. You are not confused by lights and buildings and screaming noises. I want you to talk to me.

I have not the words, I said. I am a simple man.

I have millions of words, he said. They are on paper. I could fill a room with the books they are written in, but they mean nothing. He was sitting up in the boat, shaking a hand at me. I want your words, he said. Listen. The winter is long. The nights are long. Your work then is short. Before I go I will give you white paper and you will spend the winter covering this paper with the words of your mind. You will write to me why you are what you are, Colmain. You will write a letter to me, the writing man you call Pól, whose name is Paul. Will you do this for me?

I laughed at him.

This is impossible, I said. Look at my hand, it is like the cured leg of a pig. It was not meant to bear a pen. Pens are for delicate fingers, not for this hand such things. You make me laugh.

He sank back again in the boat. I have two weeks, he said. Before I go, I will batter at you like a ram until you do what I want. I am a persuasive man. You could talk me into jumping over the cliff, I said with great determination, before I would do such a thing.

Set your lines, Colmain, he said, your deeds are sealed.

This is what I mean about a word before. So that you will understand. What a weak man I am, or what a persuader Pól is. It is winter time. The nights are long. It is great pain for me. My tongue wets my cheek. My wife says it's such a pity you can't write with your tongue, Colmain, instead of the pen, but I am doing it, the devil scald it and the man who put me up to it. I will start it, and if I don't finish it, it will be no loss and it will have passed the long nights, but what good it will do you, Pól, I truly don't know.

Monday

I, Colmain Fury, can fashion with my hands, a stool to sit on, a table to eat from, or a bed to sleep on. Many things I can fashion with my hands because I have learned to do these things of necessity, but when I am put to it to fashion the tale of my life I do not know where to begin, but since God Himself started work on Monday, I will begin there, because the old people have a telling that everything happens to a man on a working day since God made Sunday for rest and peace. I have thought about this. What are the things that happened to me that meant much to me? and I can see that they happened on the working days. With your permission I will do that now. I know that other tales are divided into divisions called Chapters, but I have no skill in that sort of confusion. My tale is of little interest. Indeed it could be told in four sentences if I was speaking face to face and had the right words. But this would displease Pól. He would not be satisfied. He would talk to me so much that I would have the thing to do all over again, so as I am at it I will do it as well as if I was making a kitchen table, choosing the timber and smoothing it and making the legs and mortising them and joining them and framing them and then nailing the top on them.

I belong to the sea. The island is not big. It is big enough to shelter a hundred people and give them land, good sweet land, but in short supply, to grow potatoes, and a little oats and green grass for the milk cows, and coarse cliff grass for the mutton sheep.

This Monday, I was fourteen. It was my birthday. That is how I remember. When you are fourteen you are finished with school. You can rejoice. I regret this feeling now thirty years later. I should have attended my books better at school. I would know more English and not be so ashamed of the way I talk it that I don't talk it, and could converse with Pól easier in his own tongue. I could read books easier too instead of being slow and painful at the reading of them. Regrets are vain. This day I was happy. I was lying on the green grass of the clifftop, with a line wound around my leg. I was fishing for pollack. The line and baited hook went down a hundred feet to the fishing rocks below. When I got a bite it would hurt my leg and I would haul up the fish. It was late summer. The sky was blue and the air was hot, but there was a sort of lace curtain strained across the sky so that the bright blue of it could only be seen in small holes. The seagulls were lazy. They sat like fat ducks on the rocks and the grass. Only one of them now and again would stir himself to fly and look for a fish to devour. I sat up. I was disturbed because the line was not hurting my leg. I hauled on it a bit to look at the bait. It was all right. The fish should have been biting. But they weren't. I lowered it again. I wondered. The sea was calm, smooth as a girl's face-glass, and gently heaving in long long swells. The fish should be biting. It was a day for them. Between me and the mainland there were six Irish miles of water. The mainland shore was hazy. I looked out into the wide sea then. I remember I had to shade my eyes from the glare of the water. Far, far out, by squinting my eyes, I could see the boats of the island, little tiny black oblong dots seeming to be raised between the sea and the sky.

If I was not doing well, I hoped they were. I turned on my belly and kept looking at them. My father was out there and my two brothers. I thought how lucky they were. I wondered how soon my father would use me for the fishing. I longed for the sea-fishing with all my heart. My second brother Tiernan often jeered at me. Get to the chickens, Colmain, he would say. I had a temper then. I would attack him, but he would put his big hand on my head and keep me at a distance from him with my arms flailing, laughing at me until I cooled off.

Girl's work! We had no sister so I had to help my mother. Drive the cattle, milk the cows, chop cabbage for the pig feed, help my mother in the meadow, all these things were not manly. But I liked being in the meadow with my mother. The saving-hay smelt nice in the sun, and my mother always brought good food in the basket, covered with a white cloth, and we ate well in the field. She would help me to turn the hay and row it and handcock it, and all the time she would be humming songs she had got from her own mother. My mother was a nice person. Secretly I was pleased to do all the lowly work, because it was for her and I felt rewarded when she smiled at me, or put her arm around me, or baked little sweet cakes with currants in them. All the same, I wanted the jump of fish, the hauling of nets, the smell of tar and guts.

I wound up my line. It was useless work. I would go home and dig a basket of potatoes for the dinner. My father and brothers would be hungry when they came in. There would be a pot of potatoes upended on the table, stealing from their jackets, and fresh boiled fish. I felt hunger thinking like that. I remember thinking coming down from the cliff that the village looked nice in the swathed sunshine. Most of the straw thatch of the houses had been renewed last year and the outside of them had been white-washed for the eyes of the summer visitors. The oats were yellowing and the after-grass of the meadows was very green. I was content to belong here.

A puff of wind coming from the sea, hit me, and I felt cold. I remember that. Why a quick cold wind on a warm day? Then it stopped and everything was the same. I caught nothing, said I, to my mother. You will never make a fisherman, she said, laughing. O, but I will! said I. I will be the best fisherman in the island. Go and get the dinner potatoes, she said, it would be more suitable for you. I remember my mother this time. She was a tall woman. Her hair was brown. Her face was coloured from the sun. There was no grey in her hair at all. Her teeth were as white as the teeth of a girl and she stood straight.

I took the basket and I went to the potato patch. This year the potatoes were good. They were big and clean and there were no worm holes riddling them, and it was the very odd one that was bad. I was careful not to cut them with the spade as I dug. My father would always joke if he came on a cut potato! Ho-ho, he would say, Colmain is bleeding the potatoes again. Never send a boy on the job of a man. This always shamed me. I had the potato-dish half full when I suddenly noticed that it was dark. My memory does not deceive me. One minute it was broad day and the next minute it was dark night. I was confused. I thought I was in a dream. But it was true. It was dark like night and there was a deep howling coming in from the sea. I was afraid. I leaned on the spade, and then I threw the spade away. I was afraid there would be lightning and I would be killed from the iron.

There was a great dark silence. I looked at my hand. In the strange light it was the colour of a crushed bilberry. Then the wind hit me. It was a terrible wind. It bowed me to the ground. And there was rain with it and then hailstones. This is true. A warm day, and then a terrible cold wind with hailstones. I had to cover my ears as I ran on account of the way they were hitting them. It was dark in the village. I could see people standing at doorways. I could hear the sound of banging doors and gates that were loosely latched. As I ran I saw people shouting at me, but there was no sound as the great wind stole it from their lips.

My mother was at the door. O, Colmain, Colmain! she cried. She rushed me in. We closed the door against the wind. It was dark in the kitchen. We looked at one another in the light of the turf fire. Her eyes were wide. We listened to the wind howling about us. We were afraid. We didn't say what we were thinking. Father and my brothers and the boat and all the other fishermen. Maybe it would be short. It wasn't short. It seemed to go on forever.

They will run before the wind, I said. I went to the wooden peg and took the oilskin hat and coat from it. Where are you going? she asked. You mustn't go out in that. I must go, I said. Down to the pier. They will be in before long. I will help them to tie off the boat. No, Colmain, she said, no, you mustn't go. I must go, Mother, I said. She tried to hold me, but I wouldn't stay. I had a job closing the door behind me against the wind. I went down to the pier that made a small bay to shelter the boats. I wasn't alone. Other people had come out too, boys and old men and a few women. At times down there, I had to cling to the rocks or I felt I might have been blown away on the wind like a straw.

We huddled at the pier. The sea was a frightening sight. It was like a boiling pot of milk mixed with black ink. My heart was low as I looked at it. Still they were stout boats. They were six-oared boats, broad-beamed. I left the pier. I heard the voices of men calling me but I paid them no attention. I crawled against the wind. I had to do this, get down on my hands and knees with the wet wind whipping me and crawl. Sometimes I found the shelter of stone walls and made a way in their shade. So I came to the place looking out at sea. I was in the cover of great grey mossgrown rocks, looking down at the shore and out at the sea. The waves were terrible. They were mounting over my head and breaking on the rocky shore with great booming explosions. They were gleaming with a sort of fairy light on them. I could see them stretching to the horizon against the black, black sky. So my stomach turned to water as I watched them and I was very afraid and I had to pray and say, O God, You made the storm, preserve my people.

What was night and what was day, I didn't know. I stayed there crouching in the shelter of the great grey rocks. I should have gone back to my mother, I know that now, but I didn't. I stayed there. I slept like the sheep would sleep under the shelter. It was the silence that brought me awake. All my limbs were cricked. They cracked as I unwound them. I was wet. The pins and needles racked me as I moved. It was dawn. I knew this by the glow from the east where the sun was burning. So the storm lasted since yesterday. It was dead now. The sky was clear enough. The wind was mild enough. I went back to the pier. There were people gathered there. I only had to look at them to know. There were no boats in. Not one of the six were in. Well, how could they be? They were in shelter. They had to be.

I ran home. The sound of the latch brought my mother's face around to me. She was on her knees. There was a difference between her face now and when I went to dig the potatoes. O, a great difference.

They will have run to shelter somewhere, I said. They will have run to shelter. She closed her lips on her teeth and shook her head and then brought up her long hands to cover her face. I got on my knees beside her. I put my arms around her.

Mother, I said, O, my mother, they will have gone to shelter. I remember this. It was the first time for me to see my mother helpless, with me, a fourteen-year-old boy trying to console her.

They didn't come back, O Pól, they didn't come back. Not alive. There were bits of boats found on the bru-fá-thír, the sea wrack.

And I myself found Tiernan. I found him on the shore where I had sheltered from the storm. He was wedged between the rocks with his face in the sand. There was seaweed in his fair hair. He seemed to be smiling. There was a blue mark on his cheek. I will never forget finding my brother, Tiernan. Sometimes, forgive me, I think it might have been better if Tiernan had stayed with my father and my brother Patrick in the sea, because when we brought him home on a board it seemed to me that the sight of him split the heart of my mother. She didn't wail, you understand, although the whole island seemed to be a lonely wail. Not she, she didn't. She brought him in and she undressed him and she washed the sea from him, and she laid him in my father's bed in the big room, and all through the waking of him and the praying of him and the burying of him, she did not cry.

I cried. There wasn't a part of the island that I didn't wet with my tears, seeking solitude, and waiting every day for the body of my father Colm, and my brother, Colm's Patrick, to come home. It was a great mercy that they never came home, for afterwards I saw many bodies coming home that had been weeks in the sea, and they were degraded by the fishes and the crabs and it would do no man good to look at them. So I thought of my father and my brother, waving like the seaweed at the bottom of the sea, waiting for the call that would raise them from the depths of the ocean, and they would be whole and entire and they could be looked upon with joy.

And my mother might have felt the same if Tiernan had not been sent home. Because the others died in a hurry, in a moment of time, tangled with nets, overborne by the great sea, but I spent three years after that watching my mother dying and it was not a good thing at all to behold.

I learned about love. I learned that love kills. I remembered my father and my mother together. To the eye there was nothing to betray the love they felt. It was a secret silent thing. It wasn't in the open for all to see. Because simple people do not behave that way. It causes us to be embarrassed when we see visitors holding hands and kissing one another in the light of the sun and under the eyes of people. The love between my father and mother was a feeling, a joke at times, a look from the eyes, sort of bantering, but it was not until he was taken away that I understood there was nothing left in life for my mother.

Not even me.

I may be truthful. This hurt me. One time only I said it to her. I said, maybe you should live for me, your last son, I said. I am sorry ever since. This was weakness. It made her cry, true enough. It released the flood of trapped tears, but it didn't do any good in the end, because her thoughts were gone away.

That's why I like to remember her the day I went home

16

to dig the potatoes and the way she looked.

Because she never looked the same again. I was over seventeen when she died. That was three years. She was a different woman. Her hair wasn't brown. Her teeth weren't white. The skin of her face wasn't brown and healthy. She did not stand straight.

This was a Monday too, queer enough, when she went. So you see what I mean about things happening to men on working days.

So, I was seventeen, and I was alone. I had no father or mother or brother or sisters.

I used to laugh a lot when I was under fourteen. I think I was a happy boy. I did funny things that boys do, and was scolded and I often felt the hand of my father on my body. He had a hard hand. It was like being hit by an oak board.

I had an empty house and six acres of land and a cow and two calves and a pig and some chickens.

But I had no people and I had no boat, and all these things happened to me on a Monday.

Tuesday

Fear can do queer things to people. Fear, they say, makes a woman of a man. I do not agree with this saying. It seems to me that women can show less fear than men at the right times. But they can coax men to be timorous. And that's a different thing. We were an island of seamen. And then we became an island of land men. All on account of personal fear and the timidity induced by the sea terror of the women. It was sad to see our island filled with fear. No boats were built. No man went to sea. The only fish we ate were the fish caught by the children fishing from the shore. We were just tillers of the soil. That was not good, because there was not enough soil. So the young men started to go away. What was there for them? There was nothing to test their courage on the sea. They could not make a living from fishing. So they went away to strange lands where they could find the challenge to living that all men must find.

Why are we here if there is no challenge? Life is useless if you can't see that.

I do not blame the women. If your husband or your brother is brought home to you on a board, or both of them, and if you have a young son who might follow in the same way you will not want him to go to sea. That's natural. They were afraid of the sea. That's natural too.

But I wasn't afraid of the sea. At this time I hated the sight of it. It seemed to be a personal enemy to me. I had no mother now where I could read fear in her eyes, or who would supplicate me to stay at home with an outstretched hand. I determined to wage war on the sea. This makes me smile now, but then I felt it deeply. It is like getting an idea to kill all the summer midges in the world one at a time, between two clapping boards. This feeling did not come over me all at once. The thought came to me when I was about eighteen years and it grew and made me restless. I hated the sight of the young men leaving. Each American wake that I attended to bid them farewell made me feel more bitter. I spoke of my idea to the old men but they just shook their heads and were silent. It was all right for them. Their working lives were over. They were going down into the twilight with their plug of tobacco and their stool at the hearth. I was determined to fight even if I had to fight on my own, as I would. There was no sea spirit left. The only thing the people felt of it now, was the crossing in the turf boat on placid days to the mainland market or travelling there to sell an animal, and buy stores. This maddened me, that a six-mile journey in a dull cow-like turf-boat should be a sea adventure for the people of our island.

The first thing I did was this. I got a stout rope and I canvas-wrapped a few yards of the end of it. Then I got my friend Tomás. We had been at school together, and played many tricks together. His father and brother had died too in the storm, but they recovered them and they were buried in the sandy graveyard near the church with a stone over them. Two other brothers were gone away. Tomás and two sisters and his mother and grandmother were left. He lived

18

so with women and they had him timorous.

I said, Tomás, come with me, I want you.

He said, Where do we go with a rope? Have you a cow in a bog-hole or fallen over the cliff.

No, I said, come with me. He came.

I led him to a lonely cove on the far side of the island. Two low cliffs stretch round on each side. The water there is always calm, like a pool. Even at low tide it is deep. You can see the sand, and the water is the colour of cats' eyes. While he watched me I took off my clothes and I tied the rope round my waist. Hold the end of this now, I said to Tomás, and then I took a straight jump and went into the sea. I did this because I was mad at the sea. I did not know how to swim. I had seen dogs swimming and summer visitors and fishes and frogs. It was a superstition that fishermen shouldn't be able to swim. I don't know why. Tempting God, they said. I didn't believe this. And I floundered around in the water splashing my arms and my legs with about thirty foot of water under me, and I was determined to swim. I read where the body is like a bottle, and your mouth is the place where the cork is. If you take out the cork the bottle will sink. If you cork the bottle it won't sink. I took big breaths and corked my bottle. And I let myself sink. And it was true. I just sank to my nose and popped up again like a bottle. Well, I let a great shout out of me, losing all the air, and I might have gone down if Tomás hadn't by this understood and took a pull on the rope. I felt joyful. I felt that I had won a battle against the sea. Thomás was laughing now, enjoying himself too, and he held the rope while I worked my arms and legs like a dog and like a frog. In three days I jumped into the pool without a rope and I could move around there at will. I'm sure I looked an ugly and awkward sight, but I was able to stay on top of the water and move around in it, and I thought I had won a great victory when I scrambled up the cliffs and leaped in again, and scrambled out and leaped in again. Why, I said to Tomás laughing, the sea is only water, and we are men. You hear that. You understand how I felt.

It took me some time, but I got Tomás to go in there too and I held the rope for him until he too was able to swim in it. So now, you see, I felt that I had doubled my victory. I stood up there naked the day he succeeded and shouted out at it: See now, here are two men that you won't find so easy to conquer. Here are two men that see you for what you are, just water, that can be whipped by the wind. We will not be easy victims.

Tomás thought I was mad, but he was pleased that I had induced him to learn how to swim.

You have an ambition in your heart and you strive for it, and you gain it. You find this is not enough. Another one grows in you. You are not satisfied with what you have gained. Now I found that my heart was crying out for a boat. I could have bought one. I had little enough money put aside, but I could have bought one. There were many lying lonely on the sands of the mainland. Fear was rotting them. I examined many of them. They were nearly all big boats that wanted repair. But I was on my own. How could I handle one of these? I did not want a canvas boat, a currach, which one man could handle if put to it, because they daren't venture far from the shore. I wanted a boat of my own, one that would grow from my own brain under my own hands. What an ambition! It is great to be young.

Down by the pier there was an old sagging shed. It was made of the stripping of tree trunks and it had a tarred roof. There was a padlock on its door. I went to the house of the Murtaghs. Only old Fionan was there. He was a very old man. He was hardly able to walk. His limbs were swollen by the damp fever. His hands were big and painful from it. I would like the key of the old shed, I said. I would be happy if you would loan it to me. He looked at me for a long time. His old blue eyes didn't look as old as himself. He spat into the fire. It was a fine long spit. He was yards from the fire. He was noted for that. Why do you want to see the shed, tell me, he asked? I will not tell you now, I said. I will look at the shed and I will tell you then. He spat again. We waited for it to hit a hot sod. The key is behind the door, he said, after his success. That door hasn't been opened since you know when. I knew. Since Fiarach and Tormey Murtagh had not come home from the sea. You must not let the wife of Fiarach see you going into that shed, he said. She will raise the roof on me and I am near death and I long for quiet. He was right and wrong. She would raise the roof but he was as far away from death as the old oak tree near the lake.

My heart was beating fast as I opened the door. I closed it after me. There was plenty of light to see by the chinks between the scantling logs and the two open windows. It was filled with cobwebs. There were still shavings on the floor. There was the beginnings of a boat clamped in the frame, with just the keel and the curved bow board fitted to it. There was quite a bit of timber. I looked at it. Thin larch boards ready for the bending. There were tools, adzes and planes and chisels, and mallets. I felt very sad. I wanted to cry. I had been in and out so often when I was young watching the Murtaghs putting the boats together. They had often let me drive the rust-proof nails. Here it was like this now and the wind whistling in it, and the cobwebs swaying and making it look desolate. I thought of Fiarach and Tormey. They had never come back. They were quiet kindly men, soft spoken, like most men who fashion wood with their hands.

I went out again. I locked the door after me. I went back to the Murtagh's house. I put back the key. Then I sat down opposite the old man. I want to make a boat, I said to him. He opened his eyes wide. You, he said. You have no skill in you. There was never a Fury that could make a coffin even out of match wood and you want to make a boat. Who else is there, I asked? Will you make a boat? He held up his hands. With these crippled things, he asked? With an old dying body bent like an S-hook? You had great skill, I said. I heard men say that there was no other like you in the whole land for shaping a boat. They said you could shape a boat like a tailor shapes a suit. It was true for them, he said, but these days are gone. They are gone like the boats I fashioned. Where are those? Driftwood on the shore, maggot-eaten pieces of washed wood, drifting here and there, making shore fires for the picnickers.

I want to make a boat to suit myself, I said. I have some money. I will pay you a fair price for the timber in the shed. I will clean the rust from the tools and I will use them, and I will pay you for the hire of them. I will also pay a rent for the shed. If you grant me all those things, I will build a boat.

He laughed. He had few teeth left in his head and I saw all of them as he laughed and the back of his ancient throat. I thank you, Colmain, he said, for making me laugh. I haven't laughed like this since before the storm. The sight of a Fury building a boat will make the cats die laughing. There won't be a cat left alive on the island. Your people could do with the money, I said. They could but they won't, he said. Can you see Fiarach's wife wishing you into the shed? No, I said. Do you like the way all the young men have fled from the sea? Cowards! Girls! Tailors! Weaklings! he shouted. His face was angry. Who actually owns the shed and the tools and the timber, I asked? He looked at me with his head on one side. I do! he said. I never abandoned my rights in them. Are you afraid of Fiarach's wife, I asked? I knew this would stir him. Is it me afraid of a woman? roared the old tyrant. It looks like that to me, I said. He fumed. May the devil water your puddings, he cursed me. Will you let me try so, for the love of God, I asked? It would be worth it, he said, to see a Fury going to sea in a tub, in a barrel, in a wooden vessel that will be the laughing stock of seven parishes. Would the sea forgive me for insulting it? It would give you cause for more laughter, I said. It might even lengthen your life. By the great God it would, he said. It will give me something to live for. Take the shed and the tools and the timber and go to. Set the angels in heaven laughing.

I was cunning. I was determined to build a boat no matter what it was like, but I thought the old craftsman's pride wouldn't let him keep away from the shed, that he might guide me. I know you, he said, but this time you are wrong. You think I'll crawl down there with my dying body and scholar you with the craft of my brain. No. You are on your own, Colmain. I will not go within spitting distance of the shed. I will not hurt the tender feelings of Fiarach's wife and Tormey's mother. Now you know. Off with you, and with the grace of God I will be dead before you injure my eyes with the sight of your invention. A Fury building a boat! He loosed a tremendous spit.

I left him, but all the same my heart was high. Hadn't I got so far?

I opened the shed to the light and I cleaned it out from its years of decay. I chased the spiders, destroyed their webs, and I cleaned the tools and ground them and freed them from their rust and I was ready to begin. I had to shorten the keel that was laid. I had in my eye a short boat with a deep keel and a strong bow with a wide stern for a rudder. And I would step a mast into it for a single sail. I knew what I wanted. But, Mother of God, how hard it was to shape it. Nobody came near the shed. They looked at me from afar. I felt I was a stranger in the midst of them. Even Tomás dodged me. It was as if I was desecrating the graves of their dead. I wanted to tell them they were wrong. I wanted to say that I felt the men who died were stirring with pleasure in the graves because a young man was trying to go to sea. It was in vain. Only one man came near me. That was the young curate.

What in the name of God are you doing, Colmain, he asked me? I was a bit angry. I am building a boat, I said loudly. He looked at me and smiled. As long as there is a bit of yourself left by the time you have finished good luck to you, he said. I had to smile myself. My hands were covered with cuts, old cuts and fresh cuts and bandaged cuts and cuts that needed to be bandaged. I even had a sore cut in my leg where the chisel slipped on me. I am going to build this damn boat, I said, if I haven't an arm or a leg left to me. Good man, he said. When you have finished, I will bless

23

it for you. If we both live that long, I said. He laughed with me and he went away but I felt encouraged and I set to, trying to get the ribs into the right shape.

After that things improved a bit. Tomás came to watch me. He laughed at me, but he held a board for me. I became a joke with the people. They laughed at the idea of Colmain building a boat. I preferred them to be laughing at me, than feeling that I was trying to hurt them.

Fionan held out a long time. I had my heart set on him, of course. But one day I looked up from my sweat and my frustration and he was there, as crooked as a thorn tree, as cantankerous as an old bull.

He looked at heaven, of course, and he walked around the thing I was shaping. What is it supposed to be, he wondered? Is it a cow stall, or maybe it is a pig's trough or is it a sort of a rat trap or is it a common cart for a donkey or what is it, whatever it is don't for the love of the great God who gives talents to all men tell me that it is supposed to be a real boat that can be launched on the waters? He hit out at all the ribs with his stick. He splintered some of them. He destroyed weeks of my work in a few minutes, and for a few seconds red rage boiled in me and I might have hit him with the mallet, but I didn't. I kept silence. So, raging he went on, you have to do this here and that there and what was I thinking of? I shouted at him too and told him the boat of my dreams. He derided it, laughed at it, scorned it, but he pointed things out to me. He wouldn't have any part in building a monster, but for the sake of the name of the community and the sacred art of boat building, do this and do that and do the other.

Really he built the boat. I was just the hands. But it was my boat. I had conceived it, and he knew it was my boat. He knew the opposition I had to fight to get it to even the wretched state it was. And every shaving off a board was done by me, and every nail driven. All, all of it was mine. The dream and the reality, but its shape was his. It had to be, so that afterwards men would look at it puzzled and say: Well, it's truly odd, but it is a Murtagh boat. So I finished her and I pared the mast and I fitted the ropes and the blocks and I sewed the sail.

This was my boat, and I was going to sail the sea in her.

I was very impatient. I would listen to nobody. She was caulked and tarred and she was ready for the sea, so I ran her down the slope and I held my breath as she went into the water. Did I expect her to sink? She didn't. She rode on the water like a bird. I stepped in the mast and locked it with the iron bolt when I had tied her to the pier. I stowed the narrow-bladed paddles, and then just for satisfaction, I fitted the sail and hoisted it. She was like a young horse tugging at the bit. There were a few people watching me. This may have led me to display pride. Tomás was up on the pier.

Cast off the rope, said I to him.

You are not going to go out in that! he protested. It was February. There was a gusty wind sweeping the water outside. I wish he had not said that. If he hadn't said it I might not have gone. If Fionan was there I might have been subdued by his scornful silence. But I was challenged and I was young so I shouted at him: Cast off the rope. Some of the people there protested. I just called: Now! Now! Tomás! so he reluctantly cast off the rope and I steered her into the sea. Ow! The way the wind took her and bowed the mast to the waves. I was sorry now I had done it. I didn't realize the wind was so strong. She was travelling sideways to it, the mast was screaming in its new step. If I went as I was going I would be over at the mainland in short time, so I shortened the rope and turned her into the wind. She came about right well. I was proud of her. She faced into the waves and headed out into the open sea, taking the beating from the waves on her broad breast. I was wet from head to foot. I could see mistily the people running down to the pier. I was full of pride. Here I was displaying to them that there was no need to be afraid of the sea. Here was one young man in one small boat who wasn't afraid of the sea. I heard voices calling over the sound of the wind. I had no

25

time to pay heed to them, because after all I didn't know enough about what I was at.

I had never sailed before. Except in a makeshift sail that one puts on a currach in a soft wind. All the rest was only dreams. My father's boat was a rowing boat. Six oars. It never carried a sail because they never went more than ten miles into the sea. I had never known what power a piece of canvas running on a rope tied to a mast could acquire in a strong wind.

I was being edged over towards the far mainland where the water was being thrown in white spray over the black rocks. So I would have to tack. This is easy if you know how to do it. I had never done it. Also there was no ballast in the boat to keep her steady. I had meant to line the bottom neatly with limestone blocks as I had seen done. But I had to do something, so I leaned on the rudder and when the sail loosened I shortened and tightened and the small boom swung over my head, the wind took the sail and stretched it, nearly breaking my arm with the strain it put on the rope and then she was bounding to the island, being battered and groaning, I thought. I had a terrible job to bring her a bit more into the wind. Another thing I didn't know, but should have known, was the sort of whirlwind water made out here, by the racing tide clashing with the rebuffed waves that were sent back from the land. It was a terrible test to put an untried boat to, and I realized that I was destroying everything from a few minutes of pride, because she couldn't last it. Something would have to go.

The sail went. It tattered. As if it had been cut with a thousand razors. O, my new sail! O, my lovely boat! Only good thing. I realized that I was a fool, and a stupid fool. I would not mind being a fool, but I felt sad that I had been stupid. I leaned on the rudder and the wind swung her about and the waves took her and tossed her with great joy. Oh, you fool, you fool! I decried myself knowing that I had earned it. She was taking a beating, with great waves going one way and smaller ones coming from the other direction. The island seemed to be coming to meet me at great speed. Now, what have you proved? I could see the people running along the tall shore of the island. Small black figures running to watch my destruction. They would say: We told you so, stupid fool! They would be right according as their eyes showed them, but they would be wrong and I could have proved them wrong. I didn't even wait to get the priest to shake holy water on the boat with tied feathers. I had to be away.

No use reaching for the paddles. The moment I let go the rudder the boat and I were lost.

I remember thinking: There is no one to bewail me, before the white water reached its arms for us and enveloped myself and the poor boat and we disappeared in its embrace.

So I could swim. Now I realized if you could swim a hundred times over, it would be no use.

I was at rest.

I opened my eyes.

I was still sitting in the boat with my arms wrapped around the rudder. The boat was still. The mast was canted. I felt the sea spray drenching me from behind. But I rose to my feet. The boat was at rest. She had been raised and tossed like you would hurl a stone in a throwing competition, from the angry water, over a belt of rocks and now she was canted on a beach of sand under a short cliff. I got out of her. I felt my feet on the sand. I walked around her in the narrow space. I probed her with my fingers. She was sound. In one place the tar of her was scraped away exposing the bare wood. But that was all. She was intact.

I looked out at the sea. It didn't want us. Scornfully, it had thrown us back, like a dead fish on the shore, food for the gulls. But I was thankful. We shouldn't have been there but we were.

Heads popped over the cliff above us, looking down at us. I waved at them. They were too amazed to wave back. I knew what they had expected to see. Not what they saw now. I was bemused, but I thought that the pride was knocked away from me. I didn't think, young and all as I was, that I would do a thing like that on the spur of the moment ever again. It wouldn't be a lot of trouble to get the boat away in the low tide. It would be a great pleasure for me to make a new sail.

This was on a Tuesday. I know this for sure. Because it was the feast of St Brigid, and that was why afterwards that was the name of my boat. I didn't deserve it, but we were preserved on a Tuesday.

Wednesday

I had a boat. I could fish. It wasn't long I was in getting to know the handling of her. She was a good boat, but she was too small to venture far. I wanted a bigger boat. But for that I would need a partner. I needed Tomás, but it was taking time to unshackle him from his unnatural fear of the sea and the gloomy cries of the womenfolk.

I wanted a wife. This was natural. I hadn't much success with the island girls. I wasn't ugly, you understand. I was big and strong and all my parts were put together favourably enough, but since I was so devout about boats and the sea, they were inclined to treat me as someone not normal minded, so there was a barrier between us. I could dance at weddings or feasts, and I could gobble a song with effect. I could play no music on any instrument, but that was no baulk as very few men are gifted that way. I went with girls, evenings on the shore in the light of the moon, or leaning against gable-ends in the dark of the moon, our faces lighted only by the glow of a cigarette tip. It was pleasant enough, but it was not vital. I knew the feel of soft lips on my mouth, the soft underarm skin of a girl beneath my coarse fingers. I knew this was not enough. There was never a great surging of the heart, or the knocking of the blood in your pulses, or deep soul knowledge, like I thought you would feel, if she was the one meant.

I didn't want to end up a bachelor either. Why would I? I wanted a woman so that we could reveal ourselves to one another, bit by bit over the years. I wanted to belong to somebody, who would worry about me, and be heart-broken if I died. I wanted to have a son, because this is the nearest that man ever approaches God in an act of creation. And, also, my son would be a fisherman! That was certain. Since I had nobody else to become a fisherman, I would have to make him. This is easier said than it is done, of course. Where was she? How would I find her? Was she there at all? Well, things happen in the strangest ways.

I had a young bull calf. I couldn't keep him. The summer before had been very dry and the hay fields were poor. They were thin, so winter feeding was restricted, and what I had I wanted for the cow and the lean pig I depended on to pay the rates and taxes. So the calf had to go. He was sturdy, red he was, with a white face. I was sorry to part with him but what could I do? This Wednesday was a market day over on the mainland, so I captured him after a bit of a chase, stalled him, roped him and brought him down to the boat. I tied his legs and stowed him in there and set out for the mainland.

It was a bright morning. The sun was shining. I re-member this day. It was a happy one. The small waves were tapping a tune on the boards of the boat. Calves have big eyes. This calf was looking at me with great sadness, I thought. Because I had taken him from his mother. You'd think he knew I was going to get rid of him. Feeling for animals, of course, is only softness, else how could we be turning around and eating them. But when you live alone like I did, animals can become companions. You look at a herd of cattle. They all look alike to you. They are not. They are odd creatures, and not one of them is the same as the next one. They can be like people in the way one is cranky and another is good-tempered and another is affec-tionate. Some are bright, some are stupid, and some have great intelligence. You would be making a mistake if you think they are all alike. This calf and I got on well together. He was a spirited animal and he constantly set up contests between us. I had to fight to make him eat, fight to get him out of the stable, fight to get him into the stable. He was a challenger, and he was to be that way to the end.

There was a good crowd at the market. Harvesting was nearly over and people had leisure. I tied off the boat at the pier and I carried my calf up the steps. He struggled a lot even while I was doing this. I had a job with him. Finally I got him down and tied a rope around his neck. He pulled hard at this until I tightened it and he had to stop or choke himself. Now, I said, we can take you to the market. We made our way through the people. I greeted those who greeted me. Not many people I knew. There was everything at the market except fish. That showed you how low we had fallen. The only fish was a barrel of salted herrings outside the post office shop. I asked. Even that had to be brought from somewhere far away. I ask you, would you believe that? It had been a long time since I was over before and the smell of fresh porter coming from the crowded pub tempted me. I captured a little boy. Hold the calf for me, son, I said, until I get a pint and I will give you three pennies. Four pennies, and a currant biscuit, he said, and I'm your man. Your father is a trader, I said. All right. I gave him the rope and went into the pub. It was crowded. Loud voices. I went to the counter and I called for a pint. I liked the smell of the pub. Porter and spices and new leather. The drink tasted good, but I wasn't fated to finish it. I heard the boy calling. He was outside the window, making faces, pointing. I left and went out to him.

The calf is gone, he said, the devil pucked me in the belly and knocked me and off with him like a greyhound. What way? I asked. I looked. There was a bit of confusion towards the top of the town in the mass of people. I set off in that direction. Hey, said the boy, he hurt me belly, I want to be compensated. I'll compensate you by hurting your backside, I said. You failed in the work. I'll tell me father on you, he said, and he'll eat you. I had to laugh. I threw him a penny and set off after my calf.

He had got to the calf market and in among the calves and when he saw me coming he set off at a run, and what happens but all the other calves, about twenty of them, follow him. Well, the place was in great confusion then with everyone chasing his own calf. Up the street and around the back of the street, racing through bonhams, upsetting potato bags, much cursing and laughing as they all ran to capture their own calves, and my fellow was a quarter mile up the road and going like a race horse on the sands before I spotted him and set out after him. Approaching people tried to turn him back so he took to the fields. They were small fields separated by stone walls. He jumped the walls and I had to jump the walls. Now and then I nearly had him cornered in a field but he'd get away from me. I soft-talked him and coaxed him and cursed him and I must have been as red in the face from the running as a sunset. The last place I tripped over a stone and fell flat on my face. I'd nearly swear the calf turned and laughed at me. Anyway, there was laughter, so I looked up and there was this girl leaning over the wall of the road. She was enjoying the sight of me spread in the field.

I was angry at this time. It's easy to amuse the simple minded, I said. You should be in a circus, Colmain of the Boat, she said. You would be a great clown. People would pay fortunes to see you chasing calves. And she laughed again. I was interested that she knew my name. I didn't know her to see. She had brown hair and because she was laughing I could see the white of her teeth. If you can afford to laugh at misfortune, I said, why don't you try and get the calf? I will do just that, she said, and she hopped over the wall as light as a feather and she approached that calf saying Suck-suck-suck, and kill me if the damn calf didn't wait for her, while she scratched his ears and got a grip on the trailing rope. Is there anything else you want me to do for you, she asked? I sat there on the grass. I had to laugh. She was smiling at me. Now all you have to do is to buy the calf, I said. I will do just that, she said. How much do you want for him? Are you mad, I asked? She considered this. I don't think so, she said. I was sent to the market to buy a calf. Name a price!

I named a price two pounds over what I thought he was

worth. My God, she said, has he diamonds in his belly or what? Is he a magic calf? Is his hoof made of gold plate? She made me laugh. She was like a jobber. I'll give you so much, she said. I forget now, naming a sum a pound under his worth. A sum like that would put you in the poorhouse, I said. Are you sure you can afford it? He is not a cast-off calf. He's not going to die tomorrow morning. Hold out your hand, she said. I held it out. She held out her own hand. She spat on it, rubbed it on her dress, and then hit my hand with a great smack. I'll give you so much, she said, naming his value. Done, I said and I closed my hand on hers. It's a time ago now, but I still remember that. My hand was much bigger than hers. It was the first time I had held anything so alive. I looked down at our hands and then I looked up at her. I am sure the same wonder was in her eyes as was in mine. Like that it happened. A drumming in my ears that shut off all other sound. Her face looked suddenly serious as I'm sure my own did. She had firm eyes. I don't know how long this period of time lasted, but in a way it was for ever. It would go on. One of us had to speak. I did. I was kind of hoarse. I had to clear my throat. How did you know my name? I asked her. I have seen you before, she said. Men have talked about you and your madness. They put Boat in as your middle name, Colmain Boat Fury. I see, I said, and what do they call you? I am Catriona O'Flaherty, she said.

Your name should only be spoken by saints, I said. Wasn't that a terrible thing to say? She looked at me. Her whole face broke up into a million laughter wrinkles. Now I know they were right, she said. You are mad. And both of us laughed senselessly there, she kneeling on the grass, and I sitting on it. Then we stopped. We said nothing for some time. I said, Are you still going to the market? No, she said, since I bought the calf. I must pay you. She dug a purse from the pocket of her dress and she counted the money into my hand. She took a long time over this and I was glad. I handed her back two half-crowns. What for, she asked? That is a luck-penny, I said. I will be pleased if you will buy a ribbon for your hair. She thought over this. I will, she said, then. What colour ribbon will I buy? Let it be blue, I said, like the colour of the sky today. I wasn't forward enough to say it was the colour of her eyes.

I said, I'd like to know what kind of a home my calf is getting so will I walk with you to your house and gauge it? She laughed at me again. Yes, she said, I think you should do that. You might not be able to sleep tonight if you didn't know.

We walked that calf three miles to her home. It was built in snugly near the sea. They were a big family. Catriona was the eldest. The others ranged down to six months, a baby in a cradle. Her mother was nice. She fed me. We laughed a lot. Her father was a tall man. Murtagh O'Flaherty. He had a lot of laughter wrinkles. He was a trickster. I think they liked me. I'm fond of children. I got on well with the young ones. It was a boon to see a house so filled with family after my own and many other raped ones I knew. I was very happy. I knew that as long as I was aware that Catriona was alive, I would be happy if we were a thousand miles apart. Just as long as I knew she was in the world. That's all.

It was late when we went back to my boat. She came with me. Mark that. And something else. I said, Are you afraid of the sea, then? She said, Yes. That was a sensible answer. But I wouldn't be afraid of the sea with you, she said, and you know what, she came out in the boat with me. There was enough light to see by, a fresh wind, and she wasn't afraid. You recognize all the questions that answers. Woman in a boat, bad omen, they say. Silly superstitions. I knew. I left her back on the pier and I crossed the sea speaking her name. You see! That is how it happened, but nothing is gained with ease. How can it be? without a struggle, and my struggle came about on account of the fact that Catriona's father was a trickster.

It happened like this.

In the village where they lived there was a young man named Paro MacDonagh. He was a very big young man with great limbs and a small brain. He was slow at school, but he was possessed of terrible strength. He became attached to Catriona's father, who was always kind to him. He had a purpose in this even if he didn't know it. Paro could get through a lot of work, and Murtagh's place was big and he ran a lobster boat, so Paro could be a great help to him in his free time. From way back, when he was helped, Murtagh would say to him, God bless you, Paro, and when you are a man I will give you my eldest daughter. This was only a joke you see, but Paro took it seriously and in order, as he thought, to retain his assistance Murtagh would keep him excited by saying such things as, She might have a feeling for you, Paro. I saw her looking after you today. He would pretend to convey messages from Paro to Catriona. This kept him amused and his invention was lively. It is a dangerous thing to play on the minds of simple men.

One Sunday evening I was going down to my boat by the pier. I noticed two men standing in the gloaming outside the pub but I didn't pay much attention to them, even when they followed me. I was going down the steps, when I heard Paro calling my name, Colmain Boat, he was shouting, stop there. I waited for him. He came close to me. He was very big. I had to look up at him and I'm not a dwarf. I said, It's a grand night, thank God, Paro, and what do you want of me? He bent down to me. He had big white teeth, that shoved out his lip. There was a smell of porter from him. You, you, he said, you do not see Catriona again. You hear that, Colmain Boat, she is for me. I am promised her of her father. The thought of Catriona, with all her fun and brightness with Paro seemed funny to me. I thought he was joking. I laughed. His big hand came down on my shoulder. It was a great weight. It bowed me. Do not laugh, he said. She has been promised to me since she was knee high. Her own father. You must not take her from me. I lost my temper. Put a hand on me again Paro, I said, and I'll break your face. Be easy, Fury, said the other one, a short butty man named Moran. Paro has the right of it. I heard her

34

father with my own ears. I didn't like Moran. I thought he was backing Paro for what he could get out of him. From what I heard he was that sort of man. You mind your own business, Moran, I said, for from what I hear it can do with minding. Listen to me! Listen to me! said Paro pounding my shoulder again. Don't do that, Paro, I shouted or you'll madden me. I warned you, he said.

Look, I said. Man is free. The girl is free. You tell me the girl wants you for a husband, and I'll never lay a track on the mainland again. That's all. When she tells you that, come and tell me. He was clenching his fists. Don't come back, Colmain, he said. Don't come back, or I'll stop you. Don't make me stop you, Paro, I said, when the drink drains out of you, then you will get sense. I will be back here next Wednesday which is a feast day and you will be sober then and we can talk together. I went down the steps. He stood on the steps looking down at me. I told you! I told you! he shouted. It was good until you came. Stay on your island, Colmain. I tell you to stay on your island. You are a person without softness or pity, Fury, Moran shouted at me. They stayed there standing on the pier until me and my boat were out of their sight.

Now this could make you laugh. I didn't know about the way Murtagh had been working Paro. I thought it was just a drunken whimsey with him, at the time. I was a little upset, in case he might do anything to Catriona, you understand. But I thought that if he and I could talk and he in his sober senses, that the thing would be eased away. There is always antagonism between island people and mainland people. One side thinks they are better than the other, more civilized, or less civilized. I don't know why this should be, but it is true and many notable fights had occurred when the islanders visited the mainland and drank a little too much. I had never been in fights myself because my nature is quiet except at times, and I was always able to talk my way out of fighting. I had a nimble brain.

So I wasn't too worried crossing to the mainland on the Wednesday night of the feast day. I didn't understand what

35

was going on, but knowing a little more now about Murtagh, I kind of guessed the trickery he had been up to, and big men like Paro are children. You talk to them quiet and slowly and they understand. Even if I had to expose Murtagh I would do so, because he is the sort of man who would talk himself out of Daniel's den. I thought the village was very quiet for a feast day. This should have warned me. It was still a bright night, summer time again. The sun was gone down but there was plenty of light in the sky. So anyone who wanted could have seen me setting out in my boat from the island. It was that sort of fine clear weather. I was thinking of Catriona. You get a book to read. The writer is skilful. He introduces the people to you and bit by bit added to her. She was who I wanted forever. Hard to discloses more and more of them to your understanding. This was such with me. I got to know her, and truly each bit added to her. She was who I wanted forever. Hard to say this. They loved her at home. She was the corner piece of the lot of them. I knew that. It would be a terrible wrench to take her from them. They were holding on to her with might. The thought of her being taken away to live on the island desolated them. They were mainland people. So I said nothing, you see. Each time I went determined to talk, but the talk left me. Sometimes I despaired that maybe I was wrong after all, and she wouldn't want to come to the island. Love is not easy when you think of other people.

A bend in the road. On one side it rose to a great rock towering in the sky. The road skipped around it. Here it was that I felt the blow on the head. It nearly took my senses from me. I fell on my hands and the stone that hit me fell with me. I heard the sound and twisted and the boot that was coming for me kicked the stone that had wounded me. I saw the boot coming again and I got to my knees and backed up against the great stone. They were facing me, panting, Moran and Paro. I knew from the look of Paro that he was drunk. A quiet sober man would never hit another on the head with a stone. There was blood on my face I knew, but my reason was coming back to me, and anger.

Paro was shouting. He came in to me with his hands out. Moran was skipping about. How will I handle two of them, I thought. Told you, told you, told you, Paro was shouting as he came to me. When he was close I dodged under his arm and ran to Moran. Moran had a rock in his hand. I was wearing my Sunday boots, not my pampooties. As Moran swung his arm I kicked him on the knee. He screamed like a female and sat in the dust, holding his leg. I was barely in time. Paro hit me. I went flying into the dust. It was like being kicked by a horse. I couldn't stay in the dust. He aimed at me again and I ducked and as he staggered past I hit him with a clenched fist on the back of the neck. It sent him farther. But he didn't fall. I should have run away. I couldn't do it. I waited for him to turn. I was trying to get my breath. When he came for me again, I hit him in the mouth. His protruding teeth cut my knuckles, but then he caught hold of the front of me with one hand and pounded at me with the other. I hit him wherever I could, in the throat and in the stomach, but I might as well have been hitting a haystack. Water will wear a stone. Paro's hand was pounding me to death. He had no aim, just to pound. To me he might have been using a sledge hammer. I remember he put both his arms around me and started to squeeze me. My breath was short. I could hear my ribs creaking. I put my hands under his jaw to squeeze back his neck and I put a foot around him and tripped him, but we fell wrong. He fell on me instead of the other way. That was the end of me. I could only lay there with his drink-laden breath in my face while his fist rose and fell, killing me, dimming my senses.

I heard her voice calling, Paro, stop it! Stop it! Stop it! I groaned then. I thought, Oh God, I'll never live this down. The blows stopped falling on me and the weight lifted off me, but I seemed to be paralysed. What I was thinking, I should have done this, I should have done that. If I hadn't been hit with the stone, I would have done this and I would have done that. Are you all right, Colmain? Colmain, are you all right? All right. I sat up, holding my head. Why

Paro, why, who set you on to it? Tell me Paro, why did you do it? Paro was sitting there too. He came for you, he said. Why wouldn't he come for me. I am his, said Catriona. No, no, your father from long ago said it so. You were thinking of me until he came. No, Paro, never, never, my father was fooling you. Do you hear. No, no, said Paro. I swear to you, she said, he was fooling you. Colmain is for me. He alone. You hear that, Paro? He is the only one in the world. Oh, no, no, it's not true. Yes, it is true. Use your senses, Paro. Why did your father say that to me. Why did he say that to me, then? Did I ever look at you, talk to you as if I favoured you? No, just that he said, you were for me. Her voice was hard. You get up and go to Murtagh, Paro. You go and ask my father why he was lying to you, Paro. You go and ask my father. Colmain is my man, for ever and ever. You hear? I hear, he said, O, I hear. I got to my feet. I leaned against the big rock. She was holding my bloodied hand. Are you all right, Colmain? Are you all right?

I couldn't help looking at Paro. He was sitting there in the dust and tears were running down his face. This is true. Of course he had been drinking. All the same. Tears were running from his eyes, and his mouth was splayed in anguish, like a child from whom a precious toy is taken. Moran was sitting on the wall at the side of the road, groaning and rubbing his knee.

Go on home, Paro, said Catriona. My father is at home. Go and talk to my father. Paro heaved himself up from the dust. I will go and talk to him, said Paro. Make him explain it all, said Catriona. I will ask him, said Paro. You have no feeling for me at all? You are a neighbour, said Catriona. You are not even my friend now. You have done what you have done. What madness got into you? Paro stood there, his hands long by his sides. He shook his head. He bent and picked his cap up from the road. He rubbed it across his eyes. I always thought. I always thought, he said. I did not hit you with the stone, Colmain Boat, he said. It was Moran used the stone. I would not use a stone. I would not use a

38

fist if I had known. It is not right. It is not right to put false dreams into the hearts of men, is it, Catriona? No, said Catriona. Tell your father then, that I will walk with him no more, said Paro. It is not right. He walked away, a big man with his shoulders sloping. I was still thinking of what I should have done. But there was Moran. I went over to him. You are on your own now, Moran man, I said. Stand up and take what is coming to you. No! No! said Moran. No! No! said Catriona. You kicked me, said Moran. You kicked me. He started to hobble away. If she hadn't held my arm I would have kicked him again. He wasn't a good man, this Moran. We watched him away.

It was God sent you, I said. I think he would have killed me.

I was uneasy, she said. My father thought of Paro as a joke. It is no joke, I said. I nearly died for his sense of humour. How soon can we be married, Colmain, she asked. That hurt my sore ribs. Three weeks from today, Catriona, I said. I owe nothing more to my father, she said. We will be married in three weeks. If only I wasn't so battered, I would dance in the dust, I said. You are sure, Catriona, you are sure. I have not so much when all is told.

I knew the day of the calf, she said, that you had more than enough for me. I laughed, and I hurt my head, but my heart was big and as she swabbed my wounds with a wetted cloth and I smelled the honey of her nearness, my life was filled, for I was no longer alone, and that's what I want to say, we were married on a Wednesday.

Thursday

I am aware that people like myself are not supposed to know beauty. I don't mean the beauty of nature, but the beauty of living. They are both bound together. People don't think of this when they come to see a countryman living in his own surroundings. Do you think a man who sells sweets knows all that goes to the making of them? They say, Well he lives in the middle of it, how then can he see it? They know that he has not had a chance to educate himself fully, being so far from all schools and universities except the prime school that teaches him to read and write and add up his simple sums. I have heard educated people when I was present pointing out to one another the beauty of a sunset, or the tracery of a cloud, or a rainbow made by the moon in showery evening weather, or a boat on a summer sea. I have been there and they speak as if I was not present. This is a mistake.

Life is a real book, you see. Once I took a man fishing. He was a professor from one of the big places. He talked philosophy to me. He had spent many years learning what he knew. He knew a lot. Yet, I could understand him. Does this seem strange? Many of the people around me could understand him. Does this surprise you? It didn't surprise him. He said, You must not wonder at your own understanding, because you live the books which people like me write. These books just put into printed words the life of men, their reason and their understanding. All men are basically the same no matter what colour they are and yet they are all different. I'm just trying honestly to tell you about myself.

I knew beauty. I saw the purple on the hills in the evening time, and stopped to stare at it. I recognized a coloured sky when the clouds are low on the horizon and the heavens are really a vault pitted with uncountable stars. I knew the feeling of eternity the day I really realized that I was fishing on water that was attached to a round planet, twirling and spinning, that my body was tied to the earth by a certain law, and that if I could fall free from the earth, I would be falling and falling in unending space for ever and for ever. So I knew eternity and I could recognize it.

I knew creation because I lived by it. The beauty of a newborn thing. A blade of green grass after the winter frosts. The first little leaf of the wild woodbine, the blossoms on the blackthorn, the oatfield with its layer of green, the first push of the potato leaf, all these I recognized with satisfaction, but because they meant food and shelter and a harvest in the end doesn't mean that I didn't see the beauty of them because they would prove useful. I saw the beauty of birth in all the animals. I felt moved by the birth of a healthy calf, not because I could later on sell this calf, but because birth is a beautiful thing and because it stirs a feeling in the heart of man that cannot be put into words.

So how much more can a man recognize beauty in human beings. I saw the small fingernails of a week-old baby and they meant wonder to me and all the other beautiful things in life seemed to me to be part of the little baby's fingernails. This was not my own baby, as you will see, but it will let you imagine how I would feel, when I would see a baby of my own that belonged to Catriona and me. I thought of this, and it seemed to me that the sight of my own baby would be the climax and reason for all the beauty in the whole world. This was a mad dream, but when you are at sea on your own, waiting for the nets to drift and fill, you have time for dreams. I would see the great mountains at the end of the troubled sea, rearing their great tops inland, and I would think, These are my baby. Glittering lakes, leaping fish, autumn heather, heat after cold, sparkling water, wild geese flying, frost cracking, snow on the hills, millions of cobwebs gleaming like diamonds in a morning of heavy dew. All these would be my baby, my son.

I can talk of these things because they are just between you and me, Pól, and you must know of them because you are a father and you know and observe beauty and God knows, you can put them into words so much better than I, because you have the gift. I will tell you this. There is no use looking and admiring beauty, unless you see what is behind it. Any man will become bored looking at beautiful things if he is just looking at them for themselves. In themselves they are poor things. It is in what they are a reflection of that their true beauty lies. You see a reflection of a wood and a mountain in a still pool. That is good. But look beyond the reflection at the real thing and the reflection pales in your eyes.

I will tell you about Catriona. It is hard to talk about her, but I will try to, because unless you know about her, you won't know much about me. Maybe I make things bigger than they are, but you will allow for this because your feet are on the ground. I was deprived and then I was filled. I had an empty house and then it was filled. It's a poor thing for a man to grow food to feed himself. He just eats to fill a gap. There is no purpose in it. A man like me is not living if he is on his own. I didn't understand this properly until Catriona came to me! That house! I mean the change in it. The ghosts of the dead who had peopled it left. How could I see the stricken face of my mother in the kitchen any longer when I knew Catriona would be there smiling at me when I came from the fields or the fishing? For a long time I went around in a state of wonder, like a half-wit, indeed. The whole place changed under her hand. Not a day passed but there wasn't a change in it. New bits of furniture and curtains on the windows and paint and whitewash, and proper delf instead of the cracked mug I used, and proper utensils. I think I lived my eating life out of one black pot that fried and stewed and baked. You will understand my wonder. I had been alone so long, eating anything, cooking it anyway. I realize now that I didn't keep the place very clean. It was something to be ordered, you see, to be made to set to and do up the stables and give them a neat appearance, and hang a gate.

All this you know yourself, I am sure. I didn't know such existed and I went about with my feet walking inches over the earth for a long time. Men in our island don't be seen much with their wives. Little enough when they are courting them and it is sort of necessary to pretend that you have no interest in them. At Mass on Sundays the women kneel one side and the men on the other. The notion of just going for a walk with your wife in free time would be so staggering that a man could hardly recover from it. I don't know why. Maybe it's to show that a man is a man and a woman is a woman and you only married her in order to have a cook and somebody (anybody would do) to breed for you. This is not true of course, and I'm afraid I broke the rules so the people regarded me as being woman-ridden, and shook their heads over my behaviour and said I would come to no good, and that Catriona wore the trousers and what could you expect from one from the mainland. Because we walked together, by the lake shore and the cliffs and we gathered sea-surf food by the shore and we ate boiled cockles and mussels and periwinkles and even bairneacs which I liked but she could not abide. Once I even took her fishing with me. This was a source of awe, and most of the people were waiting on the shore that evening to see if I would come home at all, and Tomás told me much later, that he had gone to the church and lighted a candle to a saint for my safe return, flying in the face of Providence like that.

I'm trying to tell you that I was in a state of complete happiness with Catriona. I enjoyed every moment of it, every second, seeing her smile and feeling her welcome even before I went in the door. I thought of her wonder in the potato field and in the meadows and the oatfields. At sea. You know her now, much later, but I think you can see what she meant to me then. I was holding on tightly to this happiness, because reason told me that it could not last. We are not set here for pure lasting happiness. That is not the way life is meant to be. I must have known this deep inside me all the time, and that is why I made so much of it.

She did not even feel at home when we visited her people on the mainland. She had become part of the island. She was Murtagh's favourite daughter and he missed her much, and I think he was inclined to blame me for his loss of Paro. Because he lost him. He talked him out of his fit over Catriona. He even promised to give him his second daughter, but it was no good. Paro walked with Murtagh no more. Sometimes we passed him on the mainland, and I must admit that I felt cold shivers up my spine when I turned my back on him. But he never tackled me again and our visits to the mainland became only visits of necessity. This pleased us, because we were together and uninterrupted and it is always a source of discomfort to go back to the nest from which you have torn yourself away.

So you can imagine our joy then, when we knew that we were going to have a son. It would have to be a son, I wished for one so greatly. It set my imagination on fire, I can tell you. I had him fishing with me in a new big boat with a big sail and double paddles and our voyages expanded nearly as far as Greenland in my imagination. O, I imagined him well and truly before he arrived. I cannot tell you of my heart and its choking when I could feel the kicking of him under my hand in Catriona's body. I do not have to tell you this. You know. Any man of worth will know.

The nearest I could get Tomás to the sea was in the boat shed. I saw he had a knack with his hands, and with great cunning and manœuvre I got Fionan to direct him. He was far more skilful than myself. He could use the plane with more neatness. He had an instinct for timber, you see. Under Fionan I set him to building a bigger boat. It was done in fits and starts. When I made a few shillings here and there I would buy a few boards, or a few copper nails. Fionan said that Noah built the ark quicker than Tomás was going to build this boat. Tomás hadn't the hold on his tongue that I had and he would let Fionan get under his skin and answer him back. This pleased Fionan.

It was an April evening. April is a soft month, gentle and kind. It pleases nearly everybody. But there is no rule to say that it must always be so. This evening it wasn't. The shed was shuddering under the blows of a south-westerly gale. The raindrops were like gimlets trying to pierce the roof. It was too warm for the season. But it was snug enough in the shed with a storm lantern swinging from the roof. Fionan was sitting on a box directing Tomás who was shaping the bow ribs. I was at a bench planing a board which Tomás had shaped. I remember this interlude well. It was very peaceful. I had been working late in the fields. I had done all the chores. I had had my meal with Catriona. I was conscious of all this in my background. I claimed Catriona looked well the way she was, with added flesh on her face.

44

She bemoaned it. I said, you look well with it. You are not like a rake. She said, Then did I look like a rake before, is that what you mean? I said no, you were a pretty rake. We had laughed over this. I was conscious of this in my life as I planed the board.

Fionan was saying, Are you shaping a wren's nest, or what? What the hell do you mean, asks Tomás. You'll have to put a bend in it, said Fionan. I keep telling you that. That's the way you'd shape a three-legged pot. There is a bend in it, said Tomás. There's a bend in your eye, if there is, said Fionan, come around here and look at it. Put the measuring rod on it. Why don't you go home and go to bed? Tomás shouted at him. Oul fellows like you should be in bed hours ago. If you want to built a boat and not a barn, said Fionan, you will let me guide you. You can guide me, cried Tomás, but is there any need to torture me? You are worse than a nagging woman, Fionan, go home and go to bed.

Come over here, Fury, said Fionan, and cast your eye on this rib. It's not him that's building the boat, it's me, Tomás claimed. Look along it, Fury, said Fionan. I did so. It has a bulge like the breast of a goose, I said. See said Tomás, what did I tell you. A goose can swim, can't he. Hasn't a goose the proper shape for the water. That's not the shape of a goose breast, said Fionan, unless the animal has dropsy. See the way it dips like the belly of a porter barrel. Come and look at it, Tomás. Oh, damn you, Fionan, said Tomás. He came around and hunched and closed an eye to look at it. There's nothing wrong with that rib, he said, it'll cleave the water like an ocean liner. A liner going to the bottom, said Fionan. Maybe it droops a little bit, admitted Tomás, but it's not that bad. I would have taken in the droop with the laterals. Hah-ha, said Fionan, in triumph, it'll be long until you have the true eye of the boat builder.

I heard a girl's voice calling me from the door. I turned. It was a neighbour's child Máire Fearty. I said, Yes, yes, Máire, what ails you and why are you out in the rain? She had a small shawl around her head and the rain drops were thick on her face. Mother said you must come home, Colmain, she said. She sent me for you to come home and be quick, she said.

My heart dropped. My mouth dried. I couldn't answer her. Mrs Fearty was the midwife, you see. We had no doctor. He came if we made a signal to the mainland. I ran out of the shed. The rain was very heavy. The wind nearly knocked me off my feet. I stumbled once and my hand sank in the wet mud. I wiped it off my clothes as I ran. I felt too young. I felt helpless. I wanted to go to my house and yet I wanted to run away from it. I opened the door. Some of the neighbour women were in the kitchen. I didn't like the way they looked at me. They said nothing, you see. They were silent. They looked at the closed door of the bedroom. This opened now and Mrs Fearty came out. She was a weighty woman. She was very efficient. She was good at her work. Most people praised her.

She caught my arm.

We are in trouble, Colmain, she said. It is beyond me. There is something wrong. We need a doctor. How? I asked. How in the name of God? He can't come. You hear the wind. It was howling down the chimney, scattering the ashes on the hearth. Go in with her and stay with her, she said. I will have to think. Go to her.

I went into the room. The candlelight was flickering shadows on the white walls. She was lying there. Her teeth were clenched. Her hair was splayed around her head on the pillow. It was wet with sweat. Her eyes opened and looked at me. I went beside her. Her hand reached for me. O, Colmain, she said. She tried to look brave for me, but the fear was in her. Why did Mrs Fearty tell me? Why did she tell me? It will be all right, Catriona, I said, God is good you'll see, it will be all right. She turned away from me again with clenched teeth. I was red with helplessness. Wouldn't I give an arm or a leg or an eye or a hand if it would prove its worth?

I stayed talking to her. Sometimes she turned and looked at me. She tried to reassure me with her eyes. This only made it worse.

46

The door opened. The priest stood beside me with Mrs Fearty. That nearly stopped my heart altogether. He was a good priest. A young enough man. We called him Father Very Good behind his back, because in confession as you told your sins, he would say, I know, I know. Very good! Very good! It was a habit he had. He didn't know this. It sounded as if he was praising you. But we were affectionate to him.

Bear up, now, Colmain, he said. Bear up. God is good, God is good! Go down and leave us. I let her hand go. I nearly had to use force the way she was gripping me. I went down. Mrs Fearty came after me. Will she be all right? I asked. Please God! Please God! she said. I thought she was dodging my eyes. Would she be all right if she had a doctor, I asked. He would be welcome, she said. He would be welcome. The storm will die and he can come then. It will not be too late, please God. There were drops of sweat on her upper lip.

He will come now, I said. I know him. He is a brave man. He will come now, because I will go for him. I went out the door. She tried to hold onto me, but I wouldn't let her. I heard the women calling after me, but I paid no heed to them. I ran down to the pier. How shallow your life is, bounded by such small things when you live on an island. The pier and the cliff and the lake shore. I had run to the pier before with fright in me. I remembered that. But it was nothing at all to the fright that was in me now, with the sight of Catriona lying in her hair and the agony and fear in her eyes.

The wind was whipping me off my feet. Why now? I called. Why now? A gale in April. This is not common. Why tonight of all nights in the life of a man and a woman? I was glad of the soaking I was getting. It was cooling my hot body.

I stood on the pier. I looked at the sea. It was in a terrible way. It was nearly all white with breaking waves, but here and there I could see the patches of light green. I was cool enough. I thought, even if I die then, what of it. Won't it be better that way than to see Catriona as she is. And I won't die! I won't die! They say God is good and He will smooth the way for me. They all tell me that. I was going down the steps when the hands seized me. I hadn't heard them coming behind me. But there they were, Fearty and MacDonagh and Hamilton and Tomás and other men.

They said, No, Colmain, you must not go. Look at it, man. There is nothing but death out there for you.

Let me go, I said, let me go! They didn't let me go. So I fought them. I had the strength of three men. I flung them away from me. I went down the steps to the boat, but they came after me. They held my arms and they held my legs and they dragged me out of the boat and they lay me flat on the wet pier and they held me. I was spreadeagled. The rain was on my face. I appealed to them. Please let me go! Please let me go! I know that I will get there and bring him back to her! I appeal to you by the great God of Heaven to let me go!

Tomás said, Colmain, O Colmain, you would die. Can't you see that you would die? The wind will fall. Just wait until the wind will fall. I struggled against them. I cursed them. I shouted at them all the evil things that I could think of. They would not let me go. Tomás kept saying, The wind will die, Colmain, you'll see, the wind will die.

I could struggle no more. I went lax on them. I said, I will wait for the wind to die. I went to the end of the pier and I watched the great sea. I spat at it. O, I hated it now, with all my heart and soul. The white waves, like a sea of snow between here and the mainland.

I waited one hour and two hours and then it eased. It was very dark by then and there was no moon, but I could smell my way across to the shore.

They stood away and let me go, and I bounded across.

It was no use. In my heart I knew this. Every bit of me except my eyes were weeping.

The brave man was there. He had seen the beacon. And he came with me. But I knew it was too late.

I had a son, all right, but his view of the world was of a

48

very short time, they told me. Very short. He would have been a fine son. Stout limbs he had and they said he looked like me. The priest said this who baptised him for paradise. He told me. It didn't seem to mean much to me. And they had to take Catriona away from me. She was gone for three long weeks, and when she came back she was pale, she was very pale, and her smile was dimmed and that was the reason. The little fellow, they called him Colmain, the priest said, he was her first born and he would be her last born.

I have never liked the name Thursday. I do not like it now. I don't suppose I ever will.

Friday

In a coarse way, then, I told you about beauty and what it means to us, even if we cannot word it clearly for you. The colour of the world is like the spirit of a man, a different colour for joy or laughter or pain or suffering or love or hate. Blackness alone is for evil deeds and sinfulness and despair.

The colour went out of the world for me. It was a great loss. The colour of a lake water under the laughing sky is blue. I went to the lake and I took the water in my hand, and it was not blue, just dirty brown. And the colour of the sea is different shades of green. I cupped this in my hand and it is only a dirty white. So I saw colour as a delusion. You are being deceived by something that appears good to the eye, but really it does not live at all. It is nothing.

I thought the link between Catriona and myself was forged of iron and that it was unbreakable. This was not so. She had lost her smile and she was listless. It is easy to see now that I was faulty. My efforts at rousing her were half-hearted. At a time when she really needed me, I was not there. I was away off in a world of my own choosing, filled with myself and my own sorrow. I don't suppose it was true sorrow. Real sorrow means that you are sorrowful for somebody else, not yourself. It's easy to see that now, but not then.

I was planning too much on the young Colmain. There was no reason why I shouldn't have had him that I could see. I had been bereft enough in the world, I thought, without this. Many people have lost early children, and it is very sad, but they have been consoled with the thought that the next time they will make a child that will live. So I saw that I had not even consolation. That too was taken away. You see. There would be no me after me. I was at an end. I didn't see much purpose to living so. You strive and fight for your wife and your sons and your daughters. All the worry of life is about them. That they may eat, that they may be covered, that they may learn, that they may grow. That they may be men and women. That they may be married and you see a piece of you in their children, going on and on until the end of time. Surely that is the purpose of living at all. So when there is no hope of such, what is the point of living?

I thought all this. I lost my laughter. A glum man is like an infection. He can spread this infection all about him. If he is not so taken up with himself he can see this, but he never does. I look back at myself then, and I don't feel happy. I think of Catriona and I strike my breast.

I was honest, I suppose. I stopped going to Mass. When Catriona got on her knees before the red lamp in the evening, if I was there, I would get up and walk out. This sort of behaviour marks you. In a small community actions like that can be seen by everybody. I didn't wave them like a banner, but they were there for all to see. They allowed time. It takes time for a stricken man, they say, to stop displaying his back. But time went by and I kept walking away.

I took terrible chances at sea. I went out in weather that would daunt an engined ship. I didn't care. I did it all like a machine. Death or life were all one to me. When I got safely back after these dangers and saw Catriona waiting for me to come in with terrified eyes, why, it meant nothing to me, only surprise that she should have waited up for me. I would say, You shouldn't have waited up for me. It is late. You will be tired.

Tomás would say, O, Colmain, come and look at the boat. I would say, What boat? Who cares about boats? Go and peddle the boat to some of the weak-kneed sailormen of the island. Sell a boat to them, Tomás. I could see hurt in his eyes. The boat was half finished. I didn't buy timber for him or nails. Nobody else had any interest. I suppose he went back to the part he had and rubbed it and planed it and perfected it. Time, he didn't stop to tell me. He just looked at me.

It was inevitable that the priest should have come after me. I knew this. I was his care, like everyone else. It was his duty. I wouldn't have respected him if he hadn't. I was going long-lining, when he stood on the pier. I have never been out in your boat, Colmain, he said. It is my wish to go now. I looked at the sea. It wasn't rough. You will be cold, I said, and you will get wet. It was autumn. I have been cold and wet before, he said, and it did me no harm, only made me pray harder for seamen when I am in bed and the wind is blowing strong. I said, All right. He cast off the rope and stepped in, I hoisted the sail and we made out to sea. He knew how to handle himself in a boat. He wasn't a distraction. He kept quiet for a long time. He breathed deeply. I could see he was enjoying the wind and the salt air. He was at home in a boat.

He said many things later. He said, You are nursing your sorrow, Colmain, like a mother nursing a child beyond the time when it should be taken from the breast and given solid food. I couldn't see this. I said, You are wrong. I no longer feel sorrow. How can I nurse what I do not feel? He said, Do you feel God is to blame then for the things that have happened to you? I said, No, I do not, because I am now aware that God does not exist. He is a fairy tale created by the minds of men, who need to think of somebody who is greater than themselves. Somebody not like them, a person who is strong and always successful, who can overcome everybody. That's what I think. The idea of God is a necessity for the mind, but the idea is as unreal as the colour of the sky or the lake or the sea. O, Colmain, he said.

Can you make anything, he asked? I thought over this. I can make a boat, a fishing line, a sail, harness for a pony. I can make many things, I said. No, he said, you can make nothing. To make these things you must have timber, iron, hemp, cloth, leather. You didn't make these things. Somebody had to make them in the first place. Who made them?

I said, I am an ignorant man, with little schooling. You are talking deep things of the scholar. I cannot talk these things.

I wish you were as thick as you make out, he said. I might get somewhere with you. You don't go to Mass. Do you want me to go to something in which I have no longer any belief, I asked? I do, he said. You are giving scandal, and the very thing you do not believe in, as long as you hold on to it, might be the thing to break through the hard skin of your own selfishness. You are not the only one in the world to be stricken. I said, Father, do not let us fight. Do not get angry with me. I feel nothing.

I am not angry, O, Colmain, he said, I am truly very sad. When you were bereft before, you were young and you took the blows standing. My heart admired you. You grew a kindly person who would not hurt a creature. Now you have become a man who is hurting, hurting, all around him, as if you were swinging a whip with many spiked lashes. This is not true, Father, I said. You can say many more things like that to me without hurting me. I listen to your voice. That is what I hear. But your words have no meaning for me. I am indifferent to them. I tell you this truly so that you can save breath and words. I will lay my lines.

He helped me. He enjoyed himself. His clothes were covered with sea spray and fish scales. He shared my bread and butter and cold fish and bottled tea, and he enjoyed himself, but I could look him in the eyes all the time and that seemed to dishearten him.

On the pier in the evening he said, I thank you, Colmain, for the excursion. It has given me a new lease of life. I will pray for you. That is your job, I said, and he looked at me and became sad and walked away with his head bowed and a hank of fish hanging listlessly from his arm. I felt sorry for him, but that was all.

Fionan Murtagh has a salty way of saying things, as I have tried to tell you. On the land next to us there lived a family called Cunningham. There was the father and the mother. They were quite old when a son was born to them. He was called John. He wasn't much good, I suppose because he was an only son and he came so late so they thought he was more precious than other people's children. His mother gave him great care and attention. If he sneezed she kept him in bed and killed a hen to make broth for him. She was foolish about him but who can blame her? His father was a good man, a quiet man. He partnered a boat with another family and he didn't come back from the big storm. At the time his son was not with him although he was well and able. He had a pain in his head, his mother said, although other people knew it was in his craw because he was drinking the night before. So he was spared and his father died, and most people thought the wrong man died. But not his mother. She said what a grace from God the pain in his head was that it saved him from death. Well, John was lazy. She got little help from him. The field work he found too hard for his frame, and just when his mother needed him he went away. To England they said. She got small benefit from him except tears. She haunted the post office shop waiting for letters from him. The only ones that came for her were asking for money. We knew this because she bought the pay orders to send him. She wasn't well off. It meant of course that we all had to give a hand on the place without being noticed, so that poor Margaret thought the fairies were coming in the night and doing the digging for her. She was well liked, and even if people thought she was foolish about her son, they thought well of her loyalty, which is a rare gift.

53

She died. She ailed a while before she died. The scoundrel didn't come home although he was written to. He didn't come home for the funeral even. She was well buried when he came home. He wore strange clothes. He talked about how he was married to a rich girl whose father owned a factory. He talked about selling the place, or wondering if he would keep it as a sort of country house for the summer, like the gentlemen. He spent money freely, treating people in the pub. We thought his mother could have done with the money before she died, but no matter. If a fool wants to throw away his money he will always find takers. Then he went away feeling superior to the rest of us, and saddened over our lot of having to grub a living in a bleak isle.

That's when Fionan said this. The filomin, he said, is a strange fly. It is born in dung, and lives in dung, and then one day it takes to the air and it flies. It flies very high, higher indeed than the eagle or even the wren, and then it falls, and when it falls it falls fast and it lands in the dung and there it dies. So poor John ever afterwards was known as the Filomin.

The Cunningham place grew weeds. This is an uncomfortable thing to see in an island where land is scarce and even precious. I went over there myself at times and chopped at the weeds before they seeded and contaminated my own land. Then one day Filomin came home.

He had three children with him. The eldest girl was ten, the next eight and the boy was four. Odd children. They had funny English names we found it hard to get our tongue around. They were Olive, Priscilla and Courtney. The point is they were grand children and they grew on everybody. They talked with precise English accents and they knew no Irish. Of course they had to learn Irish, because at school the other children knew very little English, and if you were in the humour it was funny to see grown people talking to the children and shouting Irish words at them as they pointed at things. Everyone was eager for them to advance. We heard later that their mother was an English girl, but of course her father was not rich. He was the same as ourselves, scraping a living. In a short time this girl who was foolish enough to marry Filomin, bore seven children and four of them died and she herself died. She wasn't well treated by Filomin. What could you expect from a fellow who wouldn't even attend his mother's funeral?

Olive was a great little girl. Man, she did over that house inside and outside. She'd shame a man the work she did. The size of her and the pride she had. She didn't want assistance, she was doing very well, her dear father was such a great help to her. She was devoted to Filomin. What is it men like that have in them that makes females so loyal to them? Many men in the island scratched their heads looking for it and they couldn't find it. He worked a bit in the fields, grew enough to keep them alive and enough grass to rear a calf or two. Everything he did he did at the last minute before he was overwhelmed by the seasons. When he made a sale of an animal, he got drunk. He was rowdy when he was drunk. Most men avoided him because their inclination was to kick sense into him, but then they were so fond of the strange little children and wanted to keep their respect.

So we come to this October evening. It was mild. Sometimes October is that way. It was dark. The moon wasn't up. I was sitting on the wall outside smoking a pipe. Sometimes the situation between Catriona and myself became such that I couldn't bear it. I would have to go out. The silence between us. Most good silences don't call for talk. You know those ones. You are silent and yet you are talking and the other person understands. But the other ones sometimes are beyond bearing.

This was one. I was sitting on the wall. The Cunningham place was a few hundred yards away from me. I could look into the open door. It was like watching a play on a stage. That little one Olive was never still. I saw her laying the place at the table for the other children and making them eat and sitting herself and eating, and then making them wash themselves and get into their night clothes, lighting a candle and bringing them up to the room. She was there for a time with them and then she came down and washed up the dishes and swept the floor into the street. She was a tall thin girl, thin limbs and a thin face and big eyes and her hair done in plaits. I thought what a boon it was to be the father of a child like that. I hoped that whatever else, Filomin knew what a jewel he had.

There had been a fair on the mainland. Filomin had been there. I had nothing for the fair this time. He had hired the turf boat with other men to bring over their animals. Now he was back. He should have been back some time ago, but he would have lodged in the pub on his way. I heard him coming home. He was singing. His singing voice was not good. It was as annoying as the rasp of a corn-crake. I saw him coming up the road. I did a mean thing. I slid down by the wall so that I was hidden and watched him pass. I covered the red bowl of the pipe with my palm. Then he was past, singing and shouting and laughing to himself. He was a big man but he had a lot of fat on him.

I sat up and watched him. I felt sorry for little Olive. Her father coming home like that. She handled him calmly. She met him at the door. He shouted. He embraced her, raising her off the ground. My own little girl. My stomach tightened. Then he put her down. I could see him at the table. There was a place laid for him. He kept his head sunk on his arms for awhile. She turned out the potatoes on the table and put a plate in front of him. I knew what it was, fried bacon and onions. His movements were slurred. He took up his knife and fork. Something disturbed him. He started shouting, pointing at his plate. I could hear no words. Then he caught the plate and flung it from him on the floor. I could hear the sound of its breaking. I could see the little girl's back. I saw his mouth opening. He half rose to his feet. His head hit the paraffin lamp on the wall. This seemed to annoy him. He reached up and took it and flung it. The light went out. Blotted out, just like that. Like a dream ends. I was white with anger. I could feel my anger.

One moment the house was dark and the next moment it

was red. It happened very quickly. The lamp had burst, I suppose, and scattered the flaming oil. There was a red blast and smoke and then I saw Filomin staggering out the door with his hands over his face. I cannot tell you how quickly that house became a bonfire. It was the straw roof of course helped. I stood up. I shouted with terror. Catriona! Catriona! and then I started to run. At another time it would be a short run. But now it seemed like a mile. Oh, I cursed him. He walked out of there, without a thought for Olive or the children. You hear that! Can you imagine it? Would you believe it? I shouted as I ran. At the top of my lungs, the names of the neighbours that might hear my bellowing.

I saw her coming out of the place, enveloped in smoke and flame. She was carrying the boy. By his size it must be. He was wrapped in a blanket. She placed him on the ground. I cried, No! No! Olive, but she paid no heed to me. She turned and she went back in again. O, God, I called, bring her out of there.

Filomin blocked me. His arms were outstretched. O, God help me, O, God help me, he was crying, my poor little house. I hit him passing. I couldn't help it. He fell away from me. The doorway was blocked with flame. I didn't feel it. I turned to the right. She was there at the bedroom door, almost on her knees with the other girl. I scooped the two of them into my arms and I turned and ran out. The fire chased me. It whooped behind me, the roof crashed. Catriona was there. She had taken the boy back from the heat. There were other people coming. Filomin was on his feet going around, saying O, O, O! Catriona came to me. Little Priscilla was fine. She was crying. The blanket around her was smouldering. I whipped it away. Catriona took her. She was grand. There wasn't a mark on her. She was just crying with fright. I took Olive in my arms and walked away with her to the road. There were many people there now. Her eyes were closed. She was moaning a bit. I had quenched her hair. Because it was tied in plaits it had not burned. Just loose bits here and there on her head. Her arms and legs were a white colour. Catriona brought a blanket.

She put it around her. Bring her home, said Catriona. I carried her. I said as I went to a man : Go to the post office. Tell them to call the doctor what we are to do. Get Mrs Fearty. For a while now we had a sort of radio telephone in the post office. Sometimes it worked. It depended on the weather.

Filomin was going around like a chicken without its head. O, what will I do? What will I do? he was calling. I looked at him. I thought, could it be possible that any man could be such a plague of self-pity? I looked at him and then I looked at Catriona. She was looking at me, not at him. For just a few seconds she was looking at me. I felt a fire in my heart. For a second I felt that Filomin, even Filomin, was a better man than I. Who was I to fault him? She didn't mean this in her look, you understand.

Mrs Fearty came. We had Olive on our bed. The instructions came from the mainland doctor, because the thing was working. The waves of the air were calm that evening. Do such and such, and then bring her. I don't know what, powder of some kind on her limbs and shut off the air. I left them and ran to prepare my boat. I was in a terrible state. I nearly gritted my teeth to destruction. I imagined pounding Filomin to pulp with my fists. I was not long getting the boat ready. There was a calm wind, steady from the north-east. It would waft us across. The doctor would be waiting, said they. All waiting.

Catriona carried Olive. I will go, she said. I didn't argue with her. We cast off and we set sail, and nearly everybody was there on the pier. The moon was coming up, as big as the world.

The little girl moaned a bit. Is she bad? I asked. Do you think she is very bad? I don't know, said Catriona. I think she is badly burned. O, God, I said pounding my fist, on the boat. Why are you moved? Catriona asked. I didn't answer her. The little girl spoke, Mrs Fury, Mrs Fury. Yes, Olive, she said. Are the children all right? she asked. Oh, yes, said Catriona, there is not a speck on them. I am so glad, said the little one. The lamp fell off the wall, she said. The lamp fell off the wall. I was so frightened. No! I wanted to shout, but I didn't. I strangled it. Daddy is fine? she asked. Isn't Daddy fine? He is, said Catriona. Only his heart is broken about you. Where are we going? she asked. To a doctor, said Catriona. He will fix your burns. They are hurting now, she said. I could see her shivering. It wasn't a cold night. Soon we will be there, said Catriona. You will be all right.

They were silent again. Nothing but the swish of the water and the creaking of the sail block. I could see her face in the light of the moon. It wasn't marked. Just very white and filled with pain. But her eyes were calm and bright. What a lovely moon, she said. It is very big. It is the harvest moon, said Catriona. It is like a lantern hanging there to guide us, said Olive. It is the colour of gold.

I looked at it. It was coloured, and it was colouring the sea around us, the short waves were glinting.

You are so kind, Mrs Fury, she said then. When I come back I will knit you a pair of gloves. I am good at gloves. Thank you, Olive, said Catriona. You will keep an eye on the children? she asked. I will, said Catriona. And a hand to Daddy, she said, men are so useless about the house. Isn't that so? That's true, said Catriona. I will keep an eye on him. The girl sighed and moaned a bit. I felt no feeling now. I felt as if I had been frozen to death.

We could see lights on the mainland pier. There was a group of people there. The doctor took her very gently. He brought her into a house. We waited. I felt most miserable, as if I had been scooped out like a turnip. He came out. Bad, he said. I will take her myself. We cannot wait for an ambulance. What in the name of God happened? How did the house go up?

Catriona looked at me. I felt her look. I knew what she was thinking. I found it terrible hard to say, but I said it. Olive says the lamp fell off the wall, I said. That's what she says. A bad nail. Damn it to hell, said the doctor. They brought her out. He had given her something. Her face was peaceful. She was not moaning. They fitted her into the back seat of the car. The nurse got in beside the doctor and they drove carefully away.

We went back to the boat. We went down the steps. I sat there with my head drooping. I hadn't enough energy to lift the sail. I knew she was sitting watching me. Then I felt her hand on mine. Just the light touch of her hand.

Let us go home, Colmain, Catriona said. Let us go home.

I paddled the boat away from the enclosing pier and when we were outside I raised the sail.

I had to tack a lot to get back into the teeth of the wind. It took us a long time to get home. I was glad. I don't remember much we said. I said, Soldiers get medals, what is there for the bravery of Olive, a little girl with pigtails? She said, A much greater reward than medals. I hope that she does not die.

I thought of this. I knew the silent shrieking and beseeching of my own heart. I calmed. I said, She will not die. I know she will not die. You cannot burn a tower like little Olive. She will come back.

The lamp didn't fall off the wall, said Catriona. She is very sharp, Catriona. She perceives. I thought over it.

The lamp fell off the wall, I said. In a way it did, I suppose. That was the way Olive wanted it.

Catriona sighed. I'll tell you something. The silence between us was again filled with understanding. I knew this. It was like coming from the darkness into the warm glow of a fire.

Colmain, she said later, it is a long time since I was with you on the sea. So it is, I said.

She put her hand into the water.

It is very pleasant being with you on the sea, Colmain, she said.

I said, You are filling my heart. It is good to be on the sea with you, Catriona. I said this with my lips. With my heart I said, Thank you, Olive. Thank you, Olive, thank you, Olive.

There is great colour in the night, I said. And there was.

So every time I hear Friday named, I think of Olive. You yourself know she came back, Pól, because you have often laughed with her. But you have never seen her arms and legs naked, or you might have wondered. Olive is a skilful girl. I think of the many laughs we got with her. She grew up into an odd girl; strange looking face she had that appealed to many men. Even fellows from the mainland came to dance at our feasts because of her. She entertained us often with accounts of the Saga of the Courting of Olive Cunningham. They had no chance because she had her course set for Tomás. This was amusing. Tomás is a few years younger than myself so when Olive was eighteen he was ten years older than the girl. He thought this made him a grandfather. Besides he was burdened with too many women at home, as I told you before, and they had him properly spancelled. But a girl like Olive who knew where she was going and who believed in direct action, as you have seen, who could withstand her once she had her compass set?

Almost my first deed after that Friday was to go to the mainland and come back loaded with timber. I can still see the bewildered face of Tomás when he came to the shed and saw it stacked there, and the cunning glint in the eyes of Fionan. I realized then that I had missed many years of pleasure and it made me sad.

So the boat was built. It took time but it was built. It was a very sound boat and solidly constructed. It wasn't as fleet as my little Brigid, nor would it ever be, but it was a good boat for a fellow like me advancing in years, who was learning from experience to treat the vagaries of the sea with more respect and caution. Not that I could ever get to love the sea. Too contrary for that. But to respect her and live at neutral with her, to go along with her in her rewarding times and to avoid her when she was really moody. So she was launched and blessed and the bottle of holy water was hooked inside her bow.

And now where was I? I was still on my own. A big boat like that couldn't be sailed single-handed except on mild days. Even then it was a labour to do everything with her for one man, unless he was armed like an octopus. I went around the island like a missionary trying to bring faith to the uncivilized, but I was only wasting my breath and my vigour. All I could recruit were young boys with the spirit still in them, but as soon as their adventure became known, they were scooped out of my boat like roasting potatoes from hot ashes.

Tomás, who was the man I wanted, wouldn't move. He was in terror of the tears of the females, and I suppose a lurking terror from his young days of the fear and terrible sights he had seen. Catriona offered to be a hand for me, but we had to laugh at what I would look like making my wife work in the boat like a sailorman. But we laughed genuinely over the idea, and that was good, because in life genuine laughter is rare.

Filomin was a subdued man after Olive came back. He didn't turn over a new leaf as they say. He just took a look at the new leaf and decided to look at it again in ten years' time. But he calmed at home. He got a fright I suppose. I'm sure he kept waking up in the night in their new-built house and sweating and saying to himself, Why, man, I might have been burned to death. I'd swear that's what he'd say. Surely nothing noble. But he knew what caused the fire and he knew that Olive knew and if right was right he should have been in a prison breaking stones. So he would never raise a hand or a shout to his children again. He wouldn't not after I talked to him and told him what I had seen and what would happen to him at my hands if he ever did such a thing again. He knew I meant it too. I did. Because I saw him as a picture of what I might have become if I went on the way I was going and I would have beaten this picture out of him. How far we are from true charity, I often thought.

Eventually he went to a fair and he never came back. The whole island held its breath for a long time, and then breathed freely again. Olive was bigger then. So were the other two. They could help and Tomás helped. That's how he came under her eye and her critical inspection and his days of freedom were numbered. He put up a big battle. I suppose he was thinking, Well, if women are like the ones I have at home, it will be grand to be a bachelor. I'm sure like all the rest of us he was racked with thoughts of love and marriage and children, but he thought the price was too high to pay.

I was one morning there in the boat preparing the lines to go to sea. It had to be lines. I couldn't work the nets on my own in the big boat. Tomás was there and Fionan. I wasn't saying anything. Tomás was becoming very uncomfortable about the big boat. He would say, It is a pity I have to do this or that, Colmain, and I might go with you. I would just say, Aye, it is a pity, Tomás. It was a fine morning with a spanking breeze, plenty of comfortable sail in the wind. It will be a great comfort to me when I am dead, Fionan said. He was looking at the sky. We knew what he meant. Tomás ignored him. This was when Olive came from behind and stood over me. God be with you, Colmain, she said. I hope you have a good day for the fishing. I said, Thank you. Are you not bringing the nets with you, she asked? She pointed to them. They were strung on wooden pegs to dry on the wall of the shed. No, then, I said. I wouldn't be able to handle them when I am bringing the big boat. It's a pity, she said, can't you go with him, Fionan? My two eyes I'd give to go, said Fionan, spitting into the sea, if my poor hands would hold a thing in them.

I'd nearly go myself, she said. Would I be any use to you, Colmain? She was winking at me. You might at that, said I, if you would take instruction. O, I would, she said, and I wouldn't get in the way. I could use your two hands, I said. Tomás shouted. Shouldn't you be at home getting the dinner? The others are big enough to get the dinner, said Olive, will we pull down the nets so, Colmain and put them in the boat? If you are intent, said I, we might as well. I started to climb the steps. What do you think you are

63

doing? Tomás asked her. I'm minding my own business, said Olive. She walked over towards the shed. He followed her. We watched. She started to take them off the pegs. You'll get them all tangled, said Tomás. Take them down the right way. He took them off the right way and put them in the folds. He shouldered them and walked to the pier. She followed him. Here, Colmain, she said. I said thanks. I took them, and carried them down the steps. Tomás, said Olive, would you go and inform the young ones that I am gone fishing with Colmain. Am I a messenger boy? he asked angrily. You are not a messenger man anyhow, she said. Are you rude to me? Tomás asked. I said nothing, she said. Will I have enough clothes on me, she asked? She hadn't a lot. It was warm weather. There are oil skins in the locker if you get cold, I said. Ah, then I'm all set so, she said, starting to come down the steps. Are you mad, Colmain, Tomás asked, taking an amadán girl to sea with you? No, I said. I took Catriona once or twice. She's as good as a man any day, at least she's as good as the kind of man we have on this island. Are you faulting me? he shouted. I said nothing unjust, I answered. Come up on the pier and fight it out, he said. His face was red. For God's sake have sense, Tomás, I said. Why would I insult you? I respect you. Didn't you build this boat? That quietened him. Even if you never knew how she behaves in the sea, I went on. He got red again. There, there, there! he said, you are calling me a coward. No, I said. Why would I? You are my friend. A fine friend you are, he said bitterly, shaming me. I'm not shaming you, I said. Tomás is not afraid of the sea, said Olive. He's afraid of the tongues of his sisters. Don't talk like that, he shouted. Who are you to talk like that? My business is my own. You are afraid, she said. Oh, God, said Tomás, I could hit you. You drive me too far. You wouldn't have the courage to hit me, said Olive. Look what you have done to me, said Tomás, you have made me to go. You don't understand. I do, she said. Deep down you always wanted to go. No, said Tomás, wind and wet and fish scales. I don't want to live like that. I have seen your

64

eyes, she said, when you watch after Colmain. This was a happy place until you came to it, said Tomás. I can easy go away and live on the mainland, said Olive. There would be many houses glad to take me in. I thought Tomás was going to say, All right, go then. But he didn't. He looked at her. You know I didn't mean that, he said. I do, she said. What do you want? he asked her. I want what your heart wants, she said. I like the sea. The sea was my salvation once. She smiled down at me. You are not your own man now, Tomás. Go to sea and you will be free. You think that? he asked. I know that, she said. I don't know why you didn't fight free before. So, said Tomás. There was something going on between them that neither Fionan nor myself could understand. We were kind of holding our breaths, waiting. There wasn't words between them, you understand, just one of those speaking silences.

Then Tomás just turned and clumped down the steps and sat into his own boat and as we cast off and turned into the wind, he was rubbing the sides of her with the palms of his hands. This trip of Tomás meant a lot to me. I will tell you more of it again, but now I want to tell you something else that meant much to me because, like Tomás, it started with the boat.

I'll tell you this about Tomás. He said afterwards (you can imagine the scene in his house when he came home in the dark from the sea) Colmain, all you have to do is shout at them. Is that all, I asked? Yes, said Tomás, you just open up your lungs and shout at them. You don't have to do anything else, just shout at them. It was a wonder to him as if he had discovered one of the great secrets of the world.

One day I found a stranger in my boat. He was sitting there winding a line. He was a small little chap. He had fair spiky hair, badly cut, and a thin shirt, and a short trousers that was much too big for him, badly patched and held up with braces and safety pins. He looked up at me. He had blue eyes. He would be about eight years old.

I said, Who are you. I am MacDara, he said. Are you going fishing? I am, I said. Would I be able to go with you?

he asked. Who belongs to you, I asked? I was trying to place him. Nobody on the island belonged to him. Tarp is my grandfather, he said. I said, O.

Tarp comes nearly every year to the island. I suppose he would be called a tinker. He brings rolls of tarpaulin and pedlar's things and he sets up a dirty brown tent and he fixes pots and kettles and does other odd skilful things around the place, and then he goes away before the winter. He is a big bulgy man, badly dressed, always wanting to be shaved, but never rowdy even in drink, fairly silent, with small eyes.

Would your grandfather mind if you went to sea? I asked. No, he said. I only see him in the evening. If I bring fish for the pot he would be pleased. I looked at him. He met my glance fairly. His clothes were not good but his body and his bare feet were clean. He wasn't beseeching me, you understand. I said, All right so, you can come. But you will have to do what you are told. I'll do that, he said. It was only the way his fingers squeezed one another, that I knew he was excited.

It was strange to drive in the boat watching this little boy. Of course I naturally said to myself, if things were different, this could be my son in the boat with me, not the grandson of a tinker. He showed no fear of the waves. The first time I went in a boat to sea, I was afraid. He said, Can I go up there? I nodded. He went to the bow and kneeled there, holding on to a rope, facing into the weather. It was a blue sky day with great white clouds running fast. He watched out. Sometimes a wave hit him. He turned back to me. His eyes were bright. I had to smile at his pleasure. But no fear at all. I thought that people who live unsheltered lives must abide without fear.

He was getting used to the boat. He came back. He looked at the can of lug-bait. He turned them over with his small fingers. They were not repulsive to him, I could see. They are to most people. Where do these go? he shouted. They go on the hooks of the lines, I said. Will I bait them for you? he asked. I nodded, thinking I will let him spoil a few if he takes pleasure in it. He didn't spoil them at all. He did one and held it up. It was good. I raised my eyebrows at him. He laughed. He was pleased. That boy baited the hooks like an expert.

He brought me luck, I tell you. The fish seemed to take delight in his baiting. I got pleasure from watching him. Each time a fish came aboard jumping and twitching it was a triumph for him. He was soon scales up to his eyes. This is good, he would say, now and again. I was a bit jaded with the sea by now, you know. It was a lonely life and very hard work once I lost all that youthful challenge that I told you about. He revived it for me. It is good to see things through the fresh eyes of other people. When we lay on the sea and ate our meal, he ate it with such great enjoyment that he might have been eating the food from a rich table. This is — good, he said, using a very dirty word, that shocked me I must say, on his young mouth. Where is your mother and father, I asked? Don't know, he said. They are gone away. They went away and left me with Tarp. How long ago? I asked. O, a year ago, he said. Where are they? I asked. O, I don't know, — them, that's what Tarp says, he said. I was silent.

It was late when we got home. I brought him to the house. He wasn't clean now. I walked him into the bright kitchen. Catriona, I said, I have brought a guest. He was helping me with the fishing. Catriona didn't start. Ah, you are welcome, she said. He is MacDara, I said. He is the grandson of Tarp. O, said Catriona, would you men like to wash yourselves before the meal. I will put hot water in the basin. He didn't object. He took care with the washing of himself, I noticed. But in the house a sort of wild caution seemed to have fallen on him. He didn't feel comfortable in the house. We sat at the meal. When we blessed ourselves, he saw and did that too. He ate with cautious enjoyment. It seemed to me though, that he was sitting on his chair ready to fly away. Do you sleep in a tent all the time, Catriona asked him? Yes, he said. Do you be cold? she asked. Sometimes, he said. But it is better than a house. You smother in a house. I see, said Catriona. I will go back with you to your grandfather, I said afterwards. If you like, he said. Come again and see us, said Catriona, and thank you for helping Colmain. That's all right, he said.

I walked beside him in the darkness. He wasn't afraid of that, naturally. He said, It was a great day. It was one of the best days I remember. Could I come with you again before we go away. Where are you going? I asked. I don't know, he said. All over the country. Do you like that? I asked. Sometimes, he said. But you get tired of travelling. Have you had any schooling? I asked. No, he said with disgust, who wants that? Tarp taught me to count. I can add sums in my head. That's the principal think to know, I said.

There was a light in the tent in the hollow near the shore where a small stream of clear water came from the hills. I stopped and said, Hello. The bulk of the man came to the opening. He squinted. Oh, he said, it's you MacDara. Then he saw me. He pulled back in. Come in, he said. I stooped and crawled in. There was a candle lantern there. It was very confused. It smelled of Tarp. He had been portering. I said, I took your grandson fishing. Is that where he was? he said. That's why I came, I said, I wanted to explain. I was choking in that tent. There was sweat all over my body under my clothes. No need, Tarp said. He is like a rabbit, a wild one. The bedclothes were tattered blankets and sacks. There were tin mugs hanging from the sally pole.

All right, I said, I must go. Goodbye, MacDara. He was sitting beside Tarp. He looked very small and tattered. He looked much better out in the boat under the sky. I'll see you again. If your grandfather doesn't mind, come and help me. Tarp scratched himself. He yawned. His mouth was full of gaps. Not mind, he said. What the hell. MacDara nodded at me. I walked home. I thought that is the way life is. I'm sure Tarp is kind to him, in his own way.

Catriona said, You left him home. I said, Home means different things to different people. He's a nice little fellow, she said. You should hear the tongue he has, I said. Does he know any better? she asked.

The next time I went fishing he entered my head. I wondered if he would be there. He was. It's funny how much pleasure I got out of the sight of him. He talked more too. He thought I was very ignorant about a lot of things, like how to snare rabbits, and to steal sheets from clothes-lines at the backs of houses in cities, and sell them in the next market place, how to beg, and look miserable when the police were not on the watch. Decent things like that. He knew how to extract potatoes from pits so that the opening would not be noticed. I said he was gifted in many ways. He said, You should get to know these things because you can't live without them.

Catriona and he became friendly. I don't know how. At least knowing Catriona I could guess. He didn't seem to want to flee the house as soon as he had eaten a meal. He even started to do little things for her about the house. I might as well pass the time, he said, and when you get food free and don't have to steal it, that's different. I said, Was that so? She got him into a decent shirt, one of mine changed I suppose for the better, and warm trousers. But it was remarkable how he always kept himself so clean. You know why that was? Well, it seems when you beg, people prefer to give money to clean children rather than dirty children. It was a mistake to be dirty and to look as if you had sores. You did that with dirt rubbed well in with a touch of the colour that women put on their mouths. O, MacDara had been around the world and knew a lot of things. Sometimes he made me feel as if I was the child and he was the man.

One night at the end of September, when Catriona was in bed, and I was raking the fire and preparing to go too, there was a sort of scratching at the door. I went and opened it. Tarp was there. He was breathing fumes at me. He said, I will talk to you. I said, Come in. He shook himself. He came in warily. He looked around him closely as he sat there on a chair, a raggedy, bulky man, unpleasant to the eye. He said, The boy likes you. I'm pleased to hear that, I said. I like him too. Will you keep him? he asked. I said,

What are you saying? Keep him, keep him, he said impatiently. He was the child of my daughter. Her man left her. I don't know where she is. Never will. Some other one. Left me holding him. Will you keep him?

You can't exchange children like animal pets, I said. He is fond of you. You mean a lot to him. Ach, he said, what's the use? Single man. Go my own road. No good for him. Am I good for him? I thought over this. If he is happy with you, you are good for him, I said. No, he said. He took to you and your woman, never like that before. He is a bright boy. He might be somebody. Not with me. You see what I am, where I go, what I do? Will you keep him?

My heart was pounding. Keep him! But this wouldn't work out. I know it wasn't possible for this to work out. It was too right, you see. How, I said. He won't stay. I cannot force him to stay.

You go fishing tomorrow, he said. How did he know? But these people seem to know everything. When you come back I will be gone. That's cruel, I said. Only way, he said. I'm not much, but I know. I feel. I like him, but I'm not one to be burthened by a child. You will take care of him. You work it and he will forget me and all about me. His mind is young. He will forget. You don't take him, I'll drop him off somewhere else, he added, the first orphan school. I mean this. I like MacDara, I said. I wouldn't want him against his will. That's up to you, he said. Do it your own way. He rose up. Goodbye, he said. I won't come back here again. This is the last. He went out. I followed after him, to call? Here come back! Come back here! But he had shuffled off into the darkness. When I turned Catriona was there in her nightdress. Her hair was down. You hear? I asked. I did, she said. What do you think? I asked. If it is meant to happen it will, she said. It would be a great blessing. I was afraid to think it might come true.

I don't think MacDara noticed anything wrong with me the next day. But there was a terrible burden on me. I felt I was taking part in a crime. The day was long and tedious for me. I welcomed the dark of the night. I thought when we went home and tidied the boat and gathered the baskets and put them in the shed and went to the bright home where the meal was waiting that he would surely mark my strangeness. But he didn't. Catriona was very good. She laughed and joked with him as if nothing had happened. Women are skilful deceivers. So the time came when I had to say, I will walk home with you, MacDara. I felt like a criminal. We walked the road and left it. There was moonlight, and we turned from the road and walked up the little bush-covered valley that led to the grassy place where the tent was. I could hear the stream before we came to it. I thought, when we turn the corner, the tent will be there and maybe I dreamed last night.

The tent was not there. We stood still. I watched him going to the place, kicking the refuse around. He didn't seem able to believe it. He came back to me. He's gone! he said, Tarp is gone! He ran back again. He put his hands around his mouth and he called, Tarp! Tarp! Tarp! Where are you? He came back to me again. Would he have changed his camping place? I asked. No, he said, no, he has left me. Tarp has left me. He ran up the hill where it made a sort of cliff over the sea. He stood there looking out. I didn't know what to do. I was in pain. I walked up after him. His small hands were clenched. Maybe he's not gone, I said, maybe he's not gone. Oh, yes, he said. I was always afraid he would. Someday I was afraid he would leave me. I watched him. He was holding back tears, but they were bursting out of his eyes slowly. I felt terrible. Look, I said, we will take the boat and I will go with you to the mainland and we will look for him.

He sat down. He didn't answer. Then he said, No good. He would hide from me. He doesn't really want me. He never wanted me. What will you do? I said. I don't know, he said. The good people will be after me. I said, For tonight we have a spare bed in the house, you can come and sleep with us. No! No! No! he said, I want Tarp. I want my grandfather. He was pounding the ground with his fists. I said, Well you know where the bed is if you want it then, and I turned and walked down and away from him. This took a lot of effort, you see, but I did it.

Catriona said, Where is he? I said, He's up on the cliff. O, said Catriona. She felt as bad as myself. We sat there in the kitchen. We have a wall clock. It beats the quarters and the halves and the hour. It was always comforting at night before. It wasn't now. We left the door open, the lamplight shining out.

We hardly needed the light by the time he came. It would soon be dawn. It was a little like a dream, from the drowsiness. One second the door was empty and then he was standing there.

O, I said, it was about time you made up your mind.

I will only sleep the night, he said, just the one night.

Whatever you like, I said. I'm going to bed, Catriona will see to you. I left them. I thought Tarp could give him many things that we could never give him. I understood that. That security and good clothes and food and a little comfort are not everything. Many millions of people have these things and it does not give them a peaceful feeling in their hearts. I understood all this. But I knew we were able to give him affection, that we could make him part of our own lives. I didn't know if this would pay him for Tarp and the free life. I didn't know only time would tell.

So MacDara stayed the night with us and he is still here and

Now something has happened, Pól. It is strange. You remember Máire Fearty, the little girl who came to me in the rain to tell me about Catriona. Well, she is in trouble. Life goes in a circle. She is in the trouble Catriona was in, only worse. It brings it all back to my mind, that terrible night. This is a terrible night too, only it is December and not April, and what's blowing out there now is not an April storm that will die in two hours. This is a dirty one.

They talked to the doctor on the radio phone. He says he will have to come over. Who will bring him? Why, nobody over there will, not even the turf boat man, so they have come to me, dripping wet from the rain of the night, and they have beseeched me, Colmain, please will you go and get him. He is willing to come. Now, isn't it strange, Pól? When I tried to go for Catriona, they held me down on the wet stones of the pier. Now nobody will hold me down. I have talked to Catriona. She says, If you must go, then go, if it feels right for you. MacDara says, I will go with you, Colmain. I say, you will not. You will stay and look after Catriona. There is no need for two of us to go. You understand. He says, with a sigh of giving in to me, I understand. Tomás has been here. He says, I will go with you, Colmain. I said, You will not go with me. So I am going. I have a picture in my eye of Catriona and my son MacDara in the kitchen. She has anxiety in her eyes, but everything will be all right. I'll be back. For I have many more things to tell you. I'm even beginning to enjoy writing these words for you. I am a happy man. I found MacDara in my boat as a little boy on a Saturday. You see him now, how big and fit he is, and you see six boats putting out from the pier on a fishing day, so I haven't really failed. If I went tonight I would be leaving something of achievement behind me. You know, you understand. So to save me time I will draw the name of Tomorrow's writing on the blank page and then all I will have to do is to fill it. Like this :

Sunday

Patter O'Rourke

HE WAS a tall thin man dressed in a black suit, a white shirt with a black tie, and a black hat with the brim all curled up. If you saw him from behind or from the side you would think he was a priest. But he wasn't. He was known as Patter O'Rourke because instead of saying 'God bless the work', or 'God bless you', he would say 'Pater bless the work', or 'Pater bless you', and since the people in our place can't say a word with one 't' without adding another to it, he was know as Patter, and that was apt too, because he came to our place periodically selling holy pictures, medals, statues and rosary beads, or enlargements of your grand-mother in gilt frames, and he could talk the leg off a pot. In fact all the houses in our place were saturated with the results of his salesmanship.

He was a likeable man. People liked to have him in their houses trying to sell them things, so he slept in the hotel and had his breakfast, dinner and tea in our houses and we were pleased to have him because he spoke in a very educated way about things, was well up on all the latest news, had views about it, and well, people just liked listening to him. His one failing was that he was very fond of betting on horses, and very unfortunate with them, so that now, although we listened to his tips about winners, we were no longer foolish enough to take his advice.

This particular time I want to tell you about, he was in our house and he was in a very despondent mood. It was October. The country was looking well as it faded away. The weather was mild. It had been a very good harvest, thank God, and everybody in the place was flush and lazy. Patter always came selling his things after the harvest, be-cause he knew that was the time when people had a surplus of time and also money.

74

We had enjoyed a very nice meal. I had killed a pig recently. We had fresh pork and beans, and blood pudding, apple pie and cream, so we were nicely stacked and sitting in front of the turf fire, smoking while the wife washed up the dishes.

'The whole country, my dear man,' he said, 'is suffering from a surfeit of materialism. It makes me shudder to think of it.'

'What's wrong with you,' I said, 'is that you have every house in the place surfeited with pictures and statues, so that they would have to build a second storey on every house to buy any more from you.' I laughed. I thought this was funny.

'You wrong me,' he said, holding up a thin white hand. 'You have known me long enough to be aware that I am a man of many talents. I don't necessarily have to devote those talents to the selling of religious objects, but I feel it is a mission in life. How can devotion among materialists be excited if they are not constantly regarding objects that remind them of sacred events? I make a living, that is true, but I feel that I perform a necessary service, and when I fail, as I seem to be failing on this journey, I know it is not because of any lack in me, since I don't change, but that it is a sinister hint of a rising lack in the people.'

'How do you make that out?' I asked.

'You are too well off,' he said. 'There is more thought about God in a year of famine, than in a year of plenty. Sometimes I wish that our country was as badly off as it was a hundred years ago. Then the people had slack bellies but their minds were filled with God. Here now I find that everybody's stomach is full and it proves the old saying: The fuller the belly the farther from the chapel.'

'G'wan, y'oul cod!' I said laughing, because now that I came to think of it, my own trousers were much tighter around the waist than they used to be, and this disturbed me a little, because I was always known to be a fine figure of a man.

'It stands to reason,' he urged. 'You don't want a new

rosary beads, nobody wants a new rosary beads. Why? I'll tell you, because you are not using your rosary beads enough to make them wear, and neither is anybody else. How many enlargements of dear, dead grandparents hang on a wall? Very few. Because people are thinking more about their own comforts than purchasing remembrances of the dear dead, who raised them and slaved for them. Why, my dear man, you can wear away even a holy picture if you give it sufficient devotion, but not here any more. I am disturbed by the smug sleek, sense of materialism, that has fallen on this whole place.'

I slapped my thigh and I laughed. 'Man,' I said, 'you'd sell an electric cooker to the devil.'

It was at this point I remember that we heard the commotion outside on the road; dogs barking and children calling and people laughing, and since exciting things don't happen often, we were soon standing at the door looking out at the scene. It was like a play in the hall.

Well, I had to laugh. There was Glugger Malone. Glugger is a bit of a half wit. His parents were very respectable people, now dead, and he had quite a few brothers and sisters. He was the only soft one of them. That's why we called him glugger from the old saying that there is often a glugger in a large hatch. He lived alone now down there in the old family house, a lonely place. He is a big man with white hair and very thick lenses of glasses he has to wear because his eyes are poor. It seems he was dozing away in the sun, sitting on the whitewashed stone outside his door when the kids crept up and tied the laces of his boots together, so now here he was trying to walk on the road and every step he would make he would fall down, his big hands keeping his body off the gravel. These kids are devils but I suppose boys will be boys. Weren't we the same ourselves when we were young?

It was very funny to see him. He was too dim-witted to figure out why he would fall every time he tried to take a step. All the people came out of their houses to look, and you really couldn't blame them for laughing at the sight of his bewilderment. Even the dogs were barking around laughing at him, and all the boys, naturally, were pleased at the success of their frolics.

Then he missed with his hands and he fell on his face. Laugh! It was one of the funniest things I've seen in years. His glasses fell off, and Glugger without his glasses is a very funny sight, believe me.

'Do you find this amusing?' I heard Patter asking me.

'Lord,' I said, 'wouldn't it make a cat laugh?'

'Are you serious?' he asked me.

'Is there a better comic than Glugger up in that big city of yours?' I asked him.

He left me then. Glugger was lying on the road, scratching around with a big hand for his glasses. What does Patter do, but go and spoil the whole thing. He bends down and he puts the glasses into the fool's hand, so that he can put them on, and then before Glugger can get up and fall again, Patter gets on his knees in the dust and unties the laces, and fixes them back separately again, neatly. Then he helps the big fellow to his feet and starts brushing him down with his hand.

'You're a proper spoil sport, Patter, damme if you aren't,' I called to him, 'and nobody will thank you for it. Glugger himself likes to make people laugh.'

The scoundrel didn't answer me. He reached in his pocket and handed Glugger something. Glugger stayed looking at it. Then Patter came back to me.

'You can't see it,' he said.

'What can't I see?' I asked.

'Your inhumanity to that poor fellow,' he said.

'Arrah, don't be cracked, Patter,' I said. 'That's Glugger. He loves things like that. It keeps him happy. What else has he to do?'

Patter shook his head, I remember.

'You are worse sunk in materialism than I ever thought,' he said. 'If you go on that way the lot of you will land in hell.'

I had to laugh at the serious face of him. This seemed to annoy him.

'Goodbye,' he said. 'I'll be back when the famine is on top of you again. You mark my words, because they are right words. Your thinking is lost in fat.'

He left then. I didn't know what he was talking about. He was acting very strange but I suppose it was because he was disappointed with sales. I called to your man. 'Come here, Glugger.'

He came over to me. His palm was open and he was looking down at the bright half-crown that was resting on it.

'So that's what he gave you. Frame it, Glugger, it's the first anyone ever saw from that Patter O'Rourke.' I had to inform the neighbours then of course, shouting it: 'Hey, Patter gave Glugger a half-crown!'

That made them laugh, before they went back in. They passed a few remarks about Patter's closeness. The little lads came up around Glugger. 'A whole half-crown,' they said.

'What are you going to do with it, Glugger?' I asked.

'Drink,' said Glugger grinning. 'Lemonade,' he said, 'and ice cream.'

He was fond of things like that.

'And sweets, Glugger,' said the children surrounding him, hanging on to his arms. 'Sweets, eh, Glugger. We'll all buy sweets.'

'Sweets and lemonade and ice cream,' said Glugger.

And off they went with him.

'Glugger 'll see very little of that half-crown,' I said to my wife laughing, as I went back into the kitchen.

Well, it was shortly after this that we were all excited about the letter that came from Dublin for Glugger. He couldn't read, of course, so he came to me with it. Being a sort of letter writer was one of my other functions in the place. It was addressed to Mister Garret Malone, if you don't mind, Esq. and who on the face of the earth would be writing to him, I couldn't know, until I opened the letter.

Well, sir, there were three names on the top of it and it was printed with a typewriter and it said that if Mister Garret Malone would travel to Dublin on a certain date and visit the address on the top of the page he would hear something of great advantage to himself re the demise of his Uncle Patrick in America. Now! Poor Glugger didn't know what it was all about, so I took him with me and called on the neighbours. Well, they were excited I can tell you, and we all tried to remember his uncle. The trouble was that if you touched anybody on the shoulder in Ireland and said : your Uncle Pat in Philadelphia or Boston or San Francisco or New York was asking for you, they'd jump a mile and pump your hand. Everybody has an Uncle Pat in America. But all the same we tickled the memory of old Matt Higgins and Sarah Meeney. They were fairly young yet, about ninety or so, but all the same after a few drinks they remembered Glugger's Uncle Pat the same as if he was standing in front of them. He had red hair and he was six foot six they said and he could lift a bullock with one hand, and was he dead the poor man and wasn't it young the Lord took him he must be only about eighty-five. So there you are. Naturally it threw the lot of us into a terrible tiswas, and we held a few meetings in Heffernan's pub and over the card games for the geese, and since Glugger hadn't a soul in sight to take care of him or guide him, it was finally settled that I myself should take the trip with him and look after him.

All this cost money, you know, but after all we were a charitable people, and Glugger was one of our own, you might say. So everybody, out of pure love, handed in money. We couldn't let him travel as he was with the knees out of his trousers and a bad patch on his britches – very poor clothes Glugger wore all round – so dammit if we didn't dress him like a bloody Lord. He had new underwear and shirts and ties and a brand new suit and good black boots and an overcoat and a cap to cover his white head. I tell you when we were finished with him, you'd nearly let him court your daughter, if it wasn't for the way he'd be peering through those thick glasses like a cannibal trout looking in a mirror.

So, off we went. I had to go with him, of course. Can you see that poor fellow wandering around there on his own? He'd never get out of it alive. It cost money but sure I didn't mind. It was in a good cause. We stayed in a hotel for a night too, and you should have seen Glugger looking around that place. He never saw such magnificence in his life, even if I thought it wasn't much of a place.

Then the next day at the right time off we went looking for this office we had to go to. Well, we had to travel more back streets and by-places before we came on it, a tall dirty building near a lot of warehouses, and we found the place, and it was up a narrow staircase that would be in danger of collapsing from the weight of a sparrow.

'This doesn't look like it,' I said to Glugger, 'but it is.'

We were about to go into the place when who do I see coming along the street with pictures under his arm, but our old friend Patter O'Rourke. Man, but he was surprised to see us, I can tell you.

'Pater bless you!' he exclaimed, 'and what are you doing in the big city? And I'm pleased to see you, and won't you come to the nearest pub and let me be host?'

'No, no, not now, Patter,' I said. 'We have a bit of business with a man here and it's very important and we don't want to be late, and I'm sorry we can't join you.'

'And how are you, Garret?' he asked Glugger shaking his hand, with Glugger grinning at him, very friendly, beaming in fact, 'and you are a different man,' he says, 'I'd hardly know you, and why are you dressed up like that? You look very well and I'm pleased to see that your circumstances have improved so vastly.'

'Well, Mister O'Rourke,' said Glugger, and the fool would have gone on to tell Patter all about us, if I hadn't pulled him by the arm and said, 'Come now, Glugger, we'll be late. We'll see you the next time you are our way, Patter, with the help of God, but we have very urgent business now.' And I pushed Glugger in the narrow door.

'Pater bless you, so,' said Patter and departed.

'But I wanted to tell him all about it,' said Glugger. 'He is a nice man. He is always very kind to me.'

'Nice man or not,' I said, 'you have to be careful. He is a city fella and if he heard you were coming in for a bit of money God knows how he would get it out of you, but he would. You can't trust any people, but the people that know you, remember that.'

Then we climbed the stairs.

It was a very shabby place and the room with the glass door was on the top of the stairs, and inside it was small and pokey and the lawyer man was small and pokey and even dirty it seemed to me, with a lot of cobwebby books on shelves, but all this didn't fool me, not for a minute. You know the old saying: The dirtier the lawyer the bigger his bank balance. These old philosophers knew what they were talking about.

Well, he was very pleasant and his news was good. He saw Glugger's birth-certificate and his baptismal certificate and we had a note from the JP too, so he couldn't refute Glugger. In all he said Glugger would be due for about three thousand pounds when all was cleared and paid and that he should have the money probated for him in a month. We signed papers. Glugger had to put an X of course, his mark, but I witnessed it and the little lawyer man did also, and when I inquired and sent Glugger out of the room and explained that he was only half there, and that there should be some stable honest man who would handle the money for him and see that he didn't squander it, this little man was very obliging and far-seeing and arranged that I should be what he called the power of attorney for the poor fellow. Glugger signed this too and after an hour we went our way, and I was pleased and took Glugger to a really posh place, and we ate a meal, and the price of it would have bought a calf, God forgive them, but it was in a good cause as I say and that evening we caught the train and we got home late at night and everybody was up to hear about Glugger's good fortune, and much porter was drunk on the strength of it, and we had a right good night, and Glugger was very respected.

After that, nothing happened. Just nothing at all. I'm nearly ashamed to say it. A month passed, and nothing, and another month and then I wrote a letter and the letter came back from the little dirty bastard's address, and NOT KNOWN HERE was stamped on it.

It was a fierce shock. It took a few months for the lot of us to realize that we had been the victims of heartless pranksters.

But who? Oh, there were glum faces in our village, I can tell you. By that time, Glugger had all the clothes well worn, so that we couldn't take them off his back.

I lost a lot of weight, worrying about man's inhumanity to man.

When Patter O'Rourke came back to us the next time, our sores weren't raw, but the scars were there.

Patter O'Rourke sold a lot of pictures this time. He had a very nice coloured picture of St Jude. I even bought one myself. St Jude is the patron of hopeless cases they say, and so far we hadn't as yet whistled goodbye to our money, and you never know. That saint has been known to work wonders.

Only last night, in the middle of the night, I awoke suddenly, and I thought, would Patter have been at the back of it all? But no, he couldn't. We treat him very well, and he's too Christian to commit a sin like that. It must have been only a coincidence that he was in the street that day we went to see that criminal in Dublin. Only a coincidence. And the fact that he had called Glugger Garret, that day too, knowing his odd name, that wasn't so strange. He had heard it here, I'm sure.

Ah, no, Patter wouldn't do a thing like that! Wouldn't it destroy your faith in human nature? Not Patter. He wouldn't do it. He believes in God. He wouldn't be doing the devil's work. I'm sure of it. Certain. Not Patter O'Rourke.

The Big Fish

EVERY day it was the same as the day before.

He would eat his breakfast; porridge with thick cream on it, freshly baked soda cake with home churned butter and good strong tea. Then he would wipe his mouth, grab his rod from beside the dresser, say: 'Goodbye now, Aunt Judy', listen while she said 'Be careful now, Joe, don't fall into the water or your mother will kill me', and then he was off. The cottage was a good way from the lake. You stepped outside the door and you saw the lake lying down below at your feet. It was a very big lake. It stretched away until it was lost in the mists of the morning. Some mornings when he came out, the mists had not completely cleared and the tree-covered islands seemed to be raised out of the water, held free from it, his Uncle Tom said, by fairies' fingers. He would pause for a while to look at it, count up how many days were left of his holidays before he would have to go back into the town and school, sigh at the fleet passing of the days and then he would run down the winding dirt road. It was easy to run because it was all downhill. It twisted and turned and was altogether hemmed in by stretching blackberry briars and tall bracken, which had filched wisps of hay from passing carts.

Then he reached the main road, paused to see if there was any traffic and darted across to the stile that went into the wood of young forest trees. Joe was ten years old, the same age as the young trees, Uncle Tom said, but they were nearly twice the size of him. The smell of pine was all about him, seeming to envelop him. He rarely hurried through the forest field, but when he climbed the stile at the other side he could see the stream that wound in the middle of the next one, and the waters of the lake gleaming through the trees at the end of it and it always made him hurry. First thing like this in the morning he was always filled with the most insane optimism, his pulse hammering. He ran by the stream, pushed through some low alders and then came out on the stone-littered shore of the lake. From here a tree-covered finger pointed out into the wind and the water and at the end of the finger he could see the big white rock where he would sit and fish. It took him ten minutes to work his way to the big white stone. He sat there.

The sun was warm already. There were white fleecy clouds in the sky drifting lazily. A south-west wind was blowing on the left side of him, splashing the big stone on which he was sitting.

His rod was simple. It was just a thick piece of bamboo with coarse brown line wound around the top of it. He freed this. There was a piece of gut tied to the hook. From his bulging trousers pocket he took the tin of worms. They were clean worms, blue-headed ones, wriggling on green moss. He fixed two of the worms on the hook. He had no feeling about this. He remembered the time he wouldn't touch a worm with his fingers if you shot him. Then he adjusted the cork on the line, threw in the worms, watched them sink into the deep water and waited tensely. He always waited tensely. He was sure every morning that a big trout was waiting to take his worm. Sure of it. In two hours he would be less certain. He would go home at one o'clock with a perch or maybe an eel, or even on one occasion a small trout, and he would be saying: Well tomorrow morning I bet you I will get a big fish. Tomorrow morning I will go home with an absolutely enormous fish. For an hour he would worry about what he would do when the big fish caught his hook. Would the bamboo break? He would have to haul him straight into the air. Would the gut break? Would the hook straighten out? He was all plans. And about that time, at almost exactly nine o'clock, Tickler would pass in his punt trawling his lines behind him.

Joe looked to his left and saw the punt coming around the point. If only, he thought, I could get stuck in an enormous fish now just as Tickler was passing, he would say that I was a real fisherman. He shook the rod impatiently, but it did nothing to the fish. He watched the slow approach of Tickler, who guided the boat along the edge of the shallows. The two ashpoles were sticking out each side of the punt, the heavy lines trailing from them, and on the tips of the rods Joe could see the bells. How he longed passionately that Tickler would stop some morning and say: 'Hey, Joe, how about hopping in and coming fishing with me!' That was a dream of course, because professional fishermen didn't care for little boys he supposed. And besides punts were only meant for one man. Single-oared boats they were, like chickens of the big two-oared ones that could handle almost any wind that blew on the lake.

Tickler came closer. He wore a cap. It was a brown nondescript cap, very old, with three or four trout flies stuck in it. He wore a heavy grey moustache and his face and hands were nearly the colour of mahogany from the burning of the sun and the wind. He always came by the white rock, and he would look at Joe, raise one hand from the oar, take the pipe from his mouth, nod gravely and say: 'Good-morning, any luck.' Joe would say: 'No, no luck. I think it's the east wind or the glare on the water maybe.' Joe had heard grown-ups talking about fishing. Then Tickler would say: 'That must be it. I had no luck either.' Many times of course when he said this, Tickler would have two or three fat trout in the boat, but it encouraged Joe to hear that a real professional wasn't catching any fish either.

This morning the procedure was changed.

Tickler paused as he came close.

'Any luck, Joe?' he asked.

'No luck,' said Joe, shaking his head. He couldn't think of any legitimate reason. The wind seemed to be right; there was no great glare on the water. 'I haven't been long at it,' he said.

'Would you like to come fishing in the boat with me?' Tickler asked then. He nearly laughed at the look on Joe's face. His mouth was wide open and his brown eyes were popping under his thatch of sun-bleached hair. Joe thought he might be dreaming. He said : 'What?' It came out in a sort of squeak.

'I thought you might like to come with me for the day,' Tickler said. 'If you are not too busy there, a change of ground might be good.'

'Oh, boy!' Joe said, and then he thought of his Aunt Judy. If he wasn't home at one o'clock as usual wouldn't she think he was drowned. 'Oh, I'd love to,' he said, his face a yard long. 'But I can't. Sure I have to be home at one, or they'd think I was dead.'

'Oh, that's all right,' said Tickler, 'I called in to them when I was coming down and asked if they minded if I took you for the day, that was of course, if you were willing.'

'Oh, boy!' said Joe again and started to wrap his line around the bamboo, furiously.

Tickler laughed quietly as he stopped the boat and started slowly and methodically to wind in his own lines, coiling them on the bottom boards. He was pleased that he had done this. The face of Joe was lighted like a torch. Every day for a week he had seen the small boy with the intense look sitting on the white rock. He had come to look for him each morning. He didn't really want anyone in the boat with him. He was happy trawling his lines, smoking his pipe, looking at the hills, killing his fish and thinking. But, he thought then, think of the second-hand pleasure I can get out of Joe. It's true that you can make yourself far happier by making other people happy first, particularly small boys like Joe.

'Leave your rod there under the trees,' he said. 'You can pick it up again.'

'I will,' said Joe and did so and then came back on the rock again and waited. Tickler steered in close to the rock, reached one hand for it and held on. 'Climb in now,' he said. He gave no warning, but he was pleased to see the careful way Joe stepped in, so that he would not rock the boat. It was very narrow, very slim, but Joe negotiated it with care and instinct. That fellow will make a good fisherman someday, Tickler thought, and then pushed away from the rock.

'You let out the lines,' Tickler said, 'if you like.'

'Oh, thanks, sure,' said Joe. He dropped in the bait. It was a real minnow mounted on a spinner and fixed with red thread. One was a copper spinner and the other was pewter. He was trembling in case he would do something wrong. But he didn't. He let out the wet lines carefully, all thirty yards of them.

'It's a good thing to have help in the boat,' said Tickler. 'Here I am like a gent, while you are doing all the work.'

Joe laughed.

'Oh, this is not work,' he said, 'Mr Murphy, this is real pleasure. Will we get a pull soon do you think?'

'We should do,' said Tickler. 'It's a good day.'

'Why don't you use real fishing rods?' Joe asked.

'No money in the rod,' Tickler chuckled. 'Rods are only for gentlemen, Joe. They don't depend on fish for a living. They can afford to play with trout and lose them. We can't afford that. We hook fish, we want to catch them. It's hard enough to hook them without letting them get away.'

'I see,' said Joe. 'No money in the rod.' He was determined to be a professional fisherman when he grew up and not a gentleman. Tickler could see the thought on his face. He could have told Joe about fishing in the Spring with showers of hailstones falling, sometimes snow, so that your fingers were petrified and it was all you could do to take the hook out of the fish. Paying for all this in the Winter with rheumatism and lumbago. Or he could tell him about the ineffable boredom of being ghillie to the gentlemen who came to fish in the summer, silently watching their blundering and ignorance, or the conversations they conducted over his head as if he wasn't there or as if he was a primitive man without intellect or intelligence.

'Do you like fishing?' Joe asked.

'Aye,' said Tickler, 'I do. Every year you swear you will never fish again; that you will work on shore. This when you wash the boat and put it away in October. Then as the Spring comes you feel a stirring in you, just the same as if it was the first year. I was your age when I started with my father. That's fifty years ago, Joe. Imagine that. I maybe have another ten in me.'

'Did you catch a big enormous fish, ever?' Joe asked.

'Salmon yes,' said Tickler. 'Many salmon. But the big trout always keep away from me. The biggest I got was six and a half pounds. That's the way I like it. Two to six is the right size. Good condition fish.'

'I see them stuffed in cases up in the town,' Joe said. 'Big enormous fish. I want one like that. Over twenty pounds. Imagine over twenty pounds!'

'Fish are better in a man's stomach than in a glass case, Joe,' Tickler said. 'What's a stuffed fish for, only for vanity? A great fish like that only comes once in a lifetime. You remember that. Ask anyone. You keep fishing long enough and you'll get a big fish sometime during your lifetime.'

The bell on the pole wagged, and tinkled. You'd swear a hand under the water was tugging it. Joe nearly jumped out of his skin.

Tickler's voice calmed him. 'Easy, Joe,' he said. 'You start pulling in the fish. I'll get in the other line.' Joe couldn't believe he heard him aright but he did. He caught the taut line. He could feel something alive at the end of it. He felt that his heart was suffocating him. Tickler could see the excitement even on the back of his neck, which was flushed. Hand over hand, he pulled the fish closer to the boat until he could see the distorted shape of him, right under him. He was sure he would lose the fish and that Tickler would be disgusted with him. Then Tickler leaned over with the big net and scooped him into the boat. He was a nice fish about two pounds. Joe gazed at the threshing body in wonder, flashing now gold now silver. It was the biggest trout Joe had ever been that close to, apart from the ones on the fishmonger's slab. Tickler killed him and he lay supine, his mouth wide open as if gasping for air, his eyes bulging. Tickler felt he had never enjoyed catching a fish so well since he was Joe's age. Joe was speechless with joy and wonder, his hands clasped between his knees.

Tickler repaired the slashed minnow and they fished again. Before lunch they had caught three more, none as big as the first. Then they went on to one of the islands and Tickler showed Joe the kind of sticks to gather and how to light them with a bit of faded bracken and he made tea in a terrible black kettle and it tasted, oh, like everything and Tickler also had thick slices of fresh cake and hard-boiled eggs, and as they sat there afterwards, Tickler smoking his pipe, Joe felt that he had never been as happy in his whole life before, and Tickler got a fresh view through Joe's eyes, of the low hills behind, and they giving way to the great valley in the mountains below; the white-faced cottages holding on to the sides of the hills like grim death and the patterned fields, forty-seven different shades of green, and the wild duck whistling by and the lake gulls wheeling, all under a blue sky flecked with white clouds.

It was as near Paradise as you could get, but then of course that's the difference between this Paradise and the real one. The earthly one always has a catch in it. There is always something in it to spoil it, so that people who think will be made aware of its unreality, and it would have been perfect for Joe (and for Tickler too in a way) if it wasn't for that bloody big fish.

They struck him late in the evening at the big black rock that raises an ugly head two hundred yards from the south side of the Island of The Great Yellow Ox. He nearly took the ashpole out of the boat, not to mind ringing the bell. Joe grabbed the line and the line cut into his fingers. He looked back over his shoulder at Tickler showing the whites of his eyes. 'Tickler!' he called forgetting to be polite and use the man's real name. 'I can't hold him! I can't hold him!'

'Get in the other line,' Tickler said, relieving him of it. Joe frantically started pulling in the free line.

Tickler felt his own old heart thumping with excitement. He gauged the tugging on his fingers in order to decide what kind of a fish it was. It wasn't a salmon. A big salmon would have had the pole overboard long ago, and he would have come out of the water leaping like a silver flame. It was not a big pike. A big pike just tugs and tugs, savagely and sullenly and chops at the line with his ugly retracted teeth. Tickler closed his eyes the better to get a feel of this one.

'Joe,' he said. 'This is a big fish. As sure as you're there, Joe, this is a big trout.' He knew it was. Fifty years of fishing would let you know from the pull of the line. He started to haul in, hand over hand. Joe, the other wet line lying around him, was on his knees, his small hands gripping the sides of the boat. Tickler was surprised then at the way the fish was coming easily towards them. Surely there should be more fight in him. He looked back and he saw the great body of the fish, flaccidly curving, surrendering lazily and almost lovingly to the pull of the hooks in its jaw. He just turned over and over without fight and came nearer and nearer and there he lay under them, flat on his side, yielding, too big, Tickler thought, to fight. He held a tight grip on the line with one hand and reached for the net with the other. He eased the net under him. It was ludicrous. The net wouldn't fit him. The net only covered his middle cut. So Tickler let down the net gently and reached for the crude gaff behind him. He fumbled for it, found it and then brought it forward.

Joe was thinking: Oh my God! please let us land this fish. Don't let this fish get away. He had his hands up to his mouth. He was biting on his knuckles with his teeth. His face was pale. He had never seen such a fish. He seemed to be half the length of the boat. He seemed to be bigger than any fish Joe had seen in the glass cases.

Tickler stretched forward with the gaff.

He was going to put it under the trout and gaff him in the belly when he thought: What am I doing? His hands were trembling. He was sure he was pale. This was the biggest trout that Tickler had ever seen or even dreamt about when he was young. Tickler thought a lot in that few seconds and then he reached the tip of the gaff to where the hooks of the spinner were caught in the trout's jaws. He tapped the hooks gently and they parted and the fish was free. It lay there unbelieving on top of the water for three seconds, lying almost belly up, then it turned slowly, slowly. Its head found the water. The great tail flicked. And it was gone.

Joe had reached a hand for it. He saw the green-black back disappearing and that was all and then he looked at Tickler.

'But you let him go!' Joe said. 'You let him go! You let the great fish go.'

It was then that Tickler realized that there was somebody in the boat with him. He winced at the accusing look in the boy's eyes. I should have thought of Joe, he realized, in complete dismay. Why didn't I think of Joe?

'Why did you do it, Tickler?' Joe asked. 'Why in the name of God did you do it?' Joe was bewildered.

'I'll tell you,' said Tickler, suddenly realizing that anything he could say wouldn't do. You couldn't explain to Joe. Not at his age. He would have to be fifty years older. 'Joe,' he said. 'I want to fish for another ten years. If I took that fish home, I would never fish again. Listen, why do you fish? So that some day somewhere you get the Big Fish. All right. You get him and what have you got to fish for? You have no purpose. That and this. You can't eat big fish like that, Joe. Their flesh is not good. You can't eat them see. So you sell them and somebody stuffs them and puts them in a glass case and there's a little card with your name on it and it tells that at such and such a time you caught this fish, and your life becomes different Joe, I tell you. You won't be the same man. They will point you out: That's him, that's the fellow that caught the twenty-five-pound trout on the lake.'

'Was he? Was he?' Joe asked. 'Was he twenty-five pounds?'

'He was,' said Tickler.

'You should have caught him,' Joe said. 'You should have caught him, Mister Murphy.'

Tickler opened his mouth to speak. And then he shut it. What's the use, he thought, how could you explain? They didn't talk any more. There seemed to be a chill on the air. The sun was dying. Tickler rowed home. The boy had turned his face away and was looking back at the mountains with unseeing eyes.

Tickler knew one thing for sure. Joe would never want to fish with him again. That saddened him. He dropped him off at the white rock. Joe didn't look back. He just went on the way home with his head down. Tickler knew that tomorrow Joe would be fishing from the white rock, but that he, Tickler, would have to find another way to the fishing grounds. He sighed, and he was very sorry and he rowed away.

Solo and the Nine Irons

SOME claimed that Garveen was the prettiest spot in the whole parish. It consisted of an area of about four hundred acres almost entirely surrounded by low hills, except where the river that drained the far side came through the gap in the hills, and dividing in two from the total inflexibility of the earth at that point, ran in two directions to meet the sea. Garveen faced the sea, then, a fairly rough coast except where the butty stone quay clove itself into the maw of the waves and on the sheltered side of itself had created a small beach of silver sand. Here the black boats and the currachs rested. Where the river divided there was a bridge, a sturdy one, of three stone arches, and in bad weather when the river was high this bridge was the only possible way of access to the place. The river was called The Gap. This sounds ugly in English, but its name in Irish has a sweeter sound.

On account of the feeling that the people had of being shut off, they were a little different from the other people. They regarded themselves as being a cut above them, and like all men who derive their livelihood from the terrors of the sea, regarded themselves as being superior to men who till and toil. There were only six houses in the place, no shop, no pub, so that when they wanted groceries or strong drink they would have to journey the few miles, over the bridge into the village of Gortshee. It was also notable for one other thing: it held the only blacksmith in the whole place. His forge was in there, a sort of boarded dirty ramshackle shed, but then who ever heard of a clean forge? His name was Tom Tate, and he would be the last blacksmith. He had no assistant. The coming of the tractor was almost putting him out of business and apart from odd horseshoes or the wheel of a cart, cleats and bolts and things for the few fishing boats, he wasn't kept very busy.

What I am going to relate would never have happened but for that freakish January storm. It came from nowhere, swept over the country, and then it was gone, leaving torrential rain and a lot of destruction in its wake. Unfortunately it coincided with a very high tide, which the wind blew even higher so that it ran up the double estuary like a scalded cat. The running tide made matchwood of three currachs and blew them half over the village, and one of the pucaun boats was neatly deposited almost uninjured in the front street of the Backs' house, which was the one nearest to the sea. It was a frightening storm. Some storms you can view from your window admiring the forked lightning against the piling, monstrously back clouds. Some storms just put the fear of God into you and leave you timorous and cowering, and this was one of those. It turned night into day and sent walls of water from the sky to the earth, almost solid walls of water that would test a strong man to get through. The river was high anyhow from the melting of the snow on the hills and the eternal draining of the deep bogs behind them; but with this rain falling and the sea contemptuously throwing back the waters of the river, it rose and rose higher and higher than the memory of man.

The wind stripped the thatched roof off one house as if it was peeling an orange and tore the galvanized roof off another with a dreadful tearing noise that rose above the screaming of the wind, so that the people of the houses came out and looked in horror and then scurried like refugee ants to the solid two-storey house of the Backs. That was the house in front of which the fishing boat eventually came to rest, without hurting anybody. But the sea, when it came, invaded the lower part of the house, so that kitchen chairs were floating and everybody was wet to the knees and it was very fortunate that little Mary Backs, since she was very sick, happened to be in the bedroom upstairs.

She was very sick, which is another and probably the

94

most important reason for what happened. Her sickness and that storm would nearly unhinge a person's mind. Certainly her mother and Jerr, her father, were practically driven out of their minds with fear. She was lying in the bed and she was very hot. Somebody said you could roast an apple on her forehead. And this sickness fell on her almost as fast as the storm had fallen on the earth. One minute just a childish ailment, and the next, people were sure she was dying. The face of her mother was stark white as she bent over her, rubbing her small forehead with a work-worn hand, crooning to her. And the other side of the bed was her grandmother saying, 'What'll we do? What'll we do?'

Jerr, a big man with grey hair, wearing a heavy blue gansey, said: 'Don't grieve, Julia, don't grieve. I will go now into Gortshee for the doctor,' and the grandmother said: 'Cross of God if you go out in that you will be kilt, Jerr. She will be fine. The fever will break in her.' 'I'm going,' he said. 'I'm going,' his heart torn watching the small pale face, the sweat-soaked brown curly hair, hoping that, like some miracle, if only he went away when he came back everything would be all right.

'How is she? How is she?' they asked him downstairs. All the people cowering in the kitchen, sitting on the table, on the backs of chairs. 'Not good,' he said. 'Not good. I will have to go into Gortshee for the doctor.' 'No you won't, Jerr Backs,' said a tall young man they knew as Boulder on account of the blackness of him and the buttiness of him and the endurance of him. 'I will go for the doctor and you stay here and keep the house,' and before Jerr could protest he was gone and the people were barricading the door behind him, cursing the inrush of water that his going bequeathed to them.

Boulder was soaked right into his skin in a few seconds. The force of the wind took his breath away until he turned his back on it and then it was like a giant hand pushing him from behind. Wasn't it great good fortune, he was thinking, that none of us was at sea when it fell? He paused a little

— 95

watching the black boat coming up on the tide. But wonders in these few hours were becoming almost commonplace so he pressed on, running. He had to stop on the bridge and watch. He couldn't believe that the river could rise so fast and with such power. His brown hands instinctively clutched the coping of the bridge. It was trembling under them. What, his mind asked, who in the name of God ever heard of a stone bridge trembling? But it was, and the roadway under his feet. The water was a monstrous maelstrom of lashing white foam and dirty brown, wicked-looking bog water. He made the sign of the Cross on himself, shaking his head. Then he ran on to the village. There wasn't a sinner to be seen in it. Slates were flying off the roofs. He kept close to the walls of the houses.

The doctor was in, young, slight, fair-haired, and already patient and unsurprised at urgent calls always coming at the most inopportune times. He questioned Boulder about Mary: her appearance. In his own mind he thought she might have pneumonia, so he packed his bag accordingly and got his car out of the garage. Boulder admired him for his lack of words and his decision. When they cleared the village and got on the open road to Garveen, the wind seemed to be slipping its palms under the car and tossing it up and down. Boulder, who would be quite calm in a small open boat in a heavy sea, was terrified at the movements of the heavy car in the wind. The wipers couldn't seem to keep the screen clear of the belting rainwater. They had to peer through the glass. When they were coming up on the bridge, Boulder opened the window his side and stuck out his head, purely from instinct, he said later, and shouted: 'Stop it! Stop it! Stop it, now!' and fortunately the doctor had the brakes clamped in a few seconds, or the car would have been into the river.

Because the heavy stone bridge was gone, just gone as if it had never existed, as if it hadn't withstood the worst that could befall for nearly two hundred years. It was gone. All that remained of it were the two pillars on which the arches had rested, and you could only see those occasionally in the swirling, chuckling, savage flood.

'My God,' the doctor said, standing there looking at it.

'I felt it in me bones,' Boulder said. 'I knew coming over. It was shaking like an old man in winter.'

They just stood there then, looking, in the rain, finding it hard to keep their feet.

'How do we get in, now?' the doctor asked, his lips at Boulder's ear.

'We don't,' said Boulder. 'No way in now at all. Until the river drops. Poor Mary, poor little Mary.' The doctor felt bad. Impotent. Angry. That little child. But there was no way now. Then they saw the figure on the opposite bank. Boulder recognized Jerr. He was cupping his hands around his mouth.

'Doctor, what can we do? What can we do?' he is calling. But his words are whipped away on the wind. And the doctor's words of advice to him. Even Boulder shouting across the mad torrent can't make himself heard. Such a helpless position to be in. Boulder ground his teeth. Then they heard Jerr saying something else. 'The nine irons,' he was calling desperately. 'It will have to be the nine irons now.' Frantically waving his fist at the sky and the storm, as if that would do any good. Then he was gone. 'What does he mean, the nine irons?' the doctor asked. 'The silly superstitious bastards!' said Boulder. 'Instead of being down on their knees. What good can those oul pishreogues do?'

'We'll get back,' said the doctor.

They went back, and they told the police the bridge was down, and Boulder told the doctor he would keep on watch and no matter what time of the day or night they could get across he would call for the doctor. It was only an after-thought on the doctor's part to call on the priest as he was passing the house. He always called and told him when a person was really ill.

He liked calling on the priest anyhow, since they were contemporaries. They had been at school together, Father John Henderson and he. They had played Gaelic football together and it was during the course of his brilliant football-ing that John Henderson had acquired the name of Solo. Many people still remembered those dashing, unstoppable solo runs of his, ball to toe, ball to hand, ball to ground, ball in the net almost before you were aware that he had started. Many fanatic football men still bemoaned his loss to the church, saying there could be many priests but only one footballer like Solo. The parish had lost a footballer, but gained a priest who could apply all his football skills to the guiding of a complex community towards a harder goal, the doctor thought, chuckling.

He found Solo out in his back yard nailing down the galvanized roof of a fuel house. He was well wet. The doctor told him about little Mary Backs and the bridge and then laughing said: 'Anyhow it'll be all right. They are going to work the nine irons on her. That ought to be better than drugs.'

He was amazed at the reactions of Solo.

'What?' he demanded. 'What did you say? What did you say?'

'Something about the nine irons, they said,' said the doctor. 'Going to work the nine irons on her. What are the nine irons?'

Solo didn't answer him. He jumped down from the ladder, and ran for the back door. The wind finished its work on his shed before he was in the house. The galvanized sheets screamed and groaned and then took to the air, leaving the joists naked looking and ashamed and exposed to the weather.

The doctor caught up with Solo outside. Solo was sitting behind the wheel of the doctor's car. The doctor just got in beside him in time before it took off.

Said Solo: 'You think the girl has pneumonia. Tell me what I have to do with her.'

'But you can't get across the river,' said the doctor.

'Tell me! Tell me!' said Solo urgently. 'I know that Thady Crumpaun. The bloody old pagan, God forgive me. Tell me calmly what I must do if I get to the girl.'

Bewildered the doctor tried to tell him, showed him the compartments in the bag and what they contained. 'But there's no use,' he said. 'Nobody can cross.'

The people of Garveen had known almost as soon as the bridge went and they brought word to the Backs' house about it, and the people of the house were thrown into utter despair. Julia Backs, always a calm almost phlegmatic woman, was on her knees by the bed, still holding the child's hand and crying, crying, enough to frighten you. Big Jerr helpless, clenching his great fists. Only Thady calm. A little randy-looking man, with a white moustache and whiskers. Small, no spare flesh at all on him and piercing pale blue eyes. Lived alone up on the far hill. A house of his own, managed on his own. Men respected Thady but they didn't love him. Too self-sufficient maybe. But they listened to him now (they would have listened to anybody at this despairing moment) when he said: 'Look, people, there is nothing left for it but the nine irons.' The grandmother looked at him and crossed herself. 'God forgive you,' she said.

'How many men who should be dead are walking about this day with the nine irons on a ring?' Thady asked them. Some of them nodded. They knew people with the nine irons. 'What hope is there else?' Thady asked. 'You hear, Julia. Let us make the nine irons.'

Julia wasn't thinking.

'Make anything, anything, anything,' she said. 'What will we do without Mary, Jerr? She is going from us.'

Thady ran to the landing outside. 'Are you there, Tom Tate?' he asked. The voice said up, 'I'm here, Thady.'

He was back in the room.

'You hear now,' he said. 'Hold on. We are away to make the irons.'

He went down the stairs. It was then Jerr left the house too and ran to the bridge to make sure for himself that it was down. He saw Boulder and the doctor on the far bank the other side of the broken bridge and he was filled with despair.

Tom Tate wasn't like a blacksmith. You expect blacksmiths to be big and broad. Tom was small and it was only when they reached the forge and he took off his coat and you could see the heavily muscled arms that you could recognize in them that he was a member of the profession.

'You name them, Thady,' he said. 'I have forgotten.' They were not alone now. A lot of the people had left the Backs' house to come with them. They were sorry, because the wind was whistling in and out of Tate's forge like demons were riding it. But said they, this was a chance that you didn't get every day – to be at the birth of the nine irons.

Thady thought. His eyes were sparkling. He was thinking. About Solo. He didn't like Solo. Thady had a good hand with sick cattle or horses or animals or humans, they said. It was mostly done by old incantations. He had the power of healing they said. In this day and age, said Solo scornfully. All you are, Thady, is a Medicine Man. You should be living in Africa with the most primitive tribe possible. You would be really big there. Thady didn't like that. People called him The Medicine Man, afterwards, his enemies with laughter and malice. That's why he thought about Solo now. Gleefully, because there was nothing Solo could do. And the nine irons were good besides. They had worked before. They would work now. 'Here it is,' he said. He spoke the names in Irish. They were:

'The plough, the harrow; spade, fork and chain;
The shovel, scythe; the axe and slean.'

'You have them now, Tom Tate?' he asked. He repeated them.

Tom Tate nodded and then he gathered from the bench nine pieces of sheet iron and he brought tools with him to the anvil, and he repeated the names and started with delicate fingers to cut the models from the sheets. And as he was at the anvil, Thady went around it, and in the old language he recited the ancient verses and this is what they meant:

Iron plough, fertile ground; let the little sick be sound.

Iron harrow, breaking soil; with your spikes her fever foil.

Iron spade, digging deep; give her rich rewarding sleep.

Iron fork, probing prongs; strike till death untie the thongs.

Iron chain, great with power; close the ring around her bower.

Iron shovel, heaping clay; let her eyes regard the day.

Iron scythe, sweet and clean; carve the fevered misty dream.

Iron axe, sharp and thick; cleave the Gaunt One's falling stick.

Iron slean, burnished bright; cut the clasping arms of night.

It was a weird scene in that forge. Some of the onlookers said afterwards that they felt the hair rising on the backs of their necks. Thady kept repeating the rhyme and walking around the anvil, with Tom crouched over it, cutting delicately at the tiny forms.

They stood on the bank watching the river and the broken bridge. There was only one alleviating feature, the wind was not as fierce by a few degrees, but the rain was very heavy and the river was beginning to cover the banks and swelling up.

'What did I tell you?' the doctor asked.

To tell the truth Solo's heart quailed as he looked at it. Boulder was there. He came up to them.

'Tell me, Boulder,' said Solo. 'Is little Mary really in danger of dying?'

'She's very bad, Father,' said Boulder, 'and no mistake, but God is good.'

'And the nine irons,' said Solo. 'What about them? Give me what I will need,' he said then to the doctor. He took out his tobacco pouch and he emptied the tobacco out of it, and he put the little bottles into it and then rolled it tightly again and put it in his inside pocket.

'What in the name of God are you going to do?' the doctor asked in amazement. 'You can't swim that river. You'll be killed.'

'I'm not going to swim it,' said Solo moving down. 'I'm going to jump it.'

'Holy Father, are you raving mad?' asked Boulder.

I probably am, Solo thought, as he regarded the river. There was the buttress near him, just under the water, and ten feet away he could see the buttress of the first arch appearing occasionally from under the torment of water. Ten feet away again there was the other arch support and ten feet away again the buttress on the other side. He didn't stop to think any more. He backed up about ten paces and ran for it, timing his take-off from the last inch of stone. The doctor turned his back to the sight of him, after shouting, but Boulder, his mouth open, his fists clenched, kept watching him. He saw his big body flying through the air and his feet landing in the welter on the stones. Now, he's gone, he thought. He nearly was. He dug his arms into the water and gripped the edges of the stones with his fingers, just to rest. The flood rose on him, dashing madly at his bent body. It went over his head, smothered him, and then it cleared again. Boulder saw him emerging like a seal, his black clothes shining wet and clinging to him. There was terrible force in the water, pulling at his fingers, pulling at his body. Lord, Solo shouted silently, I know I am brash, but it is in a good cause. He started to rise slowly, bracing his great legs well apart, stiffening the muscles of them against the current.

Now he is gone, Boulder thought.

He is still there, the doctor thought with wonder, looking, thinking about the God of drunkards and holy fools.

This is where I sink or swim now, Solo thought. He couldn't jump ten feet now to the next arch support. He would just have to throw his body at it and grip it with his hands. His heart almost failed him at the thought. His strength felt spun out already. He thought of the nine irons, the winking polished little things each as small as the fingernail of a baby and it made him so angry to think of his people putting those superstitious things before God that he leaped and his clutching hands found the edges of the rocks and held tightly as his body was swept down with the raging current.

Boulder and the doctor didn't breathe as they watched. Solo thought the stones might give under his clutching fingers. Built long, long ago they were stuck together with mortar, a mixture of lime and bullocks' blood. He prayed for the men who had mixed the mortar and hoped that they would get to Heaven if they weren't there already and he pulled himself towards the stones, groped with a heavily muscled knee, gripped with it, and slowly pulled himself on to the mass of stones. He had to keep gripping with his fingers, with his knees, with his toes, straddling them as the water flowed over him, tearing at him. When it was not covering his mouth he breathed and then slowly raised himself to his knees, then a knee and a foot and then his two feet and he stood braced to the drag, breathing very hard, and there were red spots in front of his eyes. Well, he had had red spots many times before. Playing fast, unrelenting football for a solid hour with a ten-minute interval often gave him spots in front of his eyes. And none of that was for anything but pleasure and spectator pleasure, so here now he had only one more hop to go, and he dug in and threw himself again. He only barely made it, and if the current at this side had been as great as in the middle between the two arches, that would have been the last anybody would have heard of Father Solo.

He was gripping the far buttress, and then he was lying on it and he was saying, Lord, I thank you. I didn't really mean to be brash, it was just that circumstances demanded it, and I won't do it again. The others were watching his prostrate form with their hearts in their mouths and they breathed again when they saw him slowly pulling himself to his feet. Then he turned to them, and they could see the white teeth of his smile before he turned and set off down the road, squelching wet.

Boulder sat on the wet ground. He wiped the sweat off his eyebrows.

'I don't want ever to see a thing like that again,' he said.

'Nor I,' said the doctor, 'even if it's something the like of which we could never possibly see again.' He too wiped sweat off his forehead. He felt drained as if it were he himself and not Solo who had crossed the river.

Solo went as fast as he could. He was so wet that he couldn't be any wetter, he thought, and that itself was a consolation. How long would it take them to turn out the irons? That was his problem. He would have to be there before them or his journey would have been in vain. They could always say afterwards that it was really the irons that did it.

Tom Tate was putting the finishing touches to the irons. They were all made, very neatly. He had bored tiny holes in each of them to attach them to the iron ring, but before he attached them he was polishing them with sandpaper, so that they gleamed. 'Oh, lovely, lovely, lovely,' Thady was saying to him. Thady was in no particular hurry. The little girl would keep. He knew the toughness of the human body, how hard it was to kill it. Better have everything just right. 'Now put them on the ring,' he said. 'Then we'll put the ring onto a round of fine wire to put around her neck. You'll see, the touch of the cold iron will chase the fever.'

Solo was surprised to see the boat resting in the front of the house. The tide was receding. He saw the wrecked piers, the wrecked boats. He groaned, because he would be the one who would have to set in and fight the authorities, wade through the masses of red tape to get everything repaired again. He opened the front door and went into the kitchen.

They rose and looked at him as if he was an apparition.

'Father,' said Jerr, 'you came to us. How did you come to us?'

'I crossed the river,' said Solo. 'Where is little Mary?'

'But no man could cross the river,' said Jerr. 'She is upstairs. God sent you. Everything will be fine now. I know it will.'

Solo went up the stairs. Before he did so he took off his squelching shoes and socks and rubbed his bare feet on the floor. It didn't do much good. The floor was wet from the water that had passed over it. But it felt better. He mounted the stairs. He went into the room. His heart contracted at the sight of the little girl. He closed his eyes for a moment before he went over to her. He didn't mind the adult sick and dying. But children always upset him. It always seemed such an immense break in the pattern of living. He put his hand on the mother's head. She raised it and looked at him. Amazement and acceptance and confidence blazed in her eyes. It unsettled Solo. What if the Lord meant to take the child? She released the child's hand and gripped tightly onto his own.

'It will be all right now,' said Solo. 'Everything will be all right now, Julia.'

He bent over the little one. If he could give her some of his own strength; push it into her. Not that he was as strong as he would have been normally. He took off his wet coat, extracted the bottles from the pocket and set to work.

The men came from the forge in a cavalcade. Early on they had been inclined to jeer a bit. Later their jeering became discomfort when Thady turned his pale blue eyes onto them. The way one who believes can silence the scoffers. They knew Thady's worth. He knew all the many herbs of the mountains and the streams. You remember penicillin that they were reading about? Hadn't Thady known all about that long ago, things he used to pick and boil from the spot where the mushrooms grew, and the way he could cure the horses' hooves with poultices of mouldy bread. They often felt that the doctors were only catching up on Thady's knowledge. A lot of them still wouldn't put a seed in the ground without Thady telling them the right time of the moon. And some of them wouldn't fish in the sea until Thady would tell them. He had a powerful pull over the back of their minds. And now they were not in much doubt that the nine irons would do all that Thady claimed for them.

So they followed him eagerly in a procession up the road.

And Thady stopped dead outside Backs' front door, because there was a stranger standing up there waiting for him. A very big-built, fair-haired, deep-blue-eyed stranger, dressed in old trousers and a fisherman's blue gansey and big boots on his feet and it took them a long time to realize that they were looking at Father Solo. It couldn't be him, Thady thought. How could he cross the river? But it was he. He was smiling.

'Hello, men,' said Solo. 'If you have come to ask about little Mary, she is sleeping soundly now. I think the fever has left her.'

'You couldn't have crossed the river,' said Thady. 'You couldn't have crossed it.'

'God is good, Thady,' said Solo. 'What's that strange thing you have in your hand. Do you mind if I look at it?'

He held out his big lacerated palm.

Thady looked at him. He was furious. But he had good control over his features. Only Solo could see it in his eyes. How can you fight that, Solo wondered. It's buried deep in him. He should have been living a thousand years ago. Solo was glad he had crossed the river. You cannot win, Thady, he told him with his eyes. The forces arrayed against you are too strong. Yours are wilted. Thady knew it was too late. He could never get into the house now. It was too late anyhow when he hadn't reached the house first.

He looked at the irons in his hand, then he turned and flung them from him. They rose, tinkling in an arc and then fell splashing into the waters of the sea.

'Nothing, nothing, it was nothing,' he said, and turned away from them and headed off towards the hills. They watched after him. Only Tom Tate looked with sorrow after the irons. He had taken such pains with them and they looked so neat.

Solo felt sorry for Thady. He could be happy, he thought, if only he would let me talk to him.

Then he said to them : 'The tide is going down. The river will soon be falling. Gather a lot of boards and things and we'll bridge the river as best we can and get Mary out of here into hospital. All right?'

They paused and then they said, 'All right, Father,' almost with a sigh, Solo thought. Back to the hum-drum, the commonplace things that get you to heaven. For the nine irons were colourful. They were exotic. They stirred buried things in you.

The climbing Thady was a diminishing figure on the side of the hill.

The Match Maiden

SHE lay on the bank of the river looking into the water. It was a late July morning and the sun was hot, but most of its heat was withheld from her by the low-hanging leafy branches of the giant beech tree that reared over her.

The river was shallow, but its current was swift, except near the bank where it was smooth and she could see her face and head reflected, the reflection sometimes shattered to pieces by an eddy sent in from the main flow.

The birds were very chirpy. The swallows were dipping gracefully over the water, snatching flies on the wing with almost incredible rapidity.

She heard his voice, almost in her ear, so close in fact that she could feel his warm breath on the side of her face. He was very flattering.

'It was your veiled eyes,' he said, 'that first attracted me. You can't measure the effect of eyes which are nearly always veiled, and then suddenly opened. Like an impact, a physical impact, a blow over the heart.'

She was critical. She opened her eyes and looked at them in the water. They were big and blue and could be veiled by very long dark lashes. She sighed.

'The wording of love is commonplace,' his voice went on. 'But what else can a man use but words that have been in use since the beginning of speech. The feel of your skin against the back of my hand is like the touch of a rose petal, or an infant's skin under the tips of the fingers.'

She shivered. But she was still critical. She knew. She thought she felt the momentary touch of his hand on her face; on her long dark shiny hair. I know it's not wavy, she thought, but it's long and silky. She moved her hand which was propping her pointed chin, placed it on the ground and rested her forehead on the back of it.

'The first time I said it,' his voice went on. 'I didn't want to approach you, just watch you from a distance; your form in the fields, or walking the side of a hill, or lying by the bank of the river, where you are now. All pictures shut up in the cupboard of my mind, which I would take out in secret and secretly peruse. I didn't have the courage until now.'

I can't be that attractive, she thought, and I am too shy. If I wasn't covering my face now, I couldn't even listen to him.

'If you will,' he said. 'I will always treat you with the greatest gentleness. I can't tell you how my heart is bursting to possess you. We will live far away from here. I have a place. It is by the bank of a river, like this too. And it is beautiful. It is a small house, but it is filled with sunshine. It will be like our hearts which will be filled with sunshine too, I promise you.'

Aren't promises cheap, she thought. Would it be true? Wouldn't he change when he knew me? Wouldn't I be afraid again? What do I know about him except that he is young and his hair is fair and his skin is delicately pale and not coarsened and burned by the winds and weather of the fields? His wrists are slender. In fact he is rather frail in appearance so that my heart rises to him. He would be somebody I would be able to nurse or to mind or to have depending on me. So what will I reply? But before she could reply she heard the real voice calling from behind her: 'Janey! Janey!'

It was the voice of her father and as sudden realization flooded her, the unstoppable tears flowed from her eyes. She bit into the back of her hand, but she couldn't stop them. Nor could she raise her head when she heard him behind her, standing over her, looking down at her. She could see him; the small dumpy man with pale blue watery eyes, fluttering his short weak lashes; waving his small fat hands.

'Janey! Janey!' he said. On one knee now beside her,

placing his hand on her back so that she could feel the embarrassed warmth of it through the light stuff of her wedding frock. 'Please, Janey, don't cry. Please don't cry!' he was beseeching her.

'All right, Father,' she said then. 'All right. I will be all right now,' realizing that her handkerchief was bunched in her other hand. She rubbed it fiercely on her eyes. They will be red, she thought and my nose will be red and I'll look a sight, but what does it matter?

'You are all right, Janey, all right?' He was anxious. She didn't blame him. It wasn't his fault. Just that he was weak, anything for peace, peace at any price; terrified of her mother. But then she was weak too, so what was she faulting him for? She rose to her knees and then to her feet, keeping her back to him while she dried her eyes.

'You'll really like Tom Flannagan when you get to know him better,' her father said. 'Won't you, Janey?' Wanting it to be that way.

'I'm sure I will, Father,' she said. Even though I have only spoken to him three times in my life? Even though I am nineteen and he is forty-three. Oh yes, I'll really like him when I get to know him!

'Come now,' he said. 'The car is at the door waiting. Your mother sent me to look for you. They are anxious, girl. We have only twenty minutes to get to the church.'

'I'm coming now, Father,' she said and walked with him. She was taller than he. He had to take two steps to her one. That was why they called him Dan the Dancer.

'You're a good girl, Janey, a good girl,' he said, sighing that there would be no trouble. His limited imagination had conjured up all sorts of possibilities: that he would have found her floating face down in a deep pool in the river: that he would never have found her at all: that he would have to go back to his wife and say: She is gone. I cannot find her. He patted her arm.

Jane looked over her shoulder fleetingly at the bank of the river. He might still be there under the shade of the beech tree; his shirt white; his fair hair dappled by sunlight filtering through the branches. Looking after her with sorrow; saying farewell, farewell, forever.

Somebody once said that Dan the Dancer's wife had a face that was carved out of bog oak. It was true for him. She looked hard, black and unbending, and she watched with no visible emotion her only daughter being married to Tom Flannagan who could quite easily have been her father.

Her three sons, all black-haired and seemingly as insensitive as herself, also watched, loutishly. The eldest, Dan, suffered from adenoids, and his mouth was always open like a gawk. He liked porter. He hoped it would flow freely. The other two, still in their teens, didn't like girls much anyhow, and they saw no difference between their sister Jane and a girl. Dan the Dancer, his eyes watering, sometimes nose-trumpeted into a red handkerchief.

Jane didn't know how pale she was. The priest who was marrying them kept his eyes averted from her face and prayed for her.

She was conscious of her smallness, beside the huge bulk of Tom Flannagan. Her mind was practically numbed. There was no salvation. In dreams there would have been last-minute interventions. Now none. All hope was gone.

The hand that held her own to put on the ring was enormous, with fair hairs on the back of it. The palm was as hard as a board, the nails clipped short, a very tanned useful hand, not fine and delicate.

But listen, there was a tremble in it!

That brought her eyes up in a swift look at his face.

It was a big face, square-jawed, very sunburnt, so that the crinkles around the eyes were white where they screwed against the eye-glare of the sun. Just the top of the forehead was white-skinned where the hat had protected it from the burning. The hair above that was fair, with grey hairs in the middle of the fair ones. Short fair lashes shaded his eyes. That was what she saw and then she dropped her eyes, he dropped her hand. She was Mrs Flannagan, if such a thing were possible, and she walked back to the pew and he fol-

lowed her and his big shoes banged on the kneeler as he
went into the seat and made a loud resounding noise in the
peaceful church.

She bowed her head in her hands and pressed her knees
together to try to stop the shaking of her limbs and she
prayed like this : Lord, help me, for I am alone.

The smell of stout, tapped from a barrel; the penetrating
smell of cold ham and whiskey, of fresh bread taken hot
from a pot oven. These in your nose. And in your ears,
slurred drunken conversation, or wild hurroos. A melodeon
and heavy shoes stamping on a cement floor, to bewilder
your hearing, and in your eyes, people so close, smelling of
sweat from the crowding of them, looking at them but never
at the man who was her husband, a head over the tallest of
them, until later he faced her and forced her to look at him
as he said : 'It is time now.'

She said goodbye to her room. That didn't hurt her. She
nearly always had to share it with a snoring brother with a
curtain between the beds. It wasn't her own, you see. It
wasn't even some place you could escape to, so it wasn't
hard to leave it. Her case was packed. A whole life, and she
could put it into a small case. This she said to console herself.

There was horseplay out in the bright moonlight as they
got into the car. There were lewdnesses shouted at them.
She didn't hear them. She thought : The driver is a bit drunk
and maybe he would overturn the car on the way and I
would be killed dead. That pleased her.

The road was very steep. It crawled up the side of a hill.
On one side there was a fall of several hundred feet. But
drunk or sober the driver didn't crash. He had travelled the
road so often that the car would nearly go by itself.

Then they were there, in front of the white-faced cottage
and the car had turned about and had gone away.

She felt his hand on her arm. It didn't force her.

'Would you come down here with me a minute?' he
asked.

She went to the urge of his hand. They crossed a low stone wall and walked a sloping field of short sheep-cropped grass. It was nearly as bright as day.

Then she saw the waterfall. It was above them and the spray from its waters was making odd coloured patterns over their heads. It fell to a disturbed pool at their feet. And the other side of it was closed in by rowan trees which were now red-berried.

'Oh,' she said. 'Oh!'

'Nobody much knows this is here,' he said. 'It is too far for them to come. The road is bad.'

'Oh,' she said and she lay down on the grass and put her hand into the cool water. But, why, she wondered. He sat beside her.

'You mustn't be afraid,' he said. 'Nobody will hurt you here.'

So strange. She looked around at him. He wasn't too close to her but she could feel a body warmth coming from him. And his breath was clear. No porter on his breath. This surprised her.

'I could be your father,' he said. 'But I don't want to be.' Smiling, see, the moonlight bright on his strong white teeth.

'You don't?' she asked.

'No,' he said. 'Because I'm in love with you.'

'You are?' she asked, like an idiot.

'Yes,' he said. 'I am. I think I have always been since you were a little girl. Sort of the way you cover your eyes with your lashes, like.'

'Oh,' she said.

'I haven't many words. Men who live alone rarely do, just the words they read out of books, but sometimes when they are desperate like now, words come from their insides.'

'Are you desperate?' she asked.

'Yes, I am,' he said. 'In case it should be wrong from the beginning. I don't want it to be. I've watched you often, in the fields, lying by the bank of the river near your old home where you were often. Sort of storing pictures of you like

113

that away in my mind. Saying your name: Jane, Jane, Jane.'

'But this is not real,' she said.

'It is for me,' he said. 'I want you to believe me. I knew you weren't really happy at home. You were much afeared at times. I know. So, I tell you this. You need never be afraid again as long as you live.'

She was looking at him wide-eyed in the moonlight. Am I sure this is not a fantasy she was asking herself. She did a strange thing in order to assure herself: she put up her small hand and rested the palm of it on the side of his face. He froze under her touch and then relaxed. She took away her hand.

'You are real, all right,' she said.

'I don't understand,' he said. 'Don't be afraid of me.'

'I'm not. Now,' she said.

'Man, that's good,' he said. 'And wait until you see the way I have prepared the place for you.'

She got to her knees. 'You needn't tell me,' she said. 'It is a small house by the bank of a river and it is filled with sunshine, and our hearts will be filled with sunshine too.'

'Somebody told you,' he said, disappointed. 'About the bathroom and the kitchen with the cooker in it, a real electric one. And the radio set. It all took me six months. I nearly broke me back at it, but I thought nobody knew, that it was to be a surprise.'

She got to her feet and held out her hand.

'Come on,' she said. 'Somebody knew. Come on and let's go home.'

He was staggered. He took her hand and rose to his feet. She noticed how gently he took her hand.

'And there's another thing,' she said. 'You won't vanish. You won't say, farewell, farewell, will you?'

'Oh, no,' he said. 'Bydad, no!'

'Well, come on, Tom,' she said briskly. 'It's getting late.'

The Conjugator

MY HEART nearly stopped beating when I saw him.

It was market day in the town, and they had set up stalls where men were auctioning off cheap clothes that you could wear-as-you-pay and there were vans selling fish and chips and stalls with jewellery and things like that. It was none of those made me pause but the man standing on the box sending a stream of things rising into the air in front of his face from one hand to the other, plates and coloured balls.

He was a tall man with long hands. I was too far away to hear what he was saying, but I closed on the laughing crowd that surrounded him to get a better look at his face. Maybe, I thought, it is he. I knew it couldn't be but it had always been like this. I always seemed to be searching for him, hoping, and as I moved in now towards this juggler the years seemed to fall away from me; my hair was no longer grey but brown and unruly and needing to be clipped. Sometimes it is easy to shed the weary years.

For I was young when I first met him. I remember we had all enjoyed our First Holy Communion Day a little while back and the loot we had gathered from relations and weeping sentimental women had become exhausted. It must have been summer, too, because we had discarded our shoes and stockings. I can still feel the heat of the pavement under my bare feet.

These pavements were in the poorer part of the town; long streets of houses all joined together, with doors opening on to footpaths and economically lighted with one wooden lamp-post in the middle of everything.

There was Jojo and Vincent and Daneen and myself, Tony, and it's funny how you can remember a conversation at a particular time. We were discussing where babies came from. We were doing this seriously so it will show you how much sense we had.

Daneen, who seemed to know more than the rest of us, adopted a horribly superior air, sitting on the pavement, looking knowingly out of the corner of his eye, humming and playing ceaselessly with jackstones. Now and again he would say, 'Oh, you poor ignorant children!' until we were becoming sick of him and thinking of attacking him, and we would have, but our eyes were attracted to the fellow at the lamp-post.

He had been there some time, but we had paid little attention to him. We found adults boring, and apart from mimicking a street singer, or pelting him with cabbage stalks if he was a poor singer, we never allowed them to interfere with us.

But this fellow was doing something odd. He had about six fist-sized rocks and he was throwing them into the air one after another, juggling with them, sometimes lifting a leg and juggling the rocks with his leg held up. He looked funny. Then he added a good orange to the stones and an apple, and an apple and another orange until he had four fruit and two rocks describing an unceasing circle.

'Look at the gawk,' Vincent said.

'Them's real oranges,' said Jojo.

'He's not bad,' said Daneen.

'Hard apples too,' I said.

'We'll go and look at him,' said Daneen, rising from the ground.

We walked over to him.

He was a tall skinny fellow wearing poor clothes. You could see his feet through his boots. His hair was dark and tangled and he was unshaven, but I noticed that his eyes were very blue and that his teeth were very white. You don't notice things like this about beggarmen generally. Also when you approach them you do so from the windward side because they smell of sleeping-out and unwashed clothes, but strangely enough this one smelt clean, so you could go nearer to him.

116

We ringed him but he remained unperturbed. His eyes crinkled. Suddenly one after another the fruit flew towards us and we were quick in catching our share.

He leaned against the pole and looked at us. He pointed a finger at us.

'Pixie,' he said to Jojo; 'Whitey,' to Vincent; 'Pugnose,' to Daneen; and 'Skinny,' to me. We were eating so we didn't mind. But all the same it was apt names he put on the lot of us.

I thought he was unusual, so between bites I asked, 'Who are you?'

'I am the Conjugator,' he said. 'I juggle and I conjure. Watch!' He made movements with his hands and almost as soon as you could say it he had taken a penny from Jojo's nose, a penny from Vincent's head, a penny from the bottom of Daneen's trousers, and lifting my bare foot from the dust there was a penny under it!

We laughed. He was good. You couldn't spot him at it.

Then he juggled with the pennies. 'Do you want these pennies?' he asked.

We looked at one another. Pennies weren't so easily acquired in those times.

'Do you want to drown a dog?' asked Daneen.

The Conjugator laughed. 'I want information,' he said, 'I just want to know all the soft touches in the street A bargain?'

We thought it over. Not for long. We held out our hands and he put the warm pennies in them and we sat on the road around him. We pointed out the soft-touch houses, including our own, which was a betrayal in a way. We just left in one or two old cranks because we wanted a laugh as well.

'Stout men,' he said. 'If I return to work these streets I will always consult you before my rounds.' He mooched at his clothes and a small square package appeared which he pulled at until it opened out into a sort of canvas tray. It contained ribbons and beads and gewgaws, just an excuse for begging. He was cute, you see, bribing us like that beforehand, because I suppose he knew we could make life hell for him while he was on his rounds.

So he winked at us and started.

We sat at the corner watching. He was a charmer. You would see the angry face of the woman disturbed at her work and as he talked you would see the anger melting, her face softening, until finally she would go back into the kitchen for her purse. He was a good worker. He skipped the doors we told him to skip. But all the time he was drawing close to the door of the Great Crank and we were chuckling inside with glee. We encouraged him with nods.

So he knocked at this door and the little dark-faced man appeared. He looked at the pedlar, listened to him, appearing quite amiable, then he retired and came back again waving a big blackthorn stick which he swung straight away.

The Conjugator was nimble, but all the same he got a few great whacks on the back before his running speed outdistanced the reach of the stick. The Crank stood roaring after him, cursing and shouting until he went home and banged the door. Really, it would make anyone laugh.

We weren't afraid of the Conjugator. After all we were four to one, and if we didn't wish it he couldn't be in the street at all, so we sauntered to the corner where he was sheltering.

'Aren't ye great little bastards?' he asked us.

'We forgot him,' said Daneen.

'You did like hell,' said the Conjugator. 'Is that a fair way to act?'

'Let everything calm down and start again,' I said.

'Are there many more like him?' he asked.

'No,' I said innocently. There were only two more. He sighed and produced four more pennies.

'How many?' he asked.

Glad of his intelligence, we took the pennies and told him the two houses to dodge.

Then we went off and spent the money.

We saw him several times after that. He would seek us

out, sit with us, and pretend to conjure pennies from our persons. We got to like him. He didn't talk big, like. He could have been one of ourselves. He took an interest in us, now that he was getting into our houses. He knew our mothers. Yours is the tall one and yours is the dark one and yours is the fair one and yours is the small one. We told him about our families, our brothers and sisters and how unfair our fathers were to us at times. All that.

I forgot to mention that at this time there was a sort of war going on. Arrests and shootings and raids and things, but when you are that young these things don't leave much of an impression on you.

All I remember was the terror that came over me in the middle of the night when the lorries came thundering into the street and we were all dragged out of our beds and had to stand in the kitchen while big frightening fellows with black guns in their hands searched our houses. That's the most I remember, the black guns, and the rest seemed just a nightmare you would have after going to sleep sometimes.

We talked about these things to the Conjugator and Daneen gleefully told about how his brother was up on the roof the last time, how he got out of a window and pulled himself up by the guttering.

The Conjugator praised that and said how clever it was, but unfortunately the next time they came they got Daneen's brother, because they searched the roof. It was the only time I ever saw Daneen crying and the Conjugator patted his back and told him not to worry, that everything would be all right and conjured sweets out of his pocket. They were odd times all right. Jojo's father had a rifle hidden up the chimney and they got that too and gave him a bit of a going over with Jojo's mother watching before they took him away. That was hard on Jojo as you can imagine. But I thought the Conjugator was very kind to him and seemed really sad about it because there were creases between his eyes.

Something odd happened then. My brother Joe was a big

fellow. He wasn't skinny like me. He was well filled out. He was in some sort of a job that kept him away from home a lot, selling things or something I supposed, and I remember this incident was the beginning of the end of the whole affair.

It was late evening. The sun was low in the sky and soon we would have to be off the streets. There was a curfew and you couldn't be on the streets without a pass, and you had to have lights out in the house or if you didn't they were liable to send a bullet through the window to remind you.

'The place is getting spun out for me,' the Conjugator was saying. 'Soon I won't even be able to make the bribe money that I pay you men. Today I only got elevenpence. So my profit is only sevenpence. How am I expected to live on that?'

We were a bit dismayed. 'Ah, don't give up for a while,' I said. 'You can cut the bribe money to a halfpenny a skull until times get better. We'd miss you now if you went.'

'Is it me or the money you'd miss?' he asked.

We thought this over. It was a serious question.

'Ah, we like you,' I said. 'Is that right, fellas?'

They thought it over. Daneen was chewing a bit of stick. He spat it out. 'Arrah, don't go away so soon,' he said, for them.

They meant this too. I never saw anyone they had taken to like the Conjugator. He rose to his feet.

'Sometimes the nearest and dearest must part,' he said. 'Look, Skinny, come with me a minute. I want you.' He walked me aside. His hand was tensed on my arm. He was hurting me. 'I tell you something,' he said. 'You do what I say, and don't say who.'

This was mysterious.

'What's up with you?' I asked.

'I honestly don't know what's up with me,' he said. 'Listen, tell your brother Joe not to be home tonight. Just that. That's all.' He waved to the others and went away, his tattered trousers flapping round his legs.

'What did he want, Skinny?' I was asked. 'What was the secret?'

'Ah, nothing, nothing!' I said. 'Come on and we'll race round the avenue before curfew.' And I set off, having a good start because I thought of it first, but I was worried.

Joe wasn't home. Maybe he wouldn't come home at all, I thought. I was restless. My mother was chiding me. Can't you sit quiet? What's got into you? Why didn't you eat your bread and dripping? I like bread and dripping. I don't know why I couldn't eat it then.

I was in bed when Joe came home. I heard him downstairs, so I ran down in my shirt and I shouted into the dimly-lighted kitchen, 'Joe! Joe! Go away! Don't stay home! Please don't stay home!' I can still see him, his eyes wide, staring at me.

'Go back to bed, Tony,' he said then, pulling on his coat.

My mother was standing there with her hand on her heart, but Joe was on the way out the back door. He could have hardly got out when the butts of guns were banging on the front door and I was up in bed with the blankets pulled over my head and my heart thumping.

So they didn't find him, but you can see how the trouble started. Joe was waiting for me one day when I was coming home from the school. He pulled me into a quiet way by the canal.

'Now, Tony,' he said. 'Who told you to tell me to go?'

It never entered my head to say anything but what I said.

'Who, the Conjugator,' I said. 'Wasn't he good? If it wasn't for him they would have caught you.'

'Who is the Conjugator, Tony?' he asked me.

I told him about the Conjugator, what a massive juggler he was and a super conjurer.

'When do you expect him back to the street?' he asked. 'I'd like to meet him too.'

'Oh, that's great, Joe,' I said. 'You'll love him. He's a nice fellow and he usually comes on the second Saturday.'

Then he gave me messages for my mother and we parted.

The Conjugator came back.

I thought he looked sad that day, tell you the truth. He looked around him a lot. He didn't seem at ease. But there were only the four of us in the street, sitting as usual at the lamp-post, so he came over to us, and got on his knees and started the business with the pennies. But he wasn't smiling. He had only conjured three pennies when we suddenly noticed the legs of men around us. I didn't know them but they had hard faces. They would frighten you somehow. None of them was Joe. I was wondering why Joe didn't come to meet the Conjugator. One of them said, 'Get up!'

I saw the face of the Conjugator going white in front of my eyes as he rose to his feet. Then he smiled. I saw his long hands fumbling and then they simply spouted pennies all around us in the dust like heavy raindrops.

'I have to go, fellas,' he said. 'Goodbye. Don't forget to spend the pennies for me.'

They walked away one on each side of him and one at his back.

I started up. The pennies didn't seem to matter somehow. I wanted to call out after him, 'Hey, thanks for Joe. You were right about Joe!'

But I didn't call. I didn't do anything because I was afraid of these men, dressed like ordinary men, but their faces were tight and I didn't know them.

I thought then, that maybe they were friends of the Conjugator. I walked a little after them.

Before they turned the corner the Conjugator waved his hand at me. That's what I remember so well, the long thin hands and the white teeth in his face. And then he was gone. I felt odd and lonely.

So a few days later when Daneen said, 'Did you hear? They shot the Conjugator. It's in the papers. Hey, fellas, did ye hear, they shot the Conjugator!' I wouldn't believe them. Jojo had even seen him, in a street away from ours and he had a cardboard round his neck with the word on it. I couldn't believe it.

'But I saw him,' said Jojo. 'There was a hole in his head. There was! There was! My mother nearly kilt me for looking at him.'

We spelt out the bit in the papers about an apparent itinerant and the mystery of his death, but I found it hard to believe. I still find it hard to believe it. I seem to be always looking for him.

That's why I went towards this juggler now, in case it might be he. Because whatever about him, if he died and it was he, he died from a good act. That's what troubles me. He saved my brother Joe. If he said nothing, who would have known about him? If I said nothing about him, who would have known about him? So it was me, in a way, that was responsible. Maybe that's why I am looking for him.

This fellow now wasn't he. He had black greasy hair and bad yellow teeth and there was a smell off his clothes. The Conjugator would never have had a smell off his clothes.

So I walked away from this one. I suppose that is what I will always do when I see a juggler. I will draw close to him in the hope that he will be the Conjugator, even though I know in my heart he never will be.

Solo and the Simpleton

ON THE far side of the village of Gortshee lay the sea. The coastline was rugged and ragged, but the Bay of the Mourning was very beautiful. The centre of the coastline was composed of tall cliffs, like the shoulders of a man, who encompassed the bay in two great arms, and the small battered islands at the ends of the arms were like stretching hands and fingers that never met. So it was a very sheltered bay, an almost continuous sandy beach, at least six miles in length. The sands were golden and they were blinding in the bright sun, and with the sea greeny-blue in colour and the waves, like white lace, edging the foot of the cliffs, you would travel many a long mile just to see it on a sunny day.

At the very top of the tallest cliff, built back on the spine of the hills, there was an old castle. Mangan's Castle it was called, and exactly where it was built, it looked like a head on the shoulders of the man who was embracing the bay.

All the trouble arose on account of this castle and the Sacred Cow of the Twentieth Century – the Tourist Traffic. Long ago nobody ever heard of tourists. Maybe once in a blue moon one or two would come and write a book. Earlier if the people saw a tourist they would either knock him off or hold him for ransom on the solid assurance that he was probably an enemy spy, and who knows but that was the right way to treat him. Anyhow big talk about economics and the balance of payments, new diseases infecting the body economic like polio and thrombosis the body of the new civilized man, all these way over the heads of the people, led to the trouble about Mangan's Castle.

You see, a live wire in some far-away place decided that for the love and honour of the Tourist Traffic, the present sheep track leading around the Bay of the Mourning should be turned into a first-class macadamized tourist road. On this proposal, men descended on the place with coloured poles and theodolites and measuring tapes and the devil knows what, and they set to measuring and marking and pegging as if the end of the world was due tomorrow.

Then they went away and some years later monstrous machines and men and lorries fell on the place and started taking it apart and putting it back together again. Their idea was to break out of the main tarred road leading to Gortshee, and build this ring road to the Bay of the Mourning and descend from the hills into the middle of Gortshee. The people of Gortshee approved of this. The road wasn't by-passing the village, and then it would give several months' employment to people who needed it. So everybody was happy, and they built their road up and up until they reached the top and there was Mangan's Castle standing right in the middle, and what were they going to do with the castle? Why they were going to knock it down of course. Why? because there was a deep depression in front and behind it. It would cost thousands extra to by-pass it, and since it was only an old castle of no particular beauty or merit, to hell with it, they said.

Halfway between the village of Gortshee and the cliffs, there lived what men call a simpleton, in a small cottage that looked over the village and the great lake and the plains and the blue mountains in the far distance. His name was Jeremy. He was a fairly tall man and he was strong. He was simple because he lived alone, his eyes were pale blue, misty, and always seemed to be looking through you when you talked to him, giving you an uncomfortable feeling. So men said he wasn't all there, he had a slate loose. He didn't read newspapers, had no radio set, knew nothing at all about politics. In other words he had nothing to say. He knew a lot about weather signs, about birds and fish and sheep and if you asked him he would tell you about those things. He earned a living by hiring himself out to cut turf or to help in the fields, or do any odd job that you wanted done, and while he was slow performing these tasks, he did them well and earned his pay.

It was only when the question of this road came up that people remembered that his last name was Mangan. He was the only Mangan living in the whole neighbourhood, and if anybody had thought of asking him at the time he could have told them that yes he was the last of the Mangans. As far as he knew (and on this subject he was very well informed as you will see) there wasn't another of the old Mangans living on the face of the earth.

And so, that was where they came up against trouble.

Possibly it could have all been avoided if Solo had listened attentively to Jeremy the day he came to see him, but at this time he was distracted because four of the people had stopped going to Sunday Mass; he was worried about the funds for building a new church in the hills where the people had to make do with a rather ageing school house, and his head was buzzing from the after-effects of a bout of influenza. These were all the excuses he trotted out for himself afterwards but they didn't convince him.

Besides, Jeremy was more or less inarticulate. This is the way the conversation proceeded: 'Oh, hello, Jeremy, I'm happy to see you. Won't you come in and sit down?' 'No. Wet.' It was raining hard outside even though it was almost high summer. Naturally they started building this road in the summer instead of doing it in the winter and having it ready for their precious tourists by the summer. Solo was surprised to see Jeremy, so he stood in the porch with him. The big man, his clothes inclined to steam from the wet, shuffling big feet in heavy hobnail boots; Solo thought it took an effort for him to come down here and talk. But he didn't talk. 'The road,' he said. 'Yes,' said Solo, 'that's a good road. It will be a good thing for the place.' 'No!' Jeremy exploded. 'The castle!' 'What about the castle?' Solo asked.

Jeremy pursed his thick lips and clenched his huge weathered hands, and finally said: 'You will come?' Solo was going to refuse because he really had a lot on his mind, but fortunately he didn't, so there was no need to chide himself about that. He sighed and got his hat and walked with Jeremy, out of the village and up into the hills to Jeremy's house. It was a stiff enough climb. Jeremy himself walked fast up the hills with a sort of swinging movement of the hips which Solo couldn't emulate, and what with the cold on him he was soon panting and coughing. Jeremy watched him coughing, then he grunted and hopped over a wall and strode away and bent down farther in and started digging with his fingers into the boggy soil. When Solo had recovered from the spasm, Jeremy was back with three or four roots in his hands. There was black earth clinging to them. He opened the flap of one of Solo's coat pockets with his free hand and stuffed the roots, earth and all, inside before Solo could protest. 'Boil. Stir. Strain. Drink,' said Jeremy, making the motions with his hands.

'Thanks, Jeremy,' said Solo trying not to think of the mess in his pocket, now mixed up with a tobacco pouch, a box of matches, a few mint sweets and a Rosary beads. They completed the walk to Jeremy's cottage. It was a small two-roomed thatched cottage. In the kitchen a table, four wooden chairs, a dresser with delf and a settle bed. It was clean. There was a nice turf fire burning in the open fireplace.

'You have a nice little place here, Jeremy,' said Solo, thinking that he knew a lot of women who hadn't their places half as clean. Jeremy ignored this. He took a key from the mantelpiece and went to the room door which had a very heavy lock on it and he opened it and stood back and said: 'In here.' Solo went into the room. It was lighted only by a small window. It was some time before his eyes became accustomed to the gloom of it and then he was astonished. All around the walls there were tied three heavy swords, burnished bright, two long flintlock ball guns, very old and rusted, a steel breastplate, parts of it gleaming, parts of it with holes where the rust had eaten in, and a sort of conical headpiece dented and rusted but cared for.

'Jeremy,' said Solo, 'where in the name of God did this stuff come from?'

'See,' said Jeremy thrusting a metal box into the priest's hands from where it rested on the table. 'Look.'

The box was filled with papers, some of it sheepskin parchment. Solo ruffled through them, saw the faded writing. There was a whole history there, from the Irish script and the Latin and the Old English, right up to Shakespearean English.

'My God, Jeremy,' said Solo. 'This is tremendous stuff. All this should be in the hands of scholars, in a museum.'

Jeremy understood that all right. He snatched back the box and slammed it shut. 'No!' he said. 'No!'

He tried then to explain. 'It's the castle,' he said. 'The castle. So long. So long. Forever.'

'You mean all these things came from the castle?' Solo asked.

'Mine,' said Jeremy. 'All mine.'

'I see,' said Solo, thinking, so they are all his. Let the scholars get hold of them when Jeremy is dead. 'All yours, Jeremy,' he said smiling. 'You keep them. You are the last of the Mangans? Isn't that right?'

'Yes, yes,' said Jeremy eagerly.

'Fine,' said Solo. 'Well, I am flattered that you showed them to me, and I won't say anything about them. They are your property and long may you live to enjoy them.' He turned to leave on that note. Jeremy halted him.

'But the castle,' he said, thinking that all was now clear as daylight. 'I understand,' said Solo. 'I understand.' And understanding, he went out of the house accompanied by another bout of coughing and a buzzing head, thinking perhaps that all this had not happened, that it might be a sort of flu nightmare. And he walked down the hill and when the coughing fit ended, he stopped and looked back, and saw the huge man standing at the door looking after him with the metal box still in his hands, and for a piercing moment, Solo got the feeling that he had done something wrong. Then he thought, what could I have done wrong?

Nothing that he could see, and he went his way determined to get to bed for the afternoon and even to boil Jeremy's roots, and for the record he did, and it was some sort of balsam, and it certainly cured his cough, but he was to regret his unusual stupidity.

If the spirits of the dead had been permitted to walk the battlements of the castle on this fine June morning they would have been astonished. Not at the fat contented clouds around the horizon edging the blue haze of a summer sky, with the sun shining on a placid bay, but at the monstrous armaments about to besiege the walls. The castle had been besieged before, but never with man-made tools like these, giant bulldozers and scrapers and tall, almost stately cranes with heavy iron balls swinging from them. They might have seen balls like these emerging red hot from the mouths of cannons, but they would have been less afraid of those. Looking down now from the walls they would have recognized that no valour, no tremendous acts of heroism, could save their castle from destruction at the behest of the coughing monsters below waiting to consume it.

All the activity was being directed by a big man in shirt-sleeves and dungarees who wore broad wrist straps on very thick wrists to heal pulled tendons. He was burned almost black by the sun and he had white teeth and very black hair and he had a voice like a bull. 'Up here, Joe! Back here, Martin. More, more, just a little bit more. You fellows get in there and up. Sneak a bit of the top off her before we batter her bowels.'

The men who had been chatting, nipped their cigarettes and put the butts behind their ears, took off their coats and spat on their hands, and then taking up their picks and crowbars they filed through the narrow opening of the castle.

The castle was built sloping from the base and rising about forty feet into the air. The last time it had been assaulted and conquered many hundreds of years ago, the conquerors had knocked in the roof and all the floors, drained off the moat into the sea, and destroyed most of the fortified outbuildings, so that now they were just a jumble of grey ivy-smothered stones. So the castle itself stood gaunt but very solid looking, the walls mainly pierced by slotted windows, and you could still see some of the carved buttress stones which had supported the roof. The ivy was playing hell with the walls on the far side, weaving in and out of the crevices, stretching the stones apart and bursting them where they were weak with its swelling parasitical growth.

The men climbing the winding staircase inside had to mind their steps, because some of the cut stone blocks which formed the stairs were missing. They kept close to the weeping lichen-covered walls.

'Wouldn't do to be going to bed drunk on a Saturday night of these stairs,' said Tur Folan.

'And have the wife waiting at the top with a poker,' said Paddy Prender. They laughed.

They emerged at the top into the air. The walls were very thick, even up here. They were covered with grass and even one sycamore tree which had found room for its roots. Looking down they could see the stone fireplaces still set in the walls where the rooms had been.

Joe Gately leaned over, saw all the upturned faces, cupped a hand about his mouth and shouted: 'Will we start breaking her up now, Bolger?'

The ganger below shouted: 'What the hell did you go up there for? Why don't you play ring-a-ring-a-roses?'

Tur Folan grinned. He shouted: 'All right, Bolger, if that's what you want.' He started to dance on the top of the castle. He took Paddy Prender's horny hand and did a step around him singing: 'Ring-a-ring-roses, pocket full of posies, Asha! Asha! We all fall down.' He pretended to fall.

'Here, watch it, Tur,' said Paddy alarmed.

'Don't be playing the fool, Folan,' Bolger shouted up, very annoyed.

'But you told us to, sir,' Tur shouted down sweetly. Bolger banged his boot on the ground.

'Here,' said Joe Gately then, 'do you see what I see?'

All the men below were laughing at the antics of Tur. The two men followed with their eyes Joe's pointing finger, at the figure coming up towards the castle from the side of the hill below. Tur closed his eyes and opened them again to make sure he wasn't dreaming. 'My God,' said Paddy, 'is it real?'

They could see, but the people below couldn't see the man approaching, wearing a breastplate and a battered helmet and carrying a sword in one hand and a shield in the other. The sun was glinting off the burnished parts of the metal.

'Great God,' said Tur, 'I think it's Jeremy. Look at him! It is him, isn't it?'

'It is,' said Paddy. He wanted to laugh and yet he didn't feel able to laugh.

'What's wrong with you three idiots now?' Bolger shouted at them.

'Don't look now, Bolger,' said Tur, 'but there's somebody coming up behind you.'

'Will you stop the assing around?' Bolger asked, 'and get on with the work or you'll get your cards on Friday.'

'It is Jeremy,' said Joe. 'Where did he get the yokes?'

'He looks good in the fancy dress,' said Tur laughing.

Jeremy, even from here was impressive. Under the breastplate he was wearing a shirt, and corduroy trousers over rubber boots.

'It's his castle, they say,' said Tur. 'He's probably coming up to see the end of it.'

'That's odd when you think of it,' said Paddy. 'I suppose this place does really belong to Jeremy.'

'Not now,' said Joe. 'It's only a memory. The castle belongs to the fellow who owns the grazing.'

'Well, well, well!' Bolger was shouting up at them again. He wasn't saying well well well, but the distance was muffling his language.

'There he is now, Bolger,' Tur said. 'Right behind you.'

'What kind of a fool do you take me for?' Bolger asked.

Then he looked at the faces of the bulldozer men and the scraper men and all the handlers of the machines, who were looking behind him with very broad grins on their faces, looks of delight. Bolger turned.

The eyes nearly popped out of his head. There was this half-armoured man looking huge in his rusty get-up, looking at Bolger coldly and clenching the sword in his hand. The sword wasn't rusty and it had a good edge. Bolger put the cap back on his head with a gesture of impatience.

'What kind of bloody carry-on is this?' he asked almost plaintively. He craned his neck to look up again at the men on top of the castle. 'This is some of your doing, Folan,' he shouted. 'I know damn well it is.'

Jeremy said: 'Get away from here. All. All away.'

Bolger said: 'Are you mad? Who's this nut?' he called.

Jeremy closed on him. 'Go away,' he said.

Bolger didn't like the look in his eyes, that far-away look now tinged with cold determination, but it was very hard to frighten Bolger. He moved forward and took Jeremy by the arm. It was a heavy arm.

'Look,' said Bolger. 'I don't know who you are. I can laugh at a joke as well as the next man, but every minute all this machinery is idle is costing the ratepayers hundreds of pounds, so go home now like a good lad. It's all over.'

Jeremy swung his arm and Bolger flew away from him as if he was catapulted. He fell to the ground. He was very angry. He got to his feet and ran for the strange figure intending to blot him out, but the sword swung and hissed and removed the cap from his head, and Bolger stood still. He paled.

'Back now,' said Jeremy. 'Go away. All go away now. The castle stays. Not knocked down.'

'Here,' said Bolger weakly, but not defeated, he shouted then: 'Here Martin, get that bulldozer started. Close up on your man here. You hear. Edge him away from here.'

The bulldozer grunted and started to move. Bolger backed away from Jeremy and the machine made towards him, a monstrous thing. Jeremy had to back away from it, but he backed towards the opening into the castle and beyond that the bulldozer couldn't go.

Jeremy went up the stairs carefully. The three above were waiting for him.

'Hello, Jeremy,' said Tur. 'Nice day.'

'Down, get down,' said Jeremy.

'But look here,' said Paddy.

'Get down from here,' said Jeremy.

'On your way, Tur,' said Joe. They went. Jeremy followed to make sure they left, then he climbed again until he stood tall on top of the castle. He looked below at all the upturned faces. 'Away! Go away!' he shouted waving his arm. They didn't move. Jeremy bent down and levered a boulder from the top of the wall. He raised it above his head.

'Go away!' he called.

They didn't move so he dropped the boulder. While it was falling every one of them scuttled like a disturbed ant.

The boulder turned twice and then crashed on the seat of the bulldozer below. The seat crumbled.

'My God,' said Bolger, 'the lunatic is serious!'

'Now you know,' said Tur.

So when Solo finally arrived, he found a lot of the local people gathered with the helpless workers, all of them gazing up where the heroic figure of Jeremy stood dauntless against the sky. From here you couldn't see the trousers or the rubber boots, just an armoured man. The damaged bulldozer had been hauled clear and all the rest of the machinery. Solo reflected that the cost of all the stuff would have outfitted a respectable besieging force in the olden times.

Looking up at Jeremy, Solo's heart was heavy.

He could hear the laughter and the jokes. Perhaps they had reason for joking. This time Solo felt in no mood for laughing.

'What are we going to do, Father?' Bolger asked him. 'We can't get near the idiot. We tried sending men sneaking in up the stairs, but he nearly stretched them throwing stones at them. He'd kill anybody now who got near him. What am I going to do? Amn't I being made the laughing stock of the whole country?'

'I would have thought Jeremy was the laughing stock,' said Solo.

'Not him,' said Bolger. 'He's the cock on the castle. He has me by the hasp. Short of killing him with a blow of a demolition ball, I have no out. For the love of God, talk sense to him, Father. All this is costing a lot of money.'

'Very well,' said Solo. 'I'll talk to him.'

He buttoned his black coat and started to walk towards the narrow opening of the castle.

Bolger was startled.

'Come back,' he shouted. 'I didn't mean that. Talk to him from here, I mean. He's really insane, I tell you. He'll kill you. He doesn't care.'

'Take it easy, Father,' said Tur Folan.

Solo kept walking. He only stopped when Jeremy shouted at him. Jeremy had a large stone in his hand. 'Go 'way! Go 'way!' he called. Jeremy was making no distinction. He was gone beyond that now. Solo commenced walking again and Jeremy flung down the stone. It landed almost on Solo's heels. He heard the thud of it biting into the ground behind him, but he just kept walking.

Because, he told himself, it is mainly my fault. The poor man with his weak words, his inarticulateness, came to me, making a grave effort for help, and all I could think about was my own cough. There need have been no exhibition like this if I had not been so selfish at the time, had recognized what an effort it cost him to come to me and what little help I gave him.

He paused before starting to mount the steps. All the steps went up a tower with openings into the rooms where they had been. Now the openings just led off into space. The lower place would have been a sort of storehouse and guardroom. You could see that. Now it acted as a shelter for cattle and sheep and the place was thick with their droppings. Next flight you looked into what would have been the great hall. The great stone fireplace was still there as if it were sealed to the castle walls.

Looking at it Solo could easily, with his imagination, people it with the warriors and ladies who had once possessed it, almost see them in all their savagery, all their beauty, magnificence and squalor. Determined people. Like Jeremy. Looking into that space Solo suddenly thought: Why, Jeremy is quite right not to let this castle be destroyed. Isn't it too much of our faded heritage that has been destroyed; the walls of great abbeys used to build cow byres? How often had he come on a gargoyle carved grinning on a stone set into the top part of a pig sty. And this castle was old. It wasn't as old as the hills, but it was older, far older than the memory of any living man or his father or grandfather or great-grandfather.

Then he thought, how well the castle looked when you saw it from the Bay of the Mourning, a solid, weather-worn sentinel, an ancient guardian of the bay. And what came over me, that it never entered my head that the destruction of the castle would be vandalism; that the stones of it should be used to fill in a road?

Jeremy is not the simpleton, he thought. I am the simpleton. It only took thought from me, and I could have moved long ago. I should have moved long ago. Then they would never have thought of destroying the castle if I had opposed it, and after me the people.

And Jeremy knew that. And he called to me for aid. And all I gave him was the back of my hand.

Solo groaned in real anguish.

'Jeremy! Jeremy!' he called up.

'Go 'way! Go 'way!' Jeremy shouted down at him and a stone came down the steps. Solo hugged the damp walls. The stone hopped past him and went through a gap in the stairs.

Outside, Tur Folan and Paddy and Joe, were daring Jeremy. They were coming close to the walls and shouting up at him and Tur even caught a few stones and flung them towards him. All they did was to fall short and nearly brain a few people on the other side who shouted and ran away with their hands over their heads.

'But keep it up, lads,' Tur told them. 'Divert him somehow, or he'll murder Father Solo. Who do you think you are, Jeremy?' he roared. 'An oul ass, that's all you are, Jeremy, you hear!' He shouted other things too, taunting things, hoping that Solo wouldn't hear them behind the walls. But Jeremy heard him. Jeremy started pelting them with rocks. The three of them were dodging about like rats escaping from a demolished oat stack.

But Solo got the breathing space that he needed as he ran up the stairs, noting the neat rough beauty of the masonry, how they had set the slit windows and the gutters. He could feel bowmen behind the slots, see them crouching, hear the hiss of the arrows from the windows. Old, old, so old. How many hundred years old, even a thousand years old. And all of them, except Jeremy, wanted to destroy that, without a thought for the past.

He emerged into the open air. He had lost his hat on the way. His fair hair was matted with sweat and cobwebs, his face streaked.

Jeremy faced him then. He had the sword and the buckler and his pale blue eyes were red rimmed. The look of him made Solo afraid. This is true. Solo afterwards often dreamed about his facing Jeremy, armed with a glittering sword on the shaky top of the ruined castle.

He was truly the last of the Mangans, and he was very determined that nobody should destroy their memory.

He came for Solo his face set, his teeth clenched, talking through them. He looked ferocious.

'Told you! Told you! Nobody! Nobody!' he ground out.

'Listen, Jeremy,' said Solo. 'You came to me. I didn't listen. I'm sorry, Jeremy. I should have listened. You hear?'

'Too late! Too late!' said Jeremy. 'Where they are. What they are going to do!' It drove him into a frenzy. He swung the sword and made for the big black-clothed man facing him.

'No, Jeremy,' said Solo, but that was all he had time to

say. The sword swung, and Solo dropped flat and then came up under the other's guard, rose from the ground and gripped the arm with the sword in it and the wrist with the shield. He got leverage with his feet and exerted all his strength.

The people below held their breath. Some of them didn't look. Two men locked in an embrace on top of an old castle. It was fantastic. Any moment they could have toppled over and come tumbling down, turning over once or twice before they hit the ground.

They didn't, because Solo was holding Jeremy with all the strength he possessed, and talking to him, all the time talking.

For a few desperate moments, he thought that his strength would not be sufficient. It was like holding a wriggling rock, if you could imagine such a thing. Fierce strength, fierce force, throbbing, boiling with force and determination. But Solo was strong and he had learned a lot of tricks with strength, so he could hold both of them glued to the precarious spot where they struggled; but it was his talk that gradually calmed the other.

'Jeremy, believe me, they will not destroy the castle. I swear to you that they will not destroy the castle. On your own, you can't last. You hear that. Not on your own. They can get you out of it. You may end up dead. You hear. Listen, Jeremy, calm down and it will be all right. Just listen to me and it will be all right. I swear to you that it will be all right. Jeremy, Jeremy, believe me, believe me they will not destroy the castle. They will not destroy the castle.'

Not before it was time, he saw the mad glint leaving the glaring eyes in front of his own, being replaced by disbelief and then by caution. He felt the huge trembling limbs relaxing, and almost screamed as he released his own tightened muscles.

'You say?' Jeremy asked.

'I say,' said Solo. 'They will not destroy the castle.'

'You promise?' Jeremy asked. There was a mixture of

wonder and doubt and hope in the two words.

'I promise,' said Solo. 'By all that I hold sacred, Jeremy.'

Jeremy kept looking at him, searching his eyes, his face. Then he relaxed completely. A smile lighted up his whole face.

'We go down,' he said. 'You take the sword. You won.'

'No, Jeremy,' said Solo seriously. 'You keep the sword. You won. Nobody but you won this one. You hear that. Nobody but you. You did it all on your own. You are a brave man, Jeremy. This is one battle you won against greater odds than any of your ancestors. You hear that?'

'I hear that,' said Jeremy.

'So now, we'll go down,' said Solo and turned his back on him and walked down the stairs.

He just moved a step outside the doorway. Behind him Jeremy filled the doorway. Solo called:

'Hey, Tur, and you Paddy, and Joe.'

'What's up, Father?' Tur asked coming towards him cautiously.

'Come here, Bolger,' said Solo.

Bolger came close to him but not too close, keeping an eye on Jeremy. 'Yes, Father,' he said.

'You are not going to knock down the castle,' said Solo.

'What!' Bolger ejaculated. 'But we have to knock it. It's in the plans.'

'The plans will be changed,' said Solo. 'I'm going now to see to that. But in the meantime, Tur, I think you and the lads should sit down here in front of the castle with Jeremy and see that nobody lays a hand on it or him.'

'You mean, we don't want the castle knocked down after all?' Tur asked.

'We do not,' said Solo. 'We were the simpletons, not Jeremy. We want this castle. They can build their road round it.

'Well, if that's what we want,' said Tur, 'nobody is going to knock it down, not while I can back up Jeremy. Eh, Jeremy.' Tur went up to him and put his hand on his arm. Paddy and Joe went back too.

'The castle is safe with you now so until I come back?' Solo asked.

'It's in the bank, Father,' said Tur grinning.

'God bless you,' said Solo and buttoned his coat and smoothed out his crushed hat and walked away, sunk in the ways and means of setting the acrimonious wheels in motion. It would be a tough fight, but he knew he could gather reinforcements on the way. And the castle would remain. He turned once and called back: 'Thanks, Jeremy, our thanks to you!' and then he was gone walking fast down the hill already talking into the telephone, hearing the bureaucratic gasps of surprise, amazement, disbelief, and antagonism.

Tur and Paddy and Joe sat on the grass.

'Listen, Bolger,' said Tur, 'while we're waiting why not sit down with us and we'll all play a game of jackstones.'

'Hundreds of pounds per minute!' gasped Bolger. 'Per *minute*.'

Jeremy removed his helmet and placed it softly on the green grass.

Light in the Valley

THE March sun shone coldly on the side of the great hill. This hill was on the rim of the valley that faced south so that it got the sun in the evening when the hills opposite it, craggy barren ones, were crouching in gloomy darkness. This hill was almost verdant. It bore a thin covering of soil and short grass and that was why the sheep were dotted all over it, even in its perpendicular parts.

At the foot of the hill there rested the five houses of the village, looking very tiny down below; blue smoke lazily rising from the chimneys. The floor of the valley was bisected by a meandering river that flowed from the big lake on the left to the sea on the right. A pretty river that glinted now and again and had built up at its curves round piles of yellow gravel. It was a useful river providing in spate salmon and trout, and good clean drinking water, and keeping the fields on its banks lush and green.

So, it was a peaceful scene. Even the sheep occasionally stopped from their grazing and looked below them, pleased with what they saw. A foolish thought, the man on the back of the pony mused as he came over the shoulder of the hill and paused to look. The hill contained many hundreds of acres of common grazing and many thousands of sheep. Most of them had lambed by now and these were like balls of white wool, keeping close to the hooves of their mothers.

Martin Browder, who was coming from turf-cutting at the bogs on the other side, was pleased with the view so he dismounted from the grey pony, sat on a stone, filled his pipe and took a more leisurely look from under the peak of his cap. The pony sensibly started to crop the short grass.

Yes, he thought, very pretty. Some people would call it lonely. They might even call it being buried alive in a remote valley, but he didn't think of it that way. He could count his blessings: his sheep (because they came first in sheep country), his wife, his two sons and one daughter. Enough to eat; everything owned and belonging to him and a little money in the bank. Just you had to work for it and work hard, but that was the way man was meant to be.

It's good, he thought, to take a few minutes off betimes, and count your blessings in this restful place.

And then, almost before he could inhale, the peaceful scene was shattered and the hillside was spattered with blood.

And all by two dogs who, taking advantage of the folds in the hill, came very cunningly from the far side, darted from cover about half a mile from Martin's eyes and cut their way through a flock of sheep, slashing with their long fangs. One was a black dog, he saw, and one was a long-haired brown and white collie. They had killed five lambs before he got to his feet. Maginn's black, he thought, we always knew that black was dangerous. We told him over and over again. He shouted and waved his cap, but he was too far away. The sheep were scattering in all directions and the blood-flecked dogs were after them, striking here, striking there, not pausing to tear at the tender lambflesh, just killing and killing. Later they would return to feed and would be sated with one carcase alone. But once a dog killed he didn't seem to be capable of stopping.

He jumped on the pony's back and set him off down the hill. It was a steep ride and dangerous. He didn't care. He was boiling with frustrated anger and the sure-footed pony could go faster than Martin could run. He shouted. He screamed curses at the dogs. He saw a man then on the other side of the hill, just coming over, standing to stare and then pointing a shot-gun and firing. He was too far from the dogs to hit them. But they stopped and looked at the man with the gun, and then looked towards the man on the pony, and turning they ran, boxed in, down towards the village. There was no use following them.

Martin and the man approached the scene of the

slaughter. Martin got off the pony's back and stood there.

There were seven lambs dead. There is scarcely anything in this world as pitiful-looking as a dead lamb when its neck has been snapped from the back. Two sheep had faced the dogs, just two and their throats were torn open. The mothers of the dead lambs were standing far off, bleating. Two sheep had cracked their thin shanks in crevices when they ran away. These were bleating too so the man with the gun approached and shot them. The shots sounded flat and final in the valley.

Martin, who was kneeling by one of the dead lambs, lifted his head and spoke to him.

'That was Maginn's dog, Fursey,' he said. 'The black one.'

'That's right,' said Fursey coming towards him and ejecting the spent cartridges from his gun. 'And the other one was yours, Martin.'

Martin Browder looked up at the face of the man, a very dark man, with black hair, black eyebrows and bulging jaws.

'I didn't think it was my dog,' said Martin. 'My dog is not a killer.'

'It was a brown and white long-haired collie,' said Fursey with determination. 'I saw him with my own eyes and he was yours.'

Martin rose to his feet. He was taller than the other. He didn't like him and that was one reason he couldn't lose his temper.

'I don't believe it was my dog,' he said; 'but if it was my dog, he will die, I promise you.'

'He will,' said Fursey, and he spat.

Fursey wanted to kill Maginn's dog, but Maginn wouldn't let him. He was a tall lean man, normally very quiet, but he was upset about the dog, a big black smooth-haired fellow with a bit of Labrador in him. Maginn knew he was guilty because there was still dried blood on his coat. He knew he would have to be destroyed, but it was hard to part with him all the same. He was a quiet enough dog and he was fond of Maginn and even when you knew he was a sheep killer it still wasn't easy seeing him shot and he wouldn't let Fursey kill him, because he knew Fursey liked to kill.

'It will be done legal,' Maginn said and sent one of his kids off for the police. The police barracks were some distance away so the child wobbled off on his father's bicycle.

So Maginn sat in the field behind Martin Browder's house, a rope around the neck of the black dog who lay quietly beside him, and when he thought the others weren't looking Maginn would mould the back of the dog's neck with his fingers. He was fond of him, you see.

While they were waiting, Martin Browder went into his own house again, to soften them. They were all gathered in the kitchen, white-faced and silent. The white and brown collie was stretched in front of the fire.

Martin got on a knee beside him and set to examining him again.

'There's no blood on him,' the voice of his eldest son said harshly, as if he was talking to a stranger. 'There's no sign of blood at all on him. It wasn't him. He wouldn't do it.'

Martin didn't turn around. His son Michael was eleven years old. He knew how he would look. His eyebrows would be pulled down. There would be hair falling over his eyes. He was a good boy.

'Look, Michael,' he said gently. 'I saw the dog myself.'

'Are you sure, Martin, beyond doubt?' his wife asked him.

He paused, thinking.

'It must have been him,' he said.

'Why is there no blood on him so?' his son asked. 'Is there blood on Maginn's dog?'

'Yes,' said Martin.

'Well?' Michael asked.

'He was out of the house,' said Martin. 'He's a clever dog. He's the cleverest dog in the country. He was wet when he came in. He got the blood off himself.

'I don't believe it,' said Michael.

Martin lost his temper, rose to his feet, shouted: 'I saw

him! That's enough. We cannot afford a killer in the valley. Even if there is a doubt it is better that he die than the neighbours' sheep and lambs should die. That's all. I'm going out now. Bring him when I call.

He left them abruptly. He watched them from outside. Michael knelt beside the dog, cradling his head in his palms. 'You didn't do it, did you?' he pleaded. The dog licked his hands. Martin walked away.

'Your father knows best, Michael,' his mother said, coming over beside him. She put her hand on his hair.

The policeman was young. He had never shot anything in his life before outside of the shooting range. Who cares about targets? A dog is different. He had a .45 revolver. They are heavy implements and they wobble in your hand, so his aim wasn't accurate. When his first shot missed, he panicked. It was a sad business. It would try the nerves of the most callous. He fired five shots but it was Fursey finished off the dog in the end with the shotgun and Maginn didn't stop him. It was a cold evening but they were all bathed in sweat. The face of the policeman was white and his mouth was dry and he was a very relieved young man when Martin Browder said abruptly: 'You are not going to kill my dog.'

'What do you mean, Martin?' Maginn asked. 'We killed my dog?'

'And yours deserves killing more,' said Fursey. 'He is the leader. He is the cunning one.'

'There was no blood on him,' said Martin. To tell the truth the death of Maginn's dog had revolted him.

'That proves nothing,' said Fursey. 'Bring him out and let us have a look at him.'

'Michael,' Martin called, 'bring out the dog!' knowing in his heart that once he came he would be killed. So he turned to them. 'Let the dog's guilt be proved and you can kill him.'

'Is that fair to me then, Martin?' Maginn asked.

'There was no doubt about the black dog, Maginn,' said Martin. 'There isn't another black dog like him in the country. But there are a lot of white and brown collie dogs. Before mine is killed, I want to look at a few more. Is that fair?'

'It's not,' said Fursey. 'You saw the dog!'

'But I didn't recognize him until you named him,' said Martin. 'Even in the distance I should have recognized my own dog. There's a doubt in my mind. Michael! Michael!' he called, 'bring out the dog!'

They listened. There was silence from the house. They looked at one another. Martin ran to the house. Only his wife and children were in the kitchen.

'Where's Michael?' he asked.

'He's gone,' she said quietly. 'He took the dog with him. He went the front way. I had no heart to stop him.'

Martin dashed out again. He looked up the great hill. Now! There he was. Trying to hide and failing. You could see his bobbing head and the form of the dog. They were way up, running, running towards the top of the hill.

Martin cupped his mouth with his hands and called: 'Come back! Come back!' His voice was lost in the vastness of the valley. The boy and the dog bounded on.

'He'll get lost up there,' Martin said. 'He'll keep going. It's near night. He'll be ruined if he gets into the bogs.'

'Well, let's get after him,' said Fursey impatiently. 'We'll have to get that dog or he won't leave a sheep alive on the hill.'

He didn't wait for them. He set off and began toiling up the slope. Maginn was shaking his head. 'He's a foolish boy,' he said.

But he's my son, Martin thought, sighing. I'd do the same myself.

'The young fool,' he said. 'All right, we'll go. It'll take us time to catch up with him.'

The three men set out after Fursey.

And Michael's mother stood there holding her children's hands, and she prayed they wouldn't catch him until he had done what he wanted to do, and that he would come back safe.

The side of the hill was darkened now as the light of the setting sun was abruptly cut off from the valley.

Sailor walked the slope as easily as if it was level ground. Sailor! What a silly name? Michael thought, as he panted upwards. No one of the Browders had ever had anything to do with the sea. The dog might have seen the sea from the top of the hill. He wanted to disparage the dog, because he had forced him into unusual action. They came on a flock of sheep behind a huge stone. Michael stopped. He shouted at the dog. He pointed his finger.

'Go on! Go on!' he shouted. 'Kill them! Go after them and kill them if you are a killer. I won't stop you.'

The dog looked at him with his head on one side. He was a good sheep dog. He worked on whistles he knew, and the use by his master of arms and hands. Shouting and pointing meant nothing to him. He just wagged his long tail, puzzled.

'Are you too cunning?' Michael asked him. 'Is that it? Will you not kill when there is a person to see you?'

Then he heard a shout from below. He could see the figures of the men climbing the hill behind him. He was afraid. 'Come on, Sailor,' he called and tried to improve his speed towards the top of the hill. His stomach tightened as he thought of the sounds of the shots he had heard killing Maginn's dog. 'They won't do that to you,' he said to the dog. 'They won't do that to you.'

All the same he was very tired by the time they reached the top of the hill. He had to pause, bending, his mouth open. Ahead of them was a plain stretching about four miles to craggy mountain tops. It was bad ground. There were many acres of quaking green-covered marshland that would suck you to death. He knew the way fairly well but it was getting dark now and it would be difficult to find the pathways between the hard and the soft ground. But the dog would know, he hoped, and he set off into the plain.

He wasn't far into it, when he heard the calling behind him. The pursuers had reached the top of the hill more quickly than he had thought they could. Don't let them catch the dog, Lord, he pleaded and was amazed at the prompt answer to his prayer, for the heat of the sun departing, the warmed ground suddenly threw up coiling mists that rolled in long folds between himself and the men behind. He stopped to look. The writhing mists rolled higher and higher. First the men looked like magnified giants in the distance and then they were blotted out as if they had never existed. He heard the voice of his father sounding eerily, calling his own name : 'Michael! Michael!' and then there was no more and he was running ahead in wonder, but not for long because he and the dog were soon enveloped in the white damp folds. He kept veering right where he thought the hard ground should be, but very shortly he could not move because he could not see. He was alone. He called, almost desperately : 'Sailor! Sailor!' He heard the dog bark to his right. He groped towards the sound, calling and shortly felt the muzzle of the dog in the palm of his hand. His other hand rested on a stone. He felt this. It was a huge stone. It reared away above his head, so he sought the sheltered side of it and sat there with his arm around the dog.

What am I going to do? he wondered. Why did I flee? I fled because they must not kill my dog. But if the dog *is* a killer, he must die. That is sure. So I will have to kill him gently myself. How can I do that? I don't know! I don't know! He pressed his face to the head of the dog and the dog licked it for him. 'Oh, Sailor,' he said and he was very sad.

It was cold under the rock and it became colder still as the last light departed and the thick-misted night came down on the hill. He slept fitfully, warmed by the body of the dog. Each time he awoke, he awoke panic-stricken. What had happened to the happiness of his days? And once he shouted into the darkness : 'Help me! Help me!' calling to he didn't know who, his father who loved him before all this happened. He dreamed the dog could talk and said : Nonsense, I never killed a lamb. I protect lambs. But when he awoke that time, he knew the dog was dumb. That was why men had to protect dogs if they were innocent and kill them if they were guilty.

The last time he woke, the mist was lighted from behind by the early morning sun. He was cold and he was hungry, but oddly enough he had made a decision. It was just as if somebody had had a long persuasive conversation with him during the course of the restless night. Why, I will just go back with the dog, he thought, and if he is innocent he will not have to die. He rose and stamped his feet and jumped around to get the cold from his bones and waited impatiently for the mist to rise.

Below, they were coming up from the village again as the mist dispersed. They had been a long time getting back the night before. They had found a stumbling way home by the rocky bed of a mountain stream that ran in troubled, rainy times to the river in the valley.

There was little sleep behind Martin's red-rimmed eyes. His night had been filled with nightmares of his son sinking in the bogs of the plain. It was his fault. He shouldn't have frightened him. Now maybe it was too late. He groaned. They were spread out in a line, walking behind the mist as if a gauze curtain was being continually raised ahead of them.

They must have been halfway up the hill near the scene of yesterday's killing when the mist was totally wiped away as if a giant hand swept over it, and as they paused to see the whole hill magically emerging to their view, they heard sheep bleating, and almost in front of their eyes they saw a brown and white collie closing on a mother and her lamb.

Maginn shouted.

Martin shouted too. He ran towards Fursey who held the shotgun laxly in his hands. He grabbed the gun.

'Now you see! Now you see!' he shouted at him.

In a second it had come to him. Why didn't I recognize my dog yesterday? Why was I in doubt about him? Because he was a white and brown collie and here ahead of them was a brown and white dog who had knocked over a

148

lamb and then seen them and turned to flee. He jumped from a rock and was bounding towards another when Martin, on his knee, pressed the trigger. The body of the dog was contorted in the air and when he hit the ground, he was dead and Martin was confronting Fursey, wanting to kill him.

'You knew yesterday he was your dog!' he shouted at him. 'You knew yesterday! You knew yesterday!'

The anger streaks on his cheeks frightened Fursey. He saw the finger tight on the second trigger of the gun. His face paled.

'No! No! I didn't know. On my oath I didn't know!'

When Martin saw the abject fear in his face, the anger left him. He clicked on the safety catch and threw the gun at his feet.

'I wish I could believe you,' he said tightly and walked over to the body of the dead dog.

'You needn't bother looking,' said Maginn. 'The dried blood is on him.'

Then Martin heard the shout and looked up and forgot all about them. He saw the figure of his son on the top of the hill, waving and waving and he knew that his son had seen, and Martin himself could share the overflowing joy of his heart. The dog was sitting beside him, quite placidly, his long red tongue lolling.

I knew damn well he wasn't a killer, Martin thought. I knew damn well. And he waved his arm and ran to meet his son and his dog and already the risen sun was bathing the valley with light.

This Was my Day

IT WAS hard to leave the comfort of the bed. The body of
my wife was warm. The floor was cold to my feet and I
could feel the draughts around my bare legs. I didn't switch
on the light. I didn't wish to waken her. She would be up
soon enough anyhow. She worked hard. She could do with
her sleep. So I fumbled for my clothes in the dark and got
into them. They were cold too. At least the cold wakens
you up fully. I went down to the kitchen. I didn't put on
the light here either. On account of the fox. Foxes are very
clever, almost human. A fox could see a light in a house,
miles away.

The fire was raked, so I pulled the hot coals from under
the pile of ashes, blew them to redness and banked the turf
all around them. It would be a good fire by the time she
came down. I would have boiled the kettle. I would have
liked a mug of hot tea just then, but I couldn't wait for it.

I took down the gun and put in two cartridges of heavy
shot. Two were enough. If you missed with two, you
wouldn't get the chance for a third.

I was cautious about opening the door. I opened it slowly
and carefully. I believe that when foxes are working they
have a lookout, a sentinel. Other men don't agree with me,
but they are entitled to their views. I wore rubber boots.
Hob nails would have knocked sparks and sound from the
cobble stones of the yard. I was even careful lest the but-
tons of my clothes knocked against the metal parts of the
gun.

I crept through the yard, around by the gable, through
the wicket gate and into the garden. I had oiled the hinges
of the gate. It opened very silently and I was pleased.

I crossed the garden and sat under the hawthorn hedge

near the chicken house. It was dead dark. Some men hold the fox comes at sunset; others at dawn. I consider they come when you don't expect them. I could see nothing. The roof of the chicken house was a black blur. It was very cold.

In time the white streaks appeared on the eastern horizon. My heart lifted. I felt very alone until then. In the bare bushes all around me, the little birds started to come awake. You have to smile when you hear them. They are like persons. They grumble and scold and shake their nests. Birds are cross in the mornings, like people. Isn't that funny?

My heart told me the fox was there. A dull pound. Instinct. I was watching the place where they had pulled the mesh wire from the earth. It was hardly noticeable, but it was enough for them to get through. That was the clue I had the night before. I squeezed my eyes almost shut to focus. I had the gun in position. The blood was pounding in my ears. I didn't raise the barrel to my shoulder. I directed it with my knee. I pressed the first trigger and then the second. The noise ripped hell out of the dawn. It was a very foreign sound and the red blaze from the mouth of the gun was shocking. It seemed to have startled the morning completely awake. I rose from my cramped position. I had to straighten out my legs painfully. Not as young as I was. There were two dead foxes. I couldn't miss. The big one was the vixen. The other might have been her son. A young fox.

I felt sorry looking at them, teeth bared in death. I don't really like killing. But it has to be done. Pity foxes don't eat grass. They smelled very heavy. I lifted them by their bushy tails, carried them out of the garden. The chickens were kicking up murder now. Chickens are stupid. Wise after the event like the fellows they call pundits.

I left them outside the house. Mary was up. She looked a bit sleepy. 'I heard shots,' she said, 'if that means anything.' 'I killed two of them,' I said quietly. 'Oh, the hero,' she said, a laugh in her eyes. 'It makes up for all the misses,' I said. But I could see that she was pleased, and I felt successful.

After that I turned the two cows and the calves into the ceapog field across the way, and brought in a fresh bag of turf for the fire. We ate our breakfast. Our kitchen table is big. Time was it would be filled. Three sons and one girl. All gone, scattered over the world, all that remains of them ink on paper and foreign stamps. Pleasure when they came home to visit, but like shadows that come and go with the sun. Make you feel sad if you thought of it too much. The young must have their head. Maybe one day, the eldest would come home for good.

So I took the can and went to the milking. Can between my knees, I was relieving the black poll first. A good cow. I was thinking overmuch of my absent sons. Otherwise it wouldn't have happened about Red. That's the bull. A good bull, pleasant enough, but as you know there are times when you have to be careful with them. This was the time. It was early Spring. I shouldn't have been careless. Feeling sorry for myself. That always brings its rewards. The rain of milk in the can too has a soothing effect. Makes you careless, and I didn't hear the big fellow until he was well in motion. I should have heard him snorting earlier. They always do, and rake the ground with their hooves. Should have heard that too. When I did hear the pounding I looked over my shoulder. It was almost too late. He was nearly on top of me. I just had time to dive under the poll's belly and get to the other side.

He was stalled, but the milk from the can was spilt. He drew back. He was determined on destruction. He came at me from the back, his head lowered. His eyes were wicked. I got a bit of a fright. I admit that. But I knew it wasn't his fault. He was just answering his nature. It was my own foolishness. I slapped the poll on the side and she came around. That blocked him again. He wouldn't attack the cow, but he might flick her with a horn to get her out of the way. 'Walk! Walk!' I said to the poll then, scratching her back. She hesitated, and then walked. I had my arm on her neck, pressing her towards the gate. When Red charged me again I turned her sideways to him. This way I got to the gate, opened it, and slipped out. I took off my cap to wipe the sweat off my face with it, even though it was a frosty morning. But then we are only human.

I couldn't let him get away with it. I went back to the stable, took down the long-handled crook, and came back with it. I climbed the gate and stood facing him. We eyed one another. He decided to charge me. It's a bit of a terror to see nearly a ton of beef coming at you on the hoof. It makes you realize how brave them bull fighter fellows are you read about. You want to stand stock still with fright. So I advanced on him with a shout. I hit him on the nose with the pole. That stopped him. But he stuck his ground. You have to admire his courage. I hit him again. He put his head into the air and waved it from side to side. Trying to dodge the blows on his nose. I hit him again all the time trying to get the hook into the bronze ring in his nose. Then I had it in. The poor fellow was at my mercy. I twisted the pole. You can bring him to his knees that way. I shortened my grip then and got closer to him. I kept the twist on with my left hand and reached for the curly folds of his neck with my right. I patted him. He was trembling all over with excitement, but he was feeling the hurt too. I talked a bit of blather to him, and then I made him walk. Four circles of the field we did before he became calmer. Then I freed his nose and let him go. He shook his head and snorted. I didn't show my fear. I kept on talking to him. Then he walked away and started to graze, so I knew he was all right. I heaved a sigh, got my cans and finished the milking.

These are things that happen to you that shouldn't happen. If he had killed me now, they would have said it was his fault. Not his fault at all. My own fault for being careless. God gave man the mastery over animals, but He didn't mean man to be careless.

I left the milk in the dairy for Mary. She would look after it. Then I took to the hills with my bottle of tea and the few switches of bread. It was lambing time for us and you have to keep an eye on them. I freed Collie from the barn. She doesn't like being locked up in lambing time, but I don't think any dog should be free at nights those times. How do you know your dog won't learn bad habits from sheep killers? If she's in, she can't be out. She was over-joyed to see me, and I felt a bit sorry for having her locked up, but then, like the bull, you can't be careless.

It was a pleasant day climbing the mountain. The sun was shining. The sky was steel blue. Frost in the air, but that's the right kind of day to climb the mountains. It makes it less of a task. The sheep had wandered far up. It's amazing how far they can travel in a day. Funny how you can recognize all your own sheep. Can't explain that. It's just a feeling. Wouldn't you think one sheep is just the same as another sheep? No. I suppose that's how God tells human beings apart too, able to tell one from another like a man can tell his sheep.

I looked down from the top of the mountain. On one side was the valley with mists in it now from the warming sun. On the other side was a calm sea. That was fogged up too. I wondered how my sons could live in great factory cities instead of here. That's something you have to learn, I sup-pose.

Seeing the island out on the sea then made me think of The Fault, so I crossed over and went down that way. The Fault, they say, was caused by an Irish giant losing his temper one time, scooping a bit of the mountain out with his hand, and throwing it into the sea. There are tales like that everywhere.

My heart sank all the same as I came close to it and saw the sheep on the edge of it. She was bleating and I could hear another thin bleat answering her. 'Oh, no, Collie,' I said then. 'Not now!' But it was so. The sheep didn't run from Collie and that was a bad sign. I lay on my stomach and looked over. I wasn't surprised to see the lamb down there. A good thing it was a week-old lamb. I don't know how they are not killed when they go over. But they never seem to be. Looking up at me now, and bleating plaintively as if it was my fault. You can't leave them down there too long all the same. The grey crows might tatter them. I should have gone back down the mountain for a rope.

But I didn't feel like doing that, so I started to climb down. It's not a good place for climbing. You have to be careful, tell the truth. About fifty foot down it is. I was a bit puffed. Cold down there. The spring sun can't reach to the bottom. The lamb was running halfway up the wall. Afraid of me. I had a job to catch him. But I calmed him down. Talked to him about it's all right being frisky, jumping with joy, and all that, but for the love of God not to do it near holes in the mountain. He was calm enough once I got my hands on him. I suppose they sense that you are well meaning. Then I put him around my neck like a fur collar and tied his hooves with a bit of string, since I'd want both my hands for going up.

I didn't find it easy. I suppose it's because I'm getting old and the wind is not as good as it used to be. Then the lamb was bleating close to my ear, answering his mother, and that's no pleasant sound of Spring, I can tell you. I was well washed out by the time I reached the top. When I freed the lamb I had to lie on my back until my heart stopped thumping, but at least Collie felt sorry for me, because she licked my face. Then I thought : You blame the lamb, why should you blame the lamb? There's a reason for every-thing, but it's rarely the animals are at fault. I excused myself this way. You admit it's your own fault for not fencing the hole around. That should be done, I know, and lots of other things, but when I haven't a single son to help me, how can I do everything? But that's only feeling sorry for yourself and what use is that, tell me? Some day my sons might come home for good.

It was late dark when I got home. I could smell the din-ner cooking. It was a wonderful smell.

'Well?' Mary asked.

'They dropped ten more today,' I said. 'They are doing well.'

'Thank God for that,' she said.

It was nice to eat a good dinner and to stretch your feet to the bright fire.

But then, Mary's brother came. That's why I'm at this. He has a motor car. He works in the town. He is a nice chap. He comes to see us sometimes. Stays a night or two. He works in an office. We had a pleasant drink of whiskey.

He talked about how hard his life compared to mine. His day in the office. Books and figures and things, from nine till six, he says and do I realize what a grand life I have out here. What do I do all day? Not much, he says, in comparison, just at planting time and in the harvest. But his way, working, working, working, day in day out all the year round. No ceasing. Talk like that.

So when he went to bed and Mary went to bed, I sat down at this. I was worried about what he said.

I went up to Mary, sat on the edge of the bed. We were whispering.

'What's keeping you up, until this hour?' she asks.

'About your brother,' I said. 'He has a hard life. I go over all the things I did this day and they don't amount to much.'

'Well,' she said, 'what he does all day amounts to much less. I can tell you.'

'Ah no,' I said. 'Working with your head is a very hard thing.'

'It's easy when my brother does it,' she said.

'You don't understand,' I said. 'If it's all written down, my day amounts to very little in comparison to his.'

'All right,' she said, 'if I can't talk sense to you please permit me to go to sleep.'

So I let her go to sleep and came down again. But it worries me. Did I do much or didn't I? Was my day not as important to life as his?

Maybe he is right. Maybe I do have a grand life and that I don't have much to do.

Solo and the Sinner

IT WAS a fat evening in the autumn.

The sun was fairly low in the sky which seemed to be wearing a lascivious veil over itself. It is often like that in the autumn. Poets have written about it. It is full of late buzzing bees and over-ripe orchards, stacked haggards, turning leaves and plump animals. It is a time of indolence, lazy satisfaction. God has been good; the harvest is saved and garnished and men can sit down and look around them and take an interest in their neighbours. The sun is heavily warm. Some years, this time can be a little too full blown, a shade blowsy. It can lead to trouble.

The two pubs were filled with men drinking. There had been a funeral that morning. They had buried the man in the yellow earth. Now they were burying him in porter. Women had pulled their kitchen chairs to the open front doors and were sitting there, knitting or gossiping. Most of the village dogs were stretched supine on the warm footpaths. There was a smell of cooling tar from the roads, which the hot sun had earlier set to bubbling. This lazy peace was too good to last. Tom Tormey broke it. Like a bursting bomb.

His house was almost in the centre of the village. It was a neat two-storey house, with windows gleaming; lace curtains, always clean and well starched, behind the glass. From this house there came the sound of roaring that gathered the attention of the people. And then the man himself emerged. He was a big man with a moustache and a belly full of muscle. He was wearing trousers held up by scarlet galluses, and a woollen undershirt with the sleeves rolled. He always wore this, winter and summer, never a shirt or a tie. When he went abroad he wore a waistcoat and coat over it and a bowler hat. No hat now and he had a bald white spot on his head like a minor tonsure.

He stood there on the street outside his own door and he thumped his chest resoundingly and he roared: 'Who am I? What kind of a man do ye think I am? Tell me that, ye foxes ye!' Then he walked up and down outside the door with great tenseness in him, in his legs and his clenched fists and his arms held out from his sides. If he had wanted to gather attention, he had succeeded. His roars brought him all the attention he needed, people first with wonder on their faces and then grins. Seeing Tom T., they weren't surprised. He was always a dramatic man. He bought and sold things, mainly cattle, and it was always a pleasure to sell him anything for the show he would put up, just to buy a calf: hands clasping the forehead, eyes raised to the sky, calling on God to witness, stamping his hobnail boot on the stones.

The street of Gortshee wasn't a long street. Shortly, all of them, including the men from the pubs, were well within ear-shot of him. But his glaring took the grins off them. He was pale with rage. First his face would be red flushed and then it would be as white as bleached wool.

'Which of ye did it to me?' he asked. This first to the crowded door of one pub and then he went on to the door of the other and shouted at those. 'Which of ye has betrayed me? Tell me that until I know and pull the head from his shoulders.' Nobody answered him.

'Oh, well ye might, well ye might, ye monsters!' he cried. 'Five generations the Tormeys have been with ye in Gortshee, and all that time, never have they hurt any man within reach of them. Only mercy and justice in fair dealing. Why did ye do this to me? What have I done to deserve it of ye? Have I ever injured any man of ye by thought, word or deed. Tell me that alone, can't ye. Just that is all the answer I want from ye.'

One tall young man detached himself from the crowd at the far pub and came towards him, a very tall young man with fair hair and pointed white teeth. A strong face on him, pleasant except for the thin nose with the flaring nostrils that spoke of temper that could quickly rise in him.

'What's wrong with you, Tom T.?' he asked. 'What ails you? What has somebody done to you?'

'You could be one of them, Tur Folan,' said Tom. 'If it was you, big and all as you are, I would tear the lights out of you, on my solemn oath for it! Was it you, Tur? Was it you destroyed me?'

'Damn it, I don't know what you are talking about,' said Tur.

Tom kept glaring at him for a moment, his face turned up to the face of the taller man, then quick as a ferret he was back into his house again and to everybody's shocked amazement the next moment he came from the house dragging his daughter by the arm. Then he threw her from him. If she were a less sturdy girl, she might have fallen on the pavement. But she didn't. She withstood his violence and stood there looking at the street, gently rubbing her arm where his frenzied grasp had hurt it.

'Look at her!' he shouted. 'Look at her!'

They looked at her and she was well worth looking at. A finely built girl, about nineteen, with thick red-gold naturally curly hair, black eyes, and white creamy skin. Oh, she was well worth looking at, even if her teeth were clenched and if her eyes were very defiant. All the same it was a shameful thing to do and some honest people were ashamed. Afterwards, they said that Tom T. mightn't have made such a spectacle of her if your man hadn't died and he hadn't had to have a funeral and they had to bury him and drink a few drinks over his grave, and Tom T. had drunk a lot.

There was no grinning now.

'Well,' he shouted. 'Which of ye did it to me? Come on and tell me. Which of ye monsters has destroyed me name and me fame and me reputation? Talk, if ye have courage! If ye haven't the courage may the Lord God strike ye to the ground.'

'Tom, Tom, Tom,' said his wife Winnie then from the

door, a thin woman, a very hard-working woman, a decent respectable woman.

'Shut your mouth, woman,' he said back to her. 'I'll have this out into the light of day. I won't have them sniggering and whispering behind my back. I'll lift the stone and expose the crawlers to the light of day. Do ye hear that, do ye?'

The girl was looking at Tur. She saw the sardonic delight in his face. Oh, Tur! But she hated him now. Times she loved him and times she hated him. Surges, waves of one or the other. That was always the way it had been between them. In between: Never again, darling, it must never happen again, but when two people, self-willed with good minds, personalities, when they fell out, it was never like lovers' quarrels. It was deeper, more sweeping. And now she didn't care. He didn't care. Seeing her dragged into the middle of the street like this, by her own father.

Tur spoke then, keeping his eyes on her.

'How do you know, Tom,' he said. 'Why do you blame us? She hasn't confined herself to the village. She has been abroad. Is there a dance hall within a hundred miles that hasn't known her? Are you burthening us with the sins of strangers?'

Watching her. Her face immobile. To teach her. And yet she was so beautiful, so unusual. Maybe it was true, the words he sent out as a taunt. That thought brought the blood into his face. 'How the hell do we know?' he asked. 'Why the hell should you blame any of us for it?' Maddened because she remained pale and calm.

'I don't know,' shouted Tom. 'I don't know. I know this. Never again will I trust ye. I spit on ye. You hear that. And you can have her. You have ruined her and now you can keep her. You hear that. She's yours now. Never more mine. By God I swear it. All I did for ye. What ye meant to me.'

Then the deep voice, said pleasantly from behind him, 'What is it, Tom, what's wrong?' and Tom T. turned to face Solo.

The sight of the priest didn't seem to do anything to calm him. He raised a fist towards his head in a sort of beck of acknowledgement and then he turned and went back into his house, brushing past his wife, so that she stumbled. Solo looked at the girl. Then his calm eyes looked at the curious people in the street. They remained uncomfortably under his eyes just for a little time and then they turned away. All except Tur. Tur leaned against the wall, and lighted a cigarette.

'Come on in,' said Solo to the girl. She looked up at him. She looked sullen. It ill became her, but when he went in the doorway, she followed him. Solo felt sorry for the old man. He wasn't that old, but he looked old now sitting on the low chair near the open fireplace, his head in his hands, his bald spot very exposed. Then he raised his head. He rose to his feet when he saw her standing inside the door. Solo saw the disgust and distaste and actual dislike in his face.

'Get out of here,' he said to her. 'I told you to get out of here. Into the streets where you belong.'

Solo said : 'Tom, take it easy. Don't rush things.'

'No,' said Tom. 'You know me. I am an honest man. I am just, so I am. I won't have it. She doesn't stay another minute in my house. You hear that. You are a priest of God. Well. I mean it. How can you understand how it is to feel dirty when you are clean? Now I will always feel dirty, and I did nothing to deserve it.'

'You are a Christian as well,' said Solo. 'Let the night pass and we will talk again about it.'

'No,' he shouted. He was violent. 'How do you expect me to keep my hands off her if she is here. I'm a mortal man. I haven't it in me to keep my hands off her. I'd want to smash the bones of her face, break in her white teeth, tear out her curly hair by the roots, for the rotten bitch she is to do that to her own father. Now you see. Get her out of here. I won't be responsible.'

Solo abandoned the issue.

'Tom, Tom,' said Mrs T. It was no use.

'Get her things together,' said Solo to the woman. 'Go

with her,' he said to the girl. Tom sat again. Solo sat opposite him.

'Tom,' he said gently. 'You should forgive her. Dale is your daughter.'

'Easy, easy, easy to say,' said Tom, 'until you are up against it. How do you know? That it can happen to me. Anything but that. That she might die. That she might be killed. That would be better. Not this. I can never forget this.'

'You might be partly to blame,' said Solo. 'You might, you know.'

Tom refused this. He strode around the floor. 'No, no, by Almighty God,' he shouted. 'I was a good father to her. She was like a rare fruit you would have in an orchard. I nourished that one. I was kind to her. I was good to her. She does this to me and I spit her out of my mouth. The sight of her makes me sick, in here,' banging his stomach with his fist. No reason in him, Solo thought, and yet felt sorry for him, very sorry. Tom turned away abruptly when they came down from the room. Mrs T.'s eyes were red from crying. The girl wore a coat and carried a small bag in her hand. She went to the door and stood there waiting. If only she would say : I'm sorry, Solo thought. But she didn't. She looked like a queen being sent into exile. It annoyed Solo.

'All right, Tom,' he said gently, 'I'll see you again. We'll go,' he said to the girl, very kindly, because he felt the opposite. He wanted to shake her until her head rattled on her shoulders. Outside, he paused a little to wonder, where now, running over his charitable parishioners in his mind. Then he saw Tur, leaning there against the wall, grinning. He went right up to him.

'Tur,' he asked. 'Would your mother put up Dale for a day or two until I get things settled?'

'She would not,' said Tur definitely, throwing his cigarette butt on the ground and stamping on it with his heel.

'Maybe I'll ask herself,' said Solo.

'You keep away from my mother,' said Tur.

'What have I done to you, Tur?' Solo asked.

'You keep bad company,' said Tur, looking her in the eyes. She glared back at him.

'Thanks, Tur,' said Solo and went past him.

Maybe, he thought, nobody at all will take her in. Then he chided himself for taking such a poor view of his parish. He walked to four houses. His request was met with polite refusal. He began to feel as if he himself was tainted. And Dale was no help. She just stood there like a spare appendage, waiting, silently. It was nearly dark by the time Solo felt the pilgrimage had come to an end, leaving him frustrated, slightly unbelieving. His last call was on Miss Purdon. She was a great help to him. She was the chairman of practically every lay society in the place. She was a spinster and she owned a big eight-roomed house; a well-kept place with a neat farm. A hard-working woman who found time to be charitable, but she took one look out into the falling darkness at the girl by the gate and she said: 'Have you any sense, Father? Do you know what you are doing? Certainly not!' He could hardly believe his ears. He left her with her voice following him. Perhaps it's the hot autumn, he thought.

'They call her Miss Principle,' said Dale, walking demurely beside him. 'She would never let me in.'

'She doesn't mean to be that way,' he said. 'She'll change her mind.'

'She won't,' said Dale. 'You are very innocent.'

He was annoyed. 'Aren't you sorry at all?' he asked. Then quickly before she could answer, 'I'm sorry, forgive me. It will be different in the morning. They'll come to their senses then.'

He walked back through the village with her. He was conscious of the eyes watching them. He had to hold tightly to his temper. What he felt like doing was making an exhibition of himself like Tom T. He remembered that, Tom T.'s prancing, and he had to smile in the midst of his worry. He brought her to his own house. He was well watched.

He called the girl. She was a girl of about fifty, but she

163

was always known as the priest's girl. A prim-looking woman, her hair still without grey in it, her face almost unlined, a placid woman called Kathy.

He said : 'Miss Tormey will be staying the night with us. Will you fix her up a place in your rooms. Go with her,' he said to the girl. They went.

Solo ran his hand through his hair, leaned his arms on the mantelpiece, kicked at the dying coals in the fire grate, trying not to think. Why did a thing like this have to happen, and what has it got to do with me? It has something to do with me.

Then Kathy was back. She had her hat and coat on.

'I have to go to me mother, Father,' she said. 'She's sick.'

Solo was astounded. 'It happened awful sudden, Kathy,' he said.

'I got word before you came,' she said. 'I was waiting to tell you.'

'I see,' said Solo. It was true that her mother was nearly always ailing. But this was too swift. He had a mental picture of the old ladies coming to the house and telling Kathy about the girl and the priest and what he was doing.

'When will you be back?' he asked.

'When my mother is better,' she said. Her lips tight. When you get rid of that floozy, her lips left unsaid. Who am I, a pious virgin, to be bedded down in the same room as that wan?

'All right, Kathy,' he said. Watched her wait for him to say something else. He didn't say it. She went out. She banged the front door after her. He had never heard her do that before. She was very quiet normally.

Then the girl was in the doorway. 'You can't be with pitch and not be defiled,' she said. He looked at her. She still wasn't sorry. She might be sorry for the trouble she was causing him. But that was all.

'What is your full Christian name?' he asked.

'Magdalen,' she said. 'Dale for short. Didn't you know.' She was smiling. He looked at her for the first time. She was a very good-looking girl. Her beauty was almost flawless.

He began to understand why the sudden opposition had arisen. He wondered if things would be the same if she was an ugly girl, with little personality. It must be a very welcome thing to a lot of righteous women to see beauty brought low.

'I'll go now,' she said. 'I'll find some place.'

'No,' he said, taking his decision with a sigh. 'Go now to Kathy's quarters. You'll find them nice. Tomorrow is another day. Goodnight.'

She hesitated. 'They'll make trouble for you,' she said.

'I'm often in trouble,' said Solo. 'But there are saints who get you out of trouble. This time I'll pray to St Mary Magdalen.' He looked at her kindly. He saw it hitting her eyes, then her face flamed. She dropped her head and went out. He sat down in the armchair, his legs spread out from him. Where do you go from here, Solo? he wondered.

He didn't go anywhere. For almost the first time in his life Solo seemed to be bereft of inspiration. But his opponents weren't. They began to squeeze him. There were three main squeezes inside the week.

The first was Miss Principle with a deputation. All ladies, good, honest, kind ladies, who had nothing at heart but Father Solo's best interests.

'And so,' Miss Principle ended, 'you will have to send her away. That's all. Respectfully we tell you so.'

'Thank you,' said Solo. 'Where is she to go? Her father won't have her back. She hasn't a relation on the face of the earth. I'm grateful to you all for your thoughtfulness, but I would be more than grateful if one of you would agree to take the girl into your home until plans can be made.'

No answer to that. A tightening of lips, a drawing back of cloaks.

'We don't want her in the village at all,' said Miss Principle. 'Let her go away. She is well able to look after herself. We don't want her here as an example to the young girls. Fortune favours sinners, it appears, with the priest giving her every care and shelter.'

Solo thought: You don't know she is a good cook too, ladies. Kathy's cooking was insipid. Solo only found that out when he was presented with meals cooked by the sinner. All the same, he knew that things were troublesome. Something would have to be done. But not this.

He ushered them to the door. He was polite, breezy. He didn't hurt them by telling them what he thought. He thanked them for their advice. As he saw them away from his door, he looked after them with a worried frown on his forehead. Then he noticed Tur across the street, leaning against a wall, smoking a cigarette. He wondered if Tur was his main opponent. He wondered if Tur might not be the one behind the deputation. He wondered if Tur might not be behind the whole affair. So he waved cheerfully at him and went back into the house.

The next squeeze was this, and it turned out to be more serious.

It was evening and for the past few nights Solo noticed that the people had taken to gathering more closely around his house. Closing in on him. Just a hint, sort of. No demonstration. They greeted him respectfully when he appeared, bid him the time of day, but the congregating was planned. It angered him. But what could he do? It was a free country and the harvest was in. He thought there was a lot to be said for the hard harvests. If this one had been hard they would have been too busy getting their crops home ahead of the weather to have been up to their tricks.

He was in his living-room, looking at the street from behind the lace curtains, when suddenly his blood ran cold, because there coming across the street under their eyes was Dale. She was wearing a coat and carrying a few grocery messages in her hand. She shouldn't have gone, but she had done it and now it was too late. His whole body stiffened as he watched her crossing under their eyes. He could feel the silence of them. The silence was broken by a slight whistle. It was an obscene whistle. How could that be, but it was. How inhuman a human can be with the sounds he can emit from a mouth fashioned by the Creator, Solo thought. First a whistle, then a few words spoken too low for Solo to hear. He didn't have to hear them, just watching the expression on Dale's face he knew what they might be. More calling and then as she had her hand on the gate, the stone flew through the air. Solo saw it. He saw the hand that flung it and he knew it was going to strike her. It did, on the side of the face, and then Solo was out of the room, and out of the front door and up to the gate where she was leaning with her hand up to her face and already the blood was flowing through her fingers.

He didn't wait. He went through the gate and he made for the man who had flung the stone. He didn't have time to sense the change in the silence, the sucked-in breath. The stone thrower was standing there with a stupid grin on his face, a big moron they called The Pig, because that's what he looked like with his small eyes and his drooping jowls and a big heavy body. His complexion was pale and his hair was dark so he always seemed to be wanting a shave.

Solo grabbed him in his two hands and he raised him high in the air over his head, a terrible feat of strength, and it was only when he had him there and the fellow was squealing that he remembered who he was and that the fellow was a moron and only had half a mind, so he lowered his arms and stood the fellow on his feet and said: 'Forgive me, Francis, but who told you to do that?'

There was fear in the man's eyes, terror even, and he was rubbing himself where the hands of Solo had gripped him.

'Myself,' he said. 'Only myself. She's bad. They say she's bad. See. A bitch, like you throw a stone at one.'

'All right, Francis,' said Solo. 'Go home now. There's a good man. Go home now.'

Francis went, half sideways, running like a crab.

Solo went back to Dale. She had taken her hand away from her face. All one side of it was covered with blood. It was running down her cheek over her chin into her neck. She just stood there looking at the horrified people. Only Tur had moved out from the crowd of them and stood in the roadway.

'Nobody meant this,' Tur said as Solo passed him.

'Nobody ever means anything, Tur,' said Solo. 'Just build up a force, that's all you do and it gets out of hand. Always.' He turned then and shouted across at them. 'One of you go and tell the doctor to come down here.' Then he caught Dale's arm and brought her into the house.

She was very pale. It was an ugly deep gash. It was black all around the wound. He had washed it for her, bathed it, and disinfected it, by the time the doctor came, who looked at it and said : 'Too bad, at least two stitches.'

Dale said : 'No, Doctor, no stitches.'

He said : 'But there will have to be stitches. Even with those there will be a mark. But no stitches and you will be scarred for life.'

'Please,' she said. 'No stitches.'

The doctor looked at Solo, eyebrows raised, hands spread.

'She's the patient,' said Solo.

'All right,' said the doctor, 'but what a walking adverse advertisement she is going to be for me?' Her head was bent.

Afterwards she said to Solo : 'Please, I will have to go. I am bringing terrible trouble on you.'

'Where will you go?' he asked.

'Anywhere, anywhere,' she said.

'No,' said Solo. 'No desperation. Go in desperation and God knows where you will end up. Stick it out, Dale. I have a feeling. Everything will come right.'

'I might have you destroyed by then,' she said.

'God is good,' said Solo. 'Why wouldn't you take the stitches?' he asked then, looking at the wound that had been drawn together by the dressing.

'I don't know,' she said. 'Maybe I'm getting sorry.'

'I'll think of something,' said Solo.

But he didn't.

The next squeeze, he was in facing his Lordship, the Bishop. This was a nice man, very intelligent, very learned, very human, but Solo was sitting in a chair opposite him soaking in sweat, lacking in eloquence, conscious of his enormous bulk.

The Bishop had his hand on the stack of letters.

'There are forty-five of them, Father,' he said gently. 'Only three of them are anonymous. They are all very righteous. I must say, considering the circumstances, that they are tender about your reputation. You yourself emerge very well from them, but, let us say, according to your critics, foolish. Eh?'

'Yes, My Lord,' said Solo. Why can't I talk? Why can't I think? He must think that I'm a dreadful idiot.

The Bishop didn't. He knew Solo. He had heard his story.

'It is necessary to be cautious, Father,' he said. 'Charity is cardinal, but prudence is also a virtue. One must think of things like scandal.'

'Yes, My Lord,' said Solo.

'Well, will you get rid of the girl now, as soon as you go back?' the Bishop asked. Solo thought over the question.

'No, My Lord,' said Solo.

'I see,' said the Bishop 'H'm. Well, from what I know of you, Father, you are a man not lacking in wisdom, also I might say, a man not lacking in action. The situation can't go on as it is. It's dangerous from many aspects. It should be possible to find a solution inside one more week. What do you think?'

Solo heaved a great sigh of relief.

'Oh yes, My Lord,' he said. 'Without a doubt.'

'Good,' said His Lordship, tossing the letters into the waste basket. 'I will be hearing from you so, Father.'

Solo gulped air when he got outside. Then he paused. He thought: I haven't a single solitary idea in my head. I haven't an ounce of inspiration. What am I going to do?

In the end he was saved by a woodworm.

The priest's house was very old. When he had come into it some years ago he had begged, borrowed and bought enough furniture to make it very habitable. Dale Tormey was an active girl. She didn't like being cooped up, so she started to take the place apart, cleaning it. Solo had a hard job saving some treasured possessions, but anyhow she pointed out to him that all his furniture was infected by woodworm. These worms were endemic in the old house.

Solo called in an expert from the town, who said he would treat such a piece, destroy another, dismantle and re-back other pieces and that he would send a furniture van and collect them, bring them to his workshop, kill off the woodworm in the house and return the stuff almost like new.

That was the first factor.

The second was the abstracted mood of Solo, who went around thinking furiously, because there was a time limit, and only confusing his mind all the more. Before he had just acted and things turned out right. Now he couldn't think how to act, and he kept telling himself that he was as dumb as a pool of stagnant water, so that when he was talking to people he would end up by saying: 'Goodbye now,' and shaking them heartily by the hand. This happened in a lot of cases so they began to say: Why, he must be going somewhere if he is shaking us all by the hand.

They knew about the Bishop of course and his call on him. In small places they know what you eat for your breakfast. This can be a good thing or a bad thing. On the whole I think it is a good thing. You live in a great city and you could eat cyanide for your breakfast for all anybody cares. So, they associated the two things and said: Solo must be getting shifted. This set them back. They didn't want Solo to be shifted. They liked Solo. You couldn't convince Solo that he was popular, because he was a simple man and he always seemed to be finding fault with the people, but when the rumour went around that he was being shifted, people started stirring and apportioning blame. First, the Sinner. She was the cause of it all. But then, who was at the back of the movement? That was easy. Tur was. Who got them to write all the letters to the Bishop? Tur did. And here, as a result of all this, they were about to lose forever a priest for whom they had great respect and whom they had learned to like. Gortshee without Solo, people said, would be like a body without a heart. Tur told them they were wrong. What would Solo be leaving for? There was no sense to it. He was annoyed and he went up to Francis the Pig and he gave him two hard clatters in the puss. 'That will teach you,' Tur said, 'to go around firing rocks at girls.' Francis was bewildered. But Tur was in a state too. He had meant to see her coming crawling to him, and he would be magnanimous, and she would have too, only for Solo. He knew he was right. That Solo would eventually have to get rid of her and then she would have nobody but Tur. But he didn't want Solo to be sent away.

The third factor was the driver of the furniture van who came to take away Solo's furniture. Anyone who wasn't convinced that Solo was being shifted only had to be told that there was a furniture van outside his house and then they knew. It was evening and quite a crowd began drifting down to the priest's house. It was decided to question the driver.

He was a short stocky man with a moustache and a greasy cap which he kept raising and lowering on his head, he had small twinkling eyes and he was a notorious inventor. He was well known in the town for telling tales. Even when you knew he was a tale teller you could be taken in by his sincerity.

'Where are we taking the furniture? Why, we are taking the furniture to Hong Kong,' he said. 'Didn't ye know? Here, look at all these dociments.' He fluttered a lot of forms in his hand. 'To the docks. Then the ship. Over by the Mediterranean Sea, through the Canal, into India and down the coast that way. Oh, man, what a trip this furniture is going on.'

'To China, you mean,' with amazement.

'Didn't ye know? Oh, that's sure. I don't know what the holy father done, but they're sending him. That right, Jack?' To his long skinny helper with ill-fitting false teeth.

'Yuh!' he said. 'China. That's it, Pedro. Man, I'd like to go in a wardrobe.'

'To the jungle,' said Pedro. 'That's where this stuff will end up, if you ask me. And what good there? Three months I give it there, and it will be falling apart.' He winked at Jack, who showed his teeth and they went back into the house for another article.

They're sending him to China. Who? Father Solo! Are ye mad? That's what he said. I saw the yokes. It's all written on them I tell you. That's where he's going. No wonder he's going around shaking hands with us. But they can't do that. It wasn't his fault. He oney did what he thought was the right thing. Even if he was wrong, it isn't right that they should do that to him. Now, Tur, see what you have done.

With it all, you see, Tur was simple enough. The campaign ended for him when he heard the sough of the stone hitting the face of Dale. That was the first backfire. It had amused him to see how easy it was to get people stirring; get them talking; get them doing, like writing letters to the Bishop. But none of the end results had been exactly what he wanted. He worked on impulses. He always seemed to end up sorry for his impulses. He was big, strong. He had personality to spare. That was why he could impose his wishes. He had always been able to do so. Then Dale, somebody else who wasn't willing to go along with him. She had her own. He thought of the rock hitting her and he felt a flood of shame, and throwing away his cigarette he gave way to another impulse. He strode over to the house. He stood on the steps and called out: 'Dale Tormey! Dale Tormey! Come out here!'

He called loudly. He startled the people listening. He startled Solo who was in his bedroom, looking at the one chair and the bed that was left to him. He startled Dale who was in the kitchen. Her face paled to his calling, and then became resolute. She walked up the long passage towards the door.

Solo came running down the stairs. He called to her too:

Dale, don't go out that door.' Then he came running down. What did they mean to do to her?

She was facing Tur. Tur looked over her head at Solo.

'Don't do anything, Tur,' said Solo. 'I'm warning you. My patience is limited.'

'Why, I don't want to do anything to her,' said Tur. 'All I want to know is if she will come up to stay with my mother.'

'No,' said Dale.

'Think again,' Tur shouted at her. 'It's all my fault. I know. I love you. I'm sorry for all I did to you. I want you to be big like Solo maybe, and forgive me, and come with me, and if you love me enough, maybe you'll marry me, and then they won't have to send Solo to China.'

'What?' said Solo.

'What?' said Dale.

'Excuse me,' said Pedro, passing them, carrying a small coffee table.

'Now listen to me,' said Solo.

'No, listen to me,' said Tur. 'Come out now with me, Dale. Come with me now and you'll never regret it. On my solemn oath. I swear it in front of the holy father. Will you come with me?'

'I will,' said Dale.

He took her arm and tucked it into his own and walked out the gate with her. She was bewildered too, like Francis. But she was happy. Tur stood outside the gate. His arm was around her. He shouted across at the crowd over the way.

'Miss Tormey and me,' he shouted at them menacingly, 'will be married in this church three weeks from now and ye better all be there.'

That left them with their mouths open. He walked up the street with her, his heart full, thinking how tenderly he would touch his fingers to the wound on her face, when they were alone.

Dale turned back. She saw Solo, also bewildered, looking after them. She waved at him, happily.

Solo shouted after her: 'I knew she'd do it. I don't know how she did, but I knew she would.'

'What's he talking about?' Tur asked.

'He's talking about another sinner,' said Dale.

'What on earth did he mean about going to China?' Solo mused out loud.

'Ah, pay no attention to them, Father,' said Pedro who was going back to collect a table. 'Thim country gawks get the queerest notions.'

No Medal for Matt

It was a beautiful morning. The cliff top, at the western
edge of the island, which lay some miles off the Irish coast,
was a green carpet of closely cropped grass. Five hundred
feet below, the water broke indolently over black jagged
rocks. Its sinister sound was almost soothing. Westward,
the Atlantic stretched calmly away to a limitless light-blue
horizon.

Matt came toward the cliff from the village, walking on
the enormous slabs of flat rock that covered the fields,
which sloped steeply upward. The rocks were warm to the
soles of his bare feet. Homespun trousers ending at the shin
and a heavy knitted red jersey were making him sweat
under the June sun. A canvas schoolbag flopped up and
down on his hip as he journeyed, reminding him and bringing a frown between his brown eyes.

The climb up the slope was hard enough. He had to leap
at times, and try to dodge the briars lurking in the crevices
of the rocks. Sometimes the thorns scraped at the brown
skin of his feet, leaving behind a scarlet scratch of blood.
On both sides of him, small black-faced sheep, the kind that
make such tender mutton, raised their heads to look at him
and then moved cautiously away, following him with their
eyes for a little, after he had passed, and then resuming the
search for their meagre forage.

Matt was filled with a sense of guilt and injustice, and
between the two of them his heart was very heavy. You are
in school, see, just as he was yesterday. Near the end of the
day, the sleepy part, the fellow beside him in the desk,
young Pat Mullen, suddenly gives him a fierce puck in the
ribs. Matt turns to clatter him, but before he can land even
one blow on him, down the master comes and belts Matt.

Matt protests that he is being belted in the wrong, and the master belts him again. Matt still protests, and the master, his face as red as the comb of a Christmas turkey, belts him once again and asks him does he want more. Matt says he doesn't want more. On his way home from school, burning with the injustice of it all, Matt tells himself that his father will right this wrong. His father is noted for his justice. 'All right,' says his father when Matt explains to him, 'so the master was in the wrong. What do you want me to do, go up and hit the man? If every father did that, there would be not a school left in the universe.' Couldn't he just tell him that he was in the wrong? Matt asks. No, he could not, his father says. Maybe the poor fellow was having trouble with his wife, or maybe he had an interior ailment that was persecuting him. Well, you will just have to tell him he was in the wrong, Matt says. His father gets angry then and shouts that he'll be damned if he will do anything of the sort, and even if this time Matt has been belted in the wrong, it will do him no harm, because there were times when he wasn't belted before and should have been. Matt denies this, and his father walks out of the house saying, 'If I don't go, I'll belt you, and where will you be then?' His father is upset, because he doesn't like to think of Matt's being belted, right or wrong, but, being civilized, he can't go and hammer the poor teacher.

So now Matt saw that the whole world was a place of great injustice for boys; that there was no equity in it at all when even your father refused to stand up for you. That was why he had walked past the schoolhouse door this morning, just as if it wasn't there, and had headed for the tall cliffs. He had never done this before, because he liked school, except on Mondays and the first day after holidays. And even though he knew that he was right – it is necessary for every man to make some protest against injustice – he felt that he was wrong, and it seemed to him that some of the beauty had gone out of the day, and that this freedom he had chosen had, in some odd way, a chain on it.

176

When he had cleared the last obstacles barring his way to the cliff top, he stood there and looked back. He could see the whole island sloping away from his feet. It was shaped, he thought, like the kidney of a pig. He could see the golden beaches, and the sea beyond them reaching towards the distant mainland, which was hidden in a blue haze. He couldn't see his own house, but he could see the schoolhouse, and was sorry he was out of it, because just about now they would be chanting the multiplication tables, and he liked that. He also liked going into the yard at lunchtime and wolfing his jam sandwiches, so that he would have more time to play *capaillini conemara*, a game in which small boys, mounted on the backs of larger boys, raced each other.

He sighed and his heart was heavy, but his stomach was empty, so he sat on the grass and, after removing the books from his schoolbag, took the sandwiches his mother had made for his lunch and proceeded to eat them, and it was miraculous how the seagulls knew that there was food around. They thronged about him, screaming, from the sky and from the cliffs, and he amused himself by throwing crusts into the void and watching the wonderful swerving and twisting, the grace and the beauty of the gulls as they caught the crusts in flight.

My father will kill me, Matt thought then, and he looked over the water, thinking he might see his father's lobster boat if his father was doing this side of the island today. No boat was in sight. His father wouldn't actually kill him, Matt thought. He never raised a hand to him. It was his mother who always held the threat of him over Matt's head. Someday your father will kill you, Matt, she'd say. All the same, Matt knew that his father would be hurt by what he had done, and this made him feel a bit sad. He rolled on his stomach with his face over the cliff and looked down at the waves breaking on the rocks far, far below.

It was some while before he saw the movement – a fluttering movement, about fifty feet below him, on a ledge. He thought at first it might be a young gull, but then, as he watched closely, he saw that what moved was a rabbit, a plump young rabbit. He raised himself to his knees in surprise. A rabbit fifty feet down the face of the cliff! How could he have got there? Did a big bird claw him and lose him, or was he chased by a fox so that he fell and landed on that ledge below, or what?

Will I climb down and get the rabbit? was the next thought that came into his head. A terrible thought. His eyes narrowed as he looked over every inch of the cliff to the ledge. Suppose I fall, he wondered, looking farther, to the cruel black rocks waiting below. Who would miss me? Isn't everyone against me? Even so, his heart had begun to thump excitedly. It would be a famous climb. He stood up straight now, his hands on his hips, his eyes very bright. If the rabbit was left there, he would die and become a skeleton, or a bird would scoop him. If Matt saved his life, what a hero Matt would be! I climbed down cliffs when I was smaller, he thought, but never this cliff. This was the highest on the island.

He was still standing up when the boat came around a promontory behind him. He didn't see it, of course, and he didn't hear it. The chug-chug of its diesel engine was not loud, because the boat was going slowly as it negotiated a channel through some rocks toward a cluster of bobbing buoys that marked lobster pots.

The man at the tiller raised his eyes and saw the figure of the boy up there on the cliff top. He took his pipe out of his mouth, which remained open in amazement. 'Here, Tom!' he called to the other man, who was coiling a rope in the waist. 'For the love of God, is that my Matt up there?'

Tom came back to him, shaded his eyes with his hand, and said, 'By all that's holy, it is!'

'What's he doing up there?' Matt's father asked. 'He should be at school.'

Then Matt's father opened his lungs to let a shout out of them, but it was never emitted, because Tom suddenly clapped a hard hand over his mouth and the shout died in a strangled gurgle. Tom took his hand away, and the two of them stood there, looking up, petrified with fear, the hair rising on the back of their necks at the sight of the boy casually letting himself down over the cliff.

'Oh, my God!' groaned Matt's father.

'If you shouted, you would have startled him,' Tom whispered.

'He'll fall! He's mad! What's come over him?' Matt's father asked in anguish, his eyes glued painfully to the small figure slowly descending the sheer face. In that red jersey of his, it was all too easy to see him.

'Birds' eggs or something,' said Tom. 'My God, I never saw anybody climbing that bit. He'll be kilt!'

Matt's father swung the tiller to bring the boat in toward the foot of the cliff. Tom struggled with him, and forced the tiller so that the boat turned out again. He switched off the engine.

'Are you mad?' he asked. 'You can't get within fifty yards of the place. The tide is low. Will you kill us as well?'

'He'll fall! He'll fall!' said Matt's father.

'Well, if he falls now,' said Tom, annoyed at the boy, 'you'll only get his body. The rocks are up.'

'Oh, my God!' said Matt's father.

Matt's heart was thumping and his mouth was dry. Even so, there was a soaring in his breast. He was glad he was in his bare feet. His big toes were wonderful, the way they could feel, gauge, and grip a narrow crevice. The cliff face was almost solid granite, which, for all its height, had many times been washed by enormous waves. The sea water had sought every weakness, and here and there had scooped out the poor spots in the stone. So there were cracks for Matt's thin fingers and his hardened toes. All the same, you could be frightened, he thought, if you hadn't climbed down cliffs before. He knew where he was going, but he didn't want to look down to see. Clinging like a fly, he lowered himself bit by bit, until below him, out of the corner of his right eye, he could see the end of the ledge where the rabbit crouched.

Down in the boat, Matt's father, who was in the middle

of a prayer, thought he could feel the hairs turning grey on his head. He relaxed a little as he saw his son's feet feeling for a ledge and then resting there firmly.

Matt was happy to feel his feet on solid rock, though it was a very narrow ledge. The rabbit went to the far end of it, on the right, but he was still within reach of Matt's hand. Matt lowered his body slowly, gripping the surface of the cliff with the nails of his left hand and reaching for the rabbit with his right.

He grabbed the rabbit's fur. Don't struggle, don't struggle, Matt shouted at him in his heart, or you'll have the two of us over. He gripped him tightly. The animal stiffened. Slowly, Matt lifted him, and then carefully inserted him in the open schoolbag on his hip and strapped the flap shut.

Matt rested for a moment. He felt good now. Then he took a few deep breaths and started the climb up. The rabbit remained very still in the bag.

By now, Matt's father was kneeling, his hands covering his eyes. 'What's he doing now, Tom?' he asked. 'What in the name of God is he doing now?'

'He's on his way up,' said Tom quietly. 'He'll likely make it. What scoundrels boys are! What did he do it for? He got something. I wouldn't do that to rescue a king. That fellow will be a famous man or he'll end up hung.'

'God bring him to the top,' said Matt's father.

On the cliffside, Matt whispered to himself, 'Going up is not as bad as going down.' Because you can see. It looked fierce far just the same. The granite had torn his fingers. The middle ones were bleeding. And the sides of his toes were bleeding, too. He could feel them. Above, he could see a few slivers of green grass on the very top, beckoning to him. I'm coming, he silently called up to them, laughing. Wait'll you see. But it seemed a long time to him, before his hand rested on the coolness of the grass, and he paused, breathless, and then pulled himself over the top.

It seemed a lifetime to his father before he heard Tom's pent-up breath expelled and his voice saying, with a sigh,

'He is over. He is over now.' Matt's father couldn't say anything.

Matt was now lying on the grass, feeling it with one cheek. His fist was beating the ground. 'I did it! I did it!' he said out loud. What a tale to tell, he thought, but who will believe me? But what does it matter if nobody believes me? It was a great and famous climb, so it was.

Then, from the depths below, he heard a voice hailing and hailing, so he stood up and looked over the edge. Oh, it was his father and Tom. He hoped they hadn't seen him climbing down to the ledge. His father would murder him!

'What you doing? What the hell you think you're doing?' he faintly heard Tom saying.

So they *had* seen him! Then he remembered the rabbit. The rabbit would change things. Because of the rabbit, his father would be pleased with him. He'd be pleased, you'd see, and forget all about his dodging school. He opened the schoolbag and, reaching for the rabbit with his left hand, caught him by the hind legs and extracted him. Then he expertly hit him on the back of the neck with the edge of his right hand, so that the rabbit died, swiftly executed, in a second.

And Matt waved the body of the rabbit above his head, leaning out perilously over the cliff, and, with one hand curved around his mouth, shouted down, 'Hey, Father! Father! You'll have rabbit stew tonight. You hear that? Rabbit stew tonight!'

He laughed as he waved the rabbit, because his father loved rabbit stew, he really did. Then Matt gathered up his schoolbooks and put them back in his bag, along with the rabbit, and hurried down the slope, over the long fields of great flat rocks, toward home.

And his father still sat, completely drained, completely exhausted, in the bottom of the lobster boat.

The Red Rager

TOM CLANCY was bored. He decided he was as bored as the cheese with all the holes in it. He walked slowly through the village, his hands clasped behind his back, the time-worn picture of the policeman on duty. He shouldn't have been bored. He was only twenty-five years old. It was evening. It had been a fine day. There were low plump blushing clouds around the horizon. The village was very pretty, consisting of ten houses, a small village hall, three shops, the tidy police barracks – if you could call a four-roomed house a barracks – and Bartley Finnegan's pub. All right. Nothing much if you like, but all the neatly painted houses had for a background a towering benevolent mountain, which would break the heart of the highest wind, and they looked out at a placid bay of the sea enclosed by low hills on each arm. There was a new concrete pier, admittedly not as beautiful as a stone-built pier, but the fishermen thought a lot of it, and the three masts of the fishing boats rising over the pier, the black rope-ribboned tips of them catching the light of the dying sun, looked good, but Tom Clancy would have sold you the lot of them, with the village thrown in and the mountain and the sea and all the minerals it might contain for sixpence-halfpenny.

So he strolled through the village, almost unseeing, a tall lad with wide shoulders and a slim waist, and he turned down towards the pier and his mind's eye was occupied with a far different horizon. Thousands of ragged chimney pots silhouetted against a light-green sky. Later when the sun would be lower, the clouds would be tinged with the reflected glory of neon lighting. And if you stood to listen among your chimney pots you would hear the roar, con-stant and unceasing, of heavy tyres on tarmac, and screaming brakes, and the sound of thousands of people conversing above the noise of the streets. And as he walked the stony road of the pier it seemed to give way to block pavements, that you could feel through the thin soles of your shoes. He could see all the big windows lighted up with colourful goods displayed in them and the plush inviting look of the bedecked cinemas, and the lush hotels where you would go, all dressed up with a laughing girl on your arm – she smelling like a flower garden.

He sat down on a stone bollard. Before his eyes the sky was blazing and the gentle ripple of the sea caught the colour and changed it a fraction, and threw it off differently. You could nearly touch the colour of the evening, but Tom didn't even see it.

What the hell possessed me, he was thinking? He had thought that he would have been left in the city. It never even entered his mind that he might be sent down the country, a fate worse than death. But he was. It was like being sent to Purgatory when you thought you could get to Heaven. He would go farther and say it was like being sent to hell out of which there was no redemption. Well, he didn't have to stick it. He could resign. Nobody was going to beat him over the head to get him to remain. Even if he did fail, and could never forget that he had failed, what did it matter? After all, it was only a job like other jobs and people had to leave other jobs and they didn't go around afterwards thinking there was something wrong with them.

At this moment up in Bartley Finnegan's, Mike Stranger was going mad. He didn't go mad very often, maybe once every two or three years, but when he did it was murder.

He was a very big man in his late thirties. His head looked small on a very big trunk and he had wrists that were the thickness of the butts of five-year-old willow trees. He was very kindly, very amiable, and when he was in good form he would amuse the company by lifting a black-smith's anvil in one hand or pulling a diesel lorry by a cart rope held in his strong white teeth. It was just that his eyes were small and uneasy. Men always approached him cautiously in case he might be due for another spell, but then as time went by they became less cautious, like Murt Cleaver now. Murt was a strong man too, but he was nearly fifty and his hair was grey, and his once great frame was shrinking a little on itself. He was a laugh merchant. He had a lot of laugh wrinkles around his eyes.

Mike had come in and Murt had offered to stand him a drink, and when the pints were filled Murt had raised his glass and said: 'Here's to you, Mike, and may your shadow never grow less.' This toast was a joke. Murt had one time been invited to a wedding farther back, and called on to toast the bride he had done so in a very praiseworthy speech but had finished up wishing her that her shadow would never grow less. Greeted by a dead silence, it was only afterwards he realized that the bride was expecting and that his toast was unfortunate.

He was thinking of this episode now, chuckling into his glass of porter when he heard the warning shout from Bartley: 'Murt! Murt! Murt!' At the same time Mike's glass of porter shattered on the concrete floor where he had thrown it. Bits of glass flew in all directions. Murt looked up startled, but he was too late to run. The big hands of Mike were reaching for him. 'You say that! You say that! You say that!' Mike was muttering, spitting spittle. Murt was very alarmed. He had only time for one despairing shout before one hand of the madman was clutching his crotch and the other clasping his coat. His heavy body was raised in the air and was flung at the shouting face of Bartley behind the counter. Bartley ducked and Murt closed his eyes as he met all the bottles on the shelf, paused there for a moment, like a fly swatted to a wall, and then fell a long way to the floor behind the counter while bottles and glasses clattered on top of him.

Bartley had moved out of the way and was shouting. 'Get the Guards, men, get the Guards!' There were three other men in the place. Only one of them had the courage to run for the front door, because Mike was swinging the heavy wooden bar stool at everything within sight. This man was the Tailor, a small fellow with a black suit and a pale face. The other two ran for the backquarters like ferrets going into a rabbit hole. Mike caught the Tailor a clobber of the stool as he was going out the front door and he reached the street outside, tumbling like a clown in a circus. But he wasn't very hurt so he got up and ran, but paused when way below he saw the uniformed policeman with folded arms sitting on a bollard.

He shouted at him. 'Clancy! Clancy, come up here will you! Mike Stranger is loose again!' He shouted very loudly. You would have heard him eight miles away if you were a deaf mute, but did Tom Clancy hear him? Not at all. He was in the city of his birth, being a Detective Sergeant, skilfully tracking down sophisticated murderers, commended on all sides, getting medals for subduing armed desperate men, instead of being where he was buried down here where nothing ever happened except a cow aborting or a dog killing lambs in the springtime.

The Tailor despaired of him and ran down the street to the barracks. The two escapees had already beaten him to it and were pouring their tale into the ears of the Sergeant, who was cursing and buckling on his cased baton and calling for the only other guard in the place, Morahan, who was the clerk and not very robust, but they came out and ran up the street. But when they reached the pub, Mike Stranger was gone and the place was a shambles. They ran to the road behind and looked towards the mountain and there he was, clambering up it like an over-sized goat. It was always the same way. He'd go mad and then he'd take to the mountain, and in three days he'd return, ragged but sane. Why didn't they put him away? No doctor could clamber up the mountain after him, and when he came back he was so sane that nobody could certify him, and anyhow he was useful around the place. He worked for everybody and could work harder than ten men. In fact the place would be lost without him and Bartley Finnegan was insured so what did it matter?

But it was a different situation for Clancy.

The Sergeant listened to the Tailor's tale, tightened his lips and walked down to the pier. He stood behind the immobile Clancy. He was really lighting. It was a wonder his uniform didn't smoulder.

'I hope we're not disturbing you, Mister Clancy,' he roared then and Clancy leaped a foot off the bollard. 'I hope you are enjoying the decency of the sunset, the gentle lapping of the water, the cooing of the gulls.' Clancy was a bit bemused. He laughed. 'Gulls don't coo, Sergeant,' he said.

Well, the Sergeant told him a thing or two then, I can tell you, and the worst of it was that all the inhabitants were standing around listening. Murt was still holding an empty pint glass in his hand. He was to tell this for a long time afterwards, how despite all, when he came to himself there was the pint glass intact in his hand. People said that wasn't such a wonder since he had also been born with one in his hand.

They enjoyed the spectacle of Clancy being dressed down; enjoyed the sight of his sweating face. That fella was a bit superior. Who did he think he was looking down on people? It was better than a play in the hall.

'And what's more,' said the Sergeant, 'since you were supposed to be on duty and neglecting the same, there is only one thing for you to do, to go now, as you are, take to the mountain and bring back Mike Stranger. You hear that. Now, this very minute, and nobody in this place wants to see sight or sign of you until you come back with him, and,' added the Sergeant before he turned away to go back for a drink, 'I hope he pucks the bowels out of you.'

The Sergeant went and Clancy followed him slowly. The people stood by and watched him. They were grinning. Clancy hid his feelings and walked past them, climbed a stone wall and headed towards the mountain. It was getting dark. It would be a velvety, moonless blackness. He heard them laughing behind him as he crossed the meadow towards the stream. If he had had a machine gun he would have shot the lot of them.

186

It was after midnight when the Sergeant came back to the barracks.

He looked in at Morahan, who was on night duty, and he said: 'Where the hell is Clancy?'

Morahan widened his eyes. 'But you sent him up the mountain after Mike Stranger.'

'What!' the Sergeant shouted. 'Don't tell me that idiot did what I told him. Didn't he know I was in a temper?'

Morahan wanted to point out to the Sergeant how illogical he was, but he didn't, and he was sensible.

'Who ever heard the like of that?' the Sergeant fulminated. 'Now could he find him? How could he bring him back? He should just have circled a field or two and then come back. What kind of a fool is he at all? Mike might kill him dead when he's like this.'

Morahan felt like saying: Well, it's a pity you didn't tell Clancy all this before you sent him off. But he kept his mouth shut.

The Sergeant went to bed and a troubled sleep. He woke up several times sweating. He dreamed all the time of Mike falling on Clancy, who would be like a hothouse flower in that wild terrain, and strangling him or smothering him to death. He cursed Clancy. My God, he thought, all the forms I'll have to fill in if he's killed! Then he slept again and had a nightmare about forms. But he was worried. He liked Clancy. There was something young and fresh about him. He reminded the Sergeant of his own lost youth.

Clancy was lost up on that mountain. Before the sun died and the darkness came he had a glimpse way above him of Mike's bulk. Each time Mike turned Clancy fell flat. He didn't want Mike to see him. He didn't want to be ambushed. I will try and get near him in the darkness, he thought, by sound, and if I can do that and he falls asleep, maybe after that I'll be able to do something. He was mad with the Sergeant. He was mad with trade unions. Working overtime, I am, Clancy told himself but do I get paid for it? He was mad with the girls of the village. You go to a dance. All right. They are well dressed all right and they dance fairly well, but brother, they lack polish. No repartee. Just look at you and talk staight sort of. Make you uncomfortable. Make you feel you're not a patch on the big sunburned fellows, with badly tailored suits.

He was wet up to the knees. It was a fairly dry mountain but it had its weak patches and Clancy found them every time. If only the Sergeant had given him time to put on a pair of rubber boots. But no. Talking to him like that too, before all the people. Clancy burned and kept climbing. Instinct made him keep out in the open, away from overhanging folds where he might be jumped. He was too mad to feel afraid. Mike Stranger was a lunatic, and an enormous one. All right. Clancy had been reared in a tough quarter of the city, where you fought to survive. Besides, the people, mad or sane, respected the law. He would just face up to him and say: Hey you, come on down to hell out of that! and Mike Stranger would obey like an honest citizen. Clancy hoped this.

Sheep ran ahead of him like pale white ghosts. They didn't bleat. They just moved. Whirring wings went almost from under his feet too at times, frightening him, so that he stood up, his heart beating. He didn't know what they were, some sort of birds.

But up above, Mike heard every sound, every movement of the sheep and the birds. It might as well have been broad daylight, the way he could trace the coming of Clancy. He had seen him of course in the twilight; the glint of the dying light on the chromium buckle of his belt. His small eyes were narrowed as he lay and listened. He was lying under two great rocks that met together in an arch. A deep place, well used by the sheep in the bitter winds of winter. They kept it clean. Soft green grass in it. The stones warmed by the day sun, threw off the heat slowly at night. It was a snug place. Sound came into it slightly magnified. When a sheep's hoof moved over a stone ahead of Clancy, he heard it. When a darting and frightened snipe rose from under his feet he heard it; when the brace of grouse moved from him he heard them. He had Clancy pin-pointed and he was afraid. Because this was the first time he had been followed. Mike's mind was confused. A welter of blood in front of his eyes at times like this. He sweated and then he grew cold. Before, he could come up and wallow and groan and bite the grass until the cloud moved away from his mind, the red cloud. It would go, like the burst of sunshine breaking up a morning fog. But he had to be alone. The thought of some-body coming after him terrified him. He wanted to wipe out that terror and be alone.

He began to move out from the cleft. He listened and there was no sound. He listened much longer. There was no sound. Fortunately for himself, Clancy decided that it was stupid to be going around in the dark and when he came to a place that was partly sheltered, he rested there sitting on a stone. Mike listened and listened and then pulled back silently into his nook. But he wasn't calm. He was on edge. He didn't sleep. Before, he would sleep. Now he was ter-ribly conscious of having to share the mountain with another human being.

Clancy dozed. But not much. Fortunately it was a warm night but, all the same, after a doze he would shiver and hug himself.

Later he saw a very thin white line drawn across the horizon by the invisible hand. Just a thin line, and out of that thin line there grew the morning. Clancy was affected, whether it was because of the lack of sleep and he was sensitive to anything, or because this was the first time he had ever seen the dawn without chimney pots getting in his way, he didn't know, but this was certainly the first time he had ever had a grandstand seat. Imperceptibly the light grew, until first he could just distinguish the sea from the sky and then the narrow and ragged arms of the dark earth embracing the waters. The waters were grey and changed to green and after that to pink, and the land emerged from that, brown and black and then slightly purpled. Below him the small harbour gleamed as the rising sun daubed it, and

Clancy thought with wonder, Why the damn thing looks beautiful, with the boats and the tilled fields, many coloured from the different crops, yellow oats and green potatoes dying away to browns, and the hay cocks seeming to be drowning in the green fields.

And the birds woke up too. He didn't know the names of them. Pity I don't know the names of them, he thought. I must get to know the names of them, just the lark in the clear air, that one, and all the others, and the sheep bleated, and from one of the houses below a thin ribbon of smoke arose from a chimney. Now I know what that piece of music meant, he thought, that piece the visiting symphony orchestra played in that big cinema. He could hear it.

He was standing up, silhouetted against the dawn, his freed baton held in his hand. Since that one time during the night about three, when man is supposed to be at his lowest ebb, that was the time he had grasped the baton in his hand to get courage from the smooth wood. There he was, like that, standing up, when Mike Stranger jumped on top of him. Mike's hand caught the baton and pulled it and both of them went tumbling down to the next level piece of mountain. Clancy was horrified. The hair was standing up on the back of his neck. He was very lithe. He was first on his feet. But Mike had the baton and came towards him swinging it. Why does he do that? Clancy wondered, why can't he kill me with his bare hands? Then he was angry. I was on to something there. Something unforgettable and this moron has to spoil it on me.

He ran in to Mike. Mike swung the baton. Clancy dodged, but he was sent flying and he was hurt, when the baton hit his shoulder. He landed heavily, but moved immediately and instinctively, and Mike's big boots landed where his head had been. The fellow means to kill me, Clancy thought. He couldn't believe it. These things don't happen. He had talked and joked with Mike before. But this wasn't the same Mike. His eyes were red-rimmed. There was spittle on his mouth. Clancy's hand found a stone and he raised it and flung it and it hit Mike in the face. Clancy didn't wait to feel any emotion. He could do either of two things. He could run or he could fight, but he elected to fight and he followed the stone with his head and butted the big man in the pit of the stomach. That sent him flying down the hill, falling. Clancy followed him. He scrabbled for the falling baton on the way down, and he didn't delay. There was blood on Mike's face. He was sitting up, his hand raised to the cut. Clancy hit him on the head, and he hit him again a third time and it was only then, when Mike fell over, stretched like a slaughtered bullock, that Clancy had time to feel sorry for his actions. Mike's left cheek was covered with blood and his scalp was open and pouring blood down the other side of his face, but Clancy remained unmoved by that. He freed Mike's galluses and turned him and wound them tightly around his arms, and he took his bootlaces and tied his wrists. It didn't take long. Clancy sat back then on the heather, breathing deeply. He was exhausted.

By Almighty God, he thought, he meant to kill me. And it was a near thing too. He would have killed me.

Then he moved. Mike's head was downhill. Clancy swung him around like a baulk of timber by the shoulders so that his head was uphill. Then he took a handkerchief from his pocket and wet it in a pocket of rainwater in the hollow of a rock and he bathed the blood away from his wounds. He sucked in his breath as he cleaned them and saw they were fairly deep. Did I do that? I did. Holy Mother of God!

Mike's eyes were opened. They were looking at the sky. Mike thought: The sky is clear, there are no clouds in the sky. He moved his head. Clancy's face came into his vision, hatless, wanting a shave, covered with scratches and bog mud.

'I didn't hurt you?' Mike asked.

Clancy was surprised.

'No,' he said. 'Not much. But I hurt you.'

'Ah,' Mike said. 'You don't know. Why did you come after me? You are sure I didn't hurt you?'

'Not much,' said Clancy. Mike tried to get up. He was surprised to find that he couldn't. 'I'm tied,' he said.

'That's right,' said Clancy indignantly.

'Let me up,' said Mike.

'No bloody fear,' said Clancy.

Mike smiled.

'I don't blame you,' he said. 'Weren't you a remarkable man to down me? You must be the first one that ever downed me.'

'I don't want to be remarkable,' said Clancy. 'All I want to do is to be alive.'

'I am Mike Stranger,' said Mike. 'Twenty years I am here and I am still Mike Stranger. Isn't that funny?'

'Ha-ha,' said Clancy shortly.

'But it is,' said Mike. 'I come from a city too, you know, Clancy. Not a big one like yours. But a city. Would you like to hear what drove me out of the city.'

Clancy wasn't very sensitive, but somehow it seemed to him at this moment that his attitude to Mike might be important. He wanted to be short with him. He wasn't. Was there a note of pleading in the big man's voice? The blood was welling again. Clancy dampened the handkerchief and bathed the cuts. He grunted consent.

Mike said: 'Out here people are only curious about you for awhile. Then their curiosity wears away. They only become curious about what you are now. That's good. You see me when I am a boy. Big boy. Lumbering. Not very bright. But bright enough. I am very young, Clancy, when I come from school one day and my mother is dead, see, on the kitchen floor and there is a lot of blood. She did it herself. She was nice, I tell you. She had fair hair and blue eyes, and he should have loved her very much but he was no good. He went away see. And there was just the two of us. He was no good. But she loved him. It happens often that way, doesn't it?'

'Yes,' said Clancy, 'it happens often that way.'

'So she couldn't take it. But it shocked me to find her that way. She just didn't think of that, I suppose. That it might be me to find her that way. Otherwise she would never have done it, you think?'

'She didn't think,' said Clancy. 'That was all. She just didn't think it would be you.'

'You see,' said Mike. 'That's what gets into me. Clouds of blood. I looked for your man often when I got bigger. What I would have done to him! I never found him. That was as well I suppose.'

'That's right,' said Clancy. He started to untie the bonds from Mike.

'Look,' said Mike. 'You might be taking an awful chance.'

'All right,' said Clancy. 'I can hit you again.'

'I'm glad you hit me, Clancy,' Mike said. 'Maybe you get some sense into me. Maybe you scattered the cloud. Listen, Clancy?'

'What is it?' Clancy asked.

'It might be better if people asked other people things. It might be better if people were persistently curious. Do you think?'

'Why?' Clancy asked.

'I never said before, to a single soul, what the red cloud meant,' said Mike. 'Maybe I might have, if somebody persisted. Nobody did, ever since I was young. You know, Clancy, I feel like I've been washed. Is that strange?'

'Here,' said Clancy, 'put on your galluses and let's get going.'

'Thanks, Clancy,' said Mike. 'Look at the sun. It's bright now, isn't it. The land looks good below, doesn't it?'

'Yes,' said Clancy, 'the land looks good.'

They stood up looking at it.

'I will always be grateful to you,' said Mike.

Clancy said a bad word and they headed down the mountain.

So it was that a haggard Sergeant was awakened from the only peaceful sleep he had got the whole night.

His window blind was shot up and he sat up in bed staring.

193

There was an absolutely filthy Clancy and a big, grinning, sane Mike Stranger, bandaged with strips of handkerchiefs.

Clancy saluted smartly.

'Prisoner delivered as per orders, Sergeant,' he said. Then he executed a smart about-turn, and Mike laughed at the open-mouthed look of the Sergeant.

The Lion

TIM stood patiently at the edge of the small crowd and
waited for the appearance of the man he called Putrid in his
mind.

He was a young boy. His thin hands were clasped behind
his back. He wore short trousers, neatly patched, and a red
jersey. He wore no shoes or socks. Anyway it was summer
time and the dust of the place was warm under his bare
feet. This was the third day he had come to watch the
feeding of the animals of the circus. It wasn't a big circus.
The main tent was only medium size. The garish signs were
mottled from the weather. The caravans looked tawdry in
the light of day. Tim hadn't been inside to see the circus. He
could never raise the price of it, even the matinée, but he
came faithfully, and watched the feeding and then stood
hopefully outside the tent. But no kind person had as yet
cast an eye on him and offered to take him in. The over-
worked hands just shooed at him if he got in their way.

But the feeding of the animals was for free. Anybody
could come and watch. It was a small menagerie. Just a
lioness and a tiger and a few monkeys, and Samson.

Samson was the lion. It was near his cage Tim always
stood. It wasn't a big cage. It barely fitted the body of the
lion. Tim felt his own limbs cramped when he looked at the
cage. Samson wasn't like a lion you would see in books or a
picture. His mane was not bushy. It was nearly all worn
away. There was only a bit of it left around his head, up
near his ears. He didn't roar either. Even when he was pro-
voked he would only loose off a sort of half-hearted growl.
You know the sort of small bush that a lion has near the
end of his tail. Samson didn't have that either. It was worn
away. His tail was mottled, sort of mean-looking. You

could see his ribs too. He wasn't a fat lion. Tim was very fond of Samson. He preferred him to the others; to the pacing tiger with the fearful eyes and to the yawning lioness. He even preferred him to the monkeys, although the monkeys were good fun.

The other children had run up to the far side of the field. There was Putrid coming out with the bucket. It was a bucket of meat. Raw meat. The sides of the bucket were stained with old blood and fresh blood. Tim felt the wave of dislike coming over him again at the sight of the man with the bucket.

He was a small man, very black-haired, always seeming to want a shave. He wore clothes that were too big for him; the trousers were in folds around his battered shoes. He wore a collar fastened with a tie-pin, that only creased the collar into still more dirty folds, and a string of a red tie that was greasy. He was carrying a pole in his hand with a steel prod on the end of it. Tim felt the muscles of his stomach tightening at the sight of him. Always the same. Opening the slot in the cage of the tiger and the lioness and poking in the meat to them. He talked to those nicely enough always. They grabbed the meat and held it between their claws and squatted at the eating of it. Then he turned his face towards the cage of Samson and went into his act.

Before he could start the act, Tim turned to Samson, and he said to him : 'Don't mind him, Samson. Don't mind him. He is very ignorant.' Samson may have heard him. He turned his head towards him and blinked his great eyes, and then went back to his dreaming. Almost against his will Tim turned his eyes to watch Putrid.

There he was several yards away, crouching like an ape, the bucket in one hand, the pole in the other. The kids were around about him, laughing at his antics.

'Here's the fiercest one of them all, min,' he was saying, pointing Samson with his nose, like a dog. 'Fresh outa the jungles of Africa. Looka the red in his eyes. Watch the stretch of the claws. Oney to be approached with great caution. Careful with him now. He can stretch a limb five foot through the bars to get at ye.'

He circled around as if he was stalking. Tim watched him in disgust. He knew that the best parts would be gone from the bucket. Samson never got anything from him but the bare leavings of the others. The kids were delighted with Putrid. They started to imitate him, crouching and stalking and laughing. Suddenly Putrid darted towards the cage, inserted the prod and stuck it in Samson's side. The lion moved, almost grunting. He couldn't move far. He didn't growl. He didn't roar. Tim would have given anything to hear him roaring with anger. He didn't.

'See that,' says Putrid. 'Hear the roaring of him. Waken the dead he would. Oh, a fierce, fierce animal, kids. But, you don't have to be afraid of him. Watch this.' He left down the bucket and the pole and he ran crouching behind the cage and caught hold of Samson's tail. He pulled it as hard as he could, so that the body of the lion was pulled back to the end bars.

'See that,' he was shouting. 'The oney fierce animal in captivity to be held be the tail. He'll go mad, so he will. Watch him tear the cage to pieces.'

Tim's finger-nails were biting into his palms. Samson rose almost wearily, straightening himself, crouching because he could not stand upright in the cage, pulling against the pull on his tail, almost staggering on his pads as Putrid suddenly released him. The lion's head hit the bars on the other side. He didn't object.

Because he's old, I suppose, Tim thought. He wouldn't have done that to him when he was young. He conjured up a picture of Samson meeting Putrid in a jungle clearing. Samson wouldn't be unkind then, Tim bet. He would just tear Putrid to pieces. Tim savoured that.

Putrid rubbing his hands.

'Nothin' to it, min,' he was saying. 'I've pulled lions be the tail in every continent in the world. But this one is real fierce when he's feedin'. Oh, real fierce when he's feedin'.'

He didn't open the slot. He pulled the bar and opened the

whole door of the cage. Tim wished that Samson would spring out on top of him. He didn't. Putrid hit him on the head with the prod. You could hear the sound of it. Samson just blinked his eyes and pulled back.

'No play in him at all today,' said Putrid. 'Here, Fanny, have your chips.' He up-ended the bucket and flung the contents of it straight into the lion's face. The lion must have looked funny with the things on his face. The by-standers were dying laughing. The scraps fell off his face then on to the floor of the cage.

Putrid banged the door and locked it.

'Bah,' he said. 'No play for him at all today. What a lion. Come on, we'll get to the monkeys.'

They followed him. One of them, before going, tenta-tively took a pull at the lion's tail which was still hanging through the bars. He let it go quickly and ran after them shouting, 'Hey, fellas, I did it. I pulled his tail.'

Putrid patted him on the head.

'Man,' he said, 'you'll be a lion-tamer yet, so you will.'

They laughed.

Tim was looking at Samson.

'Maybe he doesn't mean it,' he was saying to him. 'But don't mind him. He has to die sometime and then he won't be after you.'

He felt tears in his eyes. Because I'm young, he thought. Like you would cry about a drowning kitten.

Samson started to clean his face. It took him some time. Then he sniffed at the food between his paws. It didn't in-terest him. He lifted his head and looked away at the sky.

At this moment Tim got the thought that maybe Samson was sick. He knew they didn't use him in the circus. Just the lioness and the tiger. They just carted him around to be a father, they said. And suddenly in his mind's eye he saw the wood outside the town. You came down a hill to it and climbed another hill out of it, and in the hollow there was a clear stream that babbled over stones, and the wood was wide and dappled with sunlight. A place like that Samson would be at home, with the birds and the trees and the bracken, and he would get well and growl and roar and nobody would disturb him, and Putrid couldn't torture him.

On this thought, Tim reached up (he had to stretch a lot) and he pulled back the steel bolt and he opened the door of the cage.

'Come on, Samson,' he said, 'I will take you to a place that you will like. It won't be like the jungle. But it'll be nearly as good. Come on! Please come on before anybody comes.'

Samson didn't want to come.

Tim pulled himself up on to the floor of the cage until he was hanging on his chest. He stretched an arm until his hand could take hold of the remaining mane and he tugged at it gently.

'Come on, Samson,' he said. 'Come on.'

Samson resisted, but then he started to go with the pull of the boy's hand. Tim got his feet on the ground. He still kept his grip on the old lion's mane. And then Samson crouched and sprang to the earth. He stood there for a while, feeling the unaccustomed ground under his pads. Then he dutifully followed the pull of the small hand on his mane and walked beside him, past the caravans, out the gate and into the street of the town.

They walked calmly down the middle of it.

Towns are quite used to odd things walking down their streets; people, contraptions, and even animals. Runaway horses are expected and frequently make heroes. Also elephants may walk down town streets as long as they are with circuses and are parading. But this was a market-day in the town and the street was crowded, both sides of it taken up with motor-vans and lorries and asses-and-carts and horses-and-carts, the owners all going about their lawful occasions. If you can ripple a pond with a pebble you can entirely upset it by throwing a large boulder into it. The pond will explode. It was like that now with the town as the first person looked at the boy and the lion.

This was a fat woman with a shopping basket. She looked and she looked again and then she dropped her basket and opened her mouth very widely and screamed and turned and ran screaming. Her legs were fat and her stockings didn't go all the way up on her legs so that when she ran men could see where they ended and were tied just above her knees with soiled red ribbon.

Everybody claimed afterwards that it was this woman who led to the unnatural panic with her screaming. Only for her, they said, nobody would have paid the least attention to the boy and the loose lion. Perhaps, but if you are walking up a street and you see a lion walking towards you, I doubt if you will stop to ask any questions. Your skin will crawl, your mouth will dry, the hair will rise on the back of your neck and you will seek safety in flight. Everybody did now. The street, thronged with people, cleared as if a plague had swept through it. People ran into the first open shop door, fighting to get in and to bang the doors behind them, and peer out through the glass. Screaming women and shouting men, all panic-stricken. They ran into cars and closed the doors of them and shot up the windows of them, and peered palely through them. It was a shameful business but it must be recorded. They left horses and donkeys where they were. If these animals were not tied to electric-light poles or telegraph poles by the reins, they were disturbed and they took to their heels dragging the heavy carts after them. There were many unknown heroes in outlying districts that day who never got medals for stopping runaway animals but that was just their bad luck.

Tim walked solemnly on, talking to Samson, almost unconscious of the confusion and upset he was leaving behind him. He turned from the busy shopping and market street into the wide Square. This was roomier and people had more time to find safety and to reflect.

It was a Councillor who got the police on to it.

He, unfortunately, ended halfway up a pole, clinging to it by his hams. It wasn't widely known, but his wife spent some time afterwards pulling wooden chips from the inside of his thighs. (It's not part of the story, but he was ever afterwards known as The Northerner, because he was the Councillor who was up the pole. Subtle but enraging.) From his uncomfortable perch he addressed the people about how the bloody police were never where they were wanted, and then he shouted at a frightened citizen who was peering through a second-storey window to go and call the police for God's sake and tell them there was a lion loose in the town and not to be standing up there gawking like an eejit. The Councillor was mad, and no wonder, and he had to stay on the pole until somebody brought a ladder, because his position was painful but he didn't want to get more chips in him than he had now, because, he shouted at an inquirer, if he got any more of them in him, he'd float.

So it was that Tim paused at the top of the Square and became aware of all the disturbance he was causing and also became aware of the line of police gradually and very cautiously closing in on him. His hand tightened on Samson, and he stopped, and Samson stopped and looked at the circle of men approaching him. He raised a lip and snarled, and the advancing line came to a dead stop. They had no arms, just their batons held in their hands, but most of them thought that a lion could have the juggler torn out of you before you could hit him, all except the Inspector, a tall man with blue eyes, who came close to the boy and the lion with nothing under his arm except a light cane. He had sense. When he got the message he had called the circus people. Out of one corner of his eye he saw them approaching now, out of the street into the Square, loaded with ropes and bars and hauling a cage on wheels which they lifted down from a van.

'Take it easy, boy,' said the Inspector. 'Don't get excited. Nothing will happen. Don't excite him.'

Tim's mouth was dry. He was afraid of the police. Where Tim lived nobody much liked the police. They often called and politely removed sons of the people for various misdemeanours. Also he suddenly realized that his hopes were at an end. He hadn't thought of the town and the police. If he could have gone a back way, nobody might have noticed. Now, he thought sadly, Samson would never see the wood.

The Inspector was surprised as he closed on him. The boy had no fear, and as he looked closely at the lion, he saw there was no need for anybody to fear. All the same, who knew? The lion looked old and thin and helpless, but one slash at the boy was all that was needed.

The men were closing from behind, cautiously, the ropes held in loops.

'Leave the lion and come here to me,' said the Inspector. Tim shook his head.

'No, no,' he said, his small hand tightening on the lion.

'You'll have to leave him go,' said the Inspector. 'The men are behind you. They are going to throw ropes over him. You'll have to come to me.'

'Don't let Putrid touch him,' said Tim.

The Inspector didn't know what he was talking about.

'All right,' he said.

'Goodbye, Samson,' said Tim then, pressing his hand deeply into the lion's neck. He didn't look at him any more. He bent his head and walked to the Inspector. The Inspector heaved a sigh and caught his hand. He watched for a short time as the ropes landed, and the lion was secured. Like a pent-up breath relieved, there was laughter and calling and shouting. He noticed the small black dirty little fellow cavorting around the lion as they put him into the cage. He went docilely, peacefully. But this chap was acting the mickey for the surrounding people. And they were laughing at his antics.

'All right,' said the Inspector, 'let's go down and get off the streets and see what this is all about.'

Level-headed people who saw the whole thing said afterwards that it was a spectacle to see the boy and the lion frightening a whole people, and that it was as much a spectacle to see a tiny boy walking down to the police barracks surrounded by very tall men.

Tim felt that he was walking in a blue forest. All he could see were blue legs like the trunks of trees. But the hand of the Inspector was holding him gently, so he wasn't as frightened and his heart didn't thump as badly as before. Perhaps the Inspector sensed his awesome incipient fear, because Tim soon found himself alone in a small room with just a desk and a bright fire, and the Inspector who didn't seem so tall when he was sitting down.

'Now, Tim,' he said, 'tell me. Did you open the cage?'

'Yes, sir,' said Tim.

'Why?' he asked.

'I wanted to bring him out to the woods,' Tim said. 'So that he would get well, and Putrid wouldn't torture him.'

'Who's Putrid?' the Inspector asked, 'and how did he torture him?'

Tim told him about Putrid.

'I see,' said the Inspector.

'Samson is not well,' said Tim. 'You should have seen him. He wouldn't roar nor nothing. And he should have. He should have eaten Putrid. But he didn't do nothing. Just sat when he stuck things into him and pulled his tail and everything. You see, Samson should be in the woods to get well.'

'I see,' said the Inspector. He took up the telephone and called a number into it. He tapped with a pencil on the desk and he waited. His eyes were hard. Tim was frightened again.

'That you, Joe?' he asked. 'Yes, it's me. I want you down here in about ten minutes. Bring your bag of tricks with you. Yes, I'll explain to you then. It's urgent.'

He put down the phone. He pressed a button and started to write lines on a sheet of paper. Another policeman came in.

'Here,' he said. 'Go to the JP down the road and get him to sign that.' The policeman went.

'All right, Tim,' said the Inspector, 'come on and we'll go out and wait for Joe.'

'What are you going to do with me?' Tim asked. 'Will I have to go to jail?'

The Inspector looked at him for a moment, then put his hand on his head.

'No, Tim,' he said. 'No jail. On the other hand, no medal either. They don't give out medals for the kind of good deed you do. Come on.' He took his hand again and walked with him down the corridor, out into the sunshine. There were men with their coats off and wearing sandshoes playing handball in the sunlight. They stopped and looked for a time until they heard the car horn honking. Then they went out. The Inspector opened the door of the car and put Tim in before him. There was a bulky red-faced man behind the wheel.

'Hello, Joe,' said the Inspector. 'This is Tim, a friend of mine.'

'Hello, Tim,' said Joe. 'Glad the Inspector has decent friends for a change.'

The policeman came breathless then, shoved in the paper through the window.

'He made no trouble about it?' the Inspector asked.

'Not a bit,' said the policeman, laughing. 'He was up in the street when it happened. Said he had to climb a pole. He's full of splinters. Said he'd sign an order to burn the circus as well.'

The Inspector laughed.

'Fine. All right, Joe.'

The car moved away.

'What's all this about a lion?' Joe asked. 'Everybody is talking about it.'

'That's the lion you are going to see,' said the Inspector. He explained to Tim. 'Joe is a doctor of animals, Tim. He cares for animals, like a doctor cares for people.'

Tim was interested.

'Oh,' he said. 'Will you make Samson well?'

'He will, Tim, don't worry,' said the Inspector.

Joe was a bit bewildered, but kept silent under the appeal of the Inspector's wink.

The car stopped outside the circus entrance. The town had returned to normal.

'You stay here, Tim,' said the Inspector. 'We won't be long.'

They left him. Tim opened a window. He could smell the circus. He didn't want to go in there again.

Joe was looking at Samson.

'What do you think?' the Inspector asked.

'I'm afraid so,' said Joe.

'You wait here,' said the Inspector.

He found the owner. He presented him with the signed order.

'You can't do that,' he protested. 'It's illegal. There's nothing wrong with him. Just because some crazy kid let him out. That's no reason. Here, Alphonsus. Come here. He knows. He keeps them fed. You know that Samson is all right, isn't he? Isn't Samson all right?'

'Strong as a lion,' said Alphonsus, chuckling.

'You are Putrid,' said the Inspector suddenly to Alphonsus. He thought how vivid had been the boy's description of him. 'You're a dirty little sadistic bastard,' he said, 'and if a lion doesn't tear you to pieces some day, some honest man will kick your puddens out.'

Putrid's mouth was open in astonishment.

The owner protested.

'Here,' he said. 'You can't say things like that.'

'You keep that fella away from your animals,' said the Inspector, and walked away from them.

Joe was at the cage. He was putting away a syringe. Samson was lying on the floor of the cage, his legs stiffened straight out from him. His chest was not rising.

They looked at the body of the lion.

'He should have been destroyed years ago,' Joe said.

'Poor devil,' said the Inspector. He put his hand through the bars of the cage, rested it on the body of Samson.

'That's from Tim, Samson,' he said, and then they walked back to the car. They got in.

They could sense the silence of the boy.

'What happened?' he asked.

Joe started the car.

The Inspector put his arm around Tim's shoulders.

'Samson is gone back to the woods, Tim,' he said. 'You

watch. One time maybe when you are playing in that wood, you might see Samson standing in the sunlight.'

'Resting on the soft leaves,' said Tim eagerly.

'That's right,' said the Inspector.

Frank O'Connor
Day Dreams and other stories 60p

'Nowhere will you get so vivid, humorous and deeply understanding
a picture of Ireland as in these tales . . . Anyone can enjoy his
stories. All start with a bang and carry one through breathless to
the end. To me he is a man of the stature of Yeats and Swift'
JOHN BETJEMANN, DAILY TELEGRAPH

The Mad Lomasneys and other stories 60p

'Brilliant and penetrating studies of young men who are either agin
the government or agin religion, young women who have a struggle
between their good Catholic consciences and sex, or priests who
have to struggle with both' OXFORD MAIL

Masculine Protest and other stories 30p

These stories abound in colourful characters — young and old, rich
and poor, priests and parishioners, doctors and patients, postmen,
teachers and nightwatchmen. The reader is taken into their homes
and pubs, churches and wakes with a warmth, intimacy and
vitality which has never been surpassed.

'Under their quiet, intimate tone lies his deep understanding of the
way of the Irish heart' SUNDAY TIMES

Also available
Fish for Friday and other stories 60p
The Holy Door and other stories 60p
An Only Child 60p
My Father's Son 60p

Christy Brown
Down All the Days 40p

In the tradition of *Ulysses* – a distillation of Dublin, its raging men
and lusty women . . . its drunken furies and its bawdy laughter . . .
its brutal matings and its frenzied wakes are captured here in the
greatest novel of a generation.

A Shadow on Summer 75p

Christy Brown's second novel has all the vitality, power, insight
and perception to make it a more than worthy successor to his
first, *Down All the Days*.
Riley McCombe comes to America, pitchforked from total
obscurity in Dublin into fame as the brilliant author of a major
bestseller.

The Childhood Story of Christy Brown 50p

The warm, humorous autobiography of a courageous Irishman who
overcame the severest of handicaps. Beneath the shattering
exterior of a helpless, lolling baby was the racing, sensitive mind
of one of the most brilliant authors of our time.